Haunted by desire . . .

Suddenly Marcus pushed her against the wall and held her there. "You would try even Sir Galahad's patience, Henrietta Courtenay! So I am the vilest yet of all the Fitzpaines, am I?"

"Yes!" she retorted, but her heart was pounding and his touch seared her.

"Then a kiss—for old time's sake—would be meaningless?"

"Totally meaningless."

"Let us test the truth of that. . . ." he whispered, and bent his head to put his lips to hers.

He pressed her to the wall, his body to hers, and his lips were ruthless. It was a kiss that tore her heart with its wild passion. . . .

The Haunting of Henrietta

∽

Sandra Heath

A SIGNET BOOK

SIGNET
Published by the Penguin Group
Penguin Putnam Inc., 375 Hudson Street,
New York, New York 10014, U.S.A.
Penguin Books Ltd, 27 Wrights Lane,
London W8 5TZ, England
Penguin Books Australia Ltd, Ringwood,
Victoria, Australia
Penguin Books Canada Ltd, 10 Alcorn Avenue,
Toronto, Ontario, Canada M4V 3B2
Penguin Books (N.Z.) Ltd, 182–190 Wairau Road,
Auckland 10, New Zealand

Penguin Books Ltd, Registered Offices:
Harmondsworth, Middlesex, England

First published by Signet, an imprint of Dutton NAL,
a member of Penguin Putman Inc.

First Printing, December, 1998
10 9 8 7 6 5 4 3 2 1

Copyright © Sandra Wilson, 1998

Chapter One

For one hundred long years, ever since 1714, the ghostly lovers of Mulborough Abbey had been obliged to haunt the scenes of their clandestine affair. This was not from choice, but was due to a rare blunder by St. Peter, who had absentmindedly consigned them to Old Nick. Had not the good saint realized his error—in the "nick" of time, some might say—they would have been lost forever.

However, things had gone too far for him to rescue the hapless pair completely, and now the fate of Miss Jane Courtenay and Lord Kit Fitzpaine hung in the balance. Being neither redeemed or doomed, they had to perform a task in order to pass through the portals of heaven. This task was to bring about the successful union of another set of lovers from the Courtenay and Fitzpaine families. There were certain conditions by which the phantoms had to abide, such as always remaining invisible, and not under any circumstance communicating the nature of their undertaking. But if a sincere decision to marry was elicited from the chosen subjects, redemption would be achieved.

St. Peter confidently expected that within a year, two at the most, Jane and Kit, together with Jane's beloved King Charles spaniel, Rowley, who was also caught up in the tangle, would perform the necessary task. There is no doubt that it *should* have been a simple exercise, but as will unfold, it was proving a labor of Herculean, if not downright impossible, proportions.

The blame for this lay with Old Nick, who was highly annoyed at having two such quality spirits snatched from his grasp. Second-rate individuals the Master of Hades had in plenty, but prime examples were much harder to come by. Making no secret of his disgruntlement, he saw to it that circumstances were very difficult indeed for the beleaguered spirits. His infernal agents were constantly alert to act if there seemed any real likelihood of the mission succeeding, and with a little deft manipulation he made sure that the spaniel, Rowley, was an encumbrance rather than a help. He also restricted the ghosts' ability to haunt to times when—as happened in 1714— the first snow of winter fell on New Year's Day, with the further proviso that the haunting could only endure while it remained on the ground.

Now, snow cannot be relied upon to fall at all in England's moderate climate, let alone on a certain day. Nor, when it does fall, can it be expected to remain for long, certainly not long enough to bring about a successful courtship! Year after year therefore passed without the unfortunate lovers having many opportunities to carry out their mission. St. Peter's embarrassment was manifest and Old Nick's mean delight huge.

It seemed this state of affairs might continue indefinitely, but then at the end of 1813 began the coldest winter in memory. The freeze was intense, but snow didn't fall until the early hours of New Year's Day, 1814. It was destined to remain until the middle of February—ample time for the increasingly frustrated ghosts to do what was required in order to pass through the gates of heaven.

The advent of such a winter displeased Old Nick. For a century he had been enjoying himself at St. Peter's expense, and he had no intention of permitting a long period of snow to interfere with this amusement. So he considered the situation a little more carefully. Every year at the festive season, Mulborough Abbey was filled with guests, and he secretly examined Lady Mulborough's invitation list. He soon perceived that although there were half a dozen unattached Fitzpaines, there was only one unmarried Courtenay, a young lady who was betrothed to a man she did not love. Old Nick knew only too well that if Cupid's arrow should strike, loveless betrothals could be abandoned, so he decided that Miss Henrietta Courtenay had to be eliminated from the proceedings. There would have been little sport in doing this himself, so he stirred one of his agents to perform the task for him. This wicked person, who secretly felt immense animosity toward the unfortunate Miss Courtenay, was the perfect weapon. The vendetta against Henrietta started before she left London, and had continued at the abbey. A succession of alarming "accidents" had already befallen her, but so far she had escaped. However, with weeks of snow to come, more so-called accidents lay ahead, and sooner or later one was bound to succeed.

Mulborough Abbey stood high on the sheer cliffs of a Yorkshire headland, overlooking the fishing town and bay with which it shared its name. Having ceased to be a place of worship during the seventeenth century, it was now the residence of the lords of Mulborough, and in the festive season was always filled with fashionable guests. A New Year's Eve ball was in progress as the first snowflakes began to fall, and no one sensed anything as the invisible specters stepped onto the ballroom staircase.

Kit was a handsome young man of twenty-eight, with quick, light blue eyes, tanned clean-cut features, and long fair hair he tied back with a black ribbon. He wore a full-skirted brick-colored coat and buckled black shoes, with a fine dress sword slung low on his left hip. However, the garb of early eighteenth-century England could not disguise the Norse in him. Back in the mists of time, his ancestors had landed in longboats to pillage Saxon settlements, and the Viking raider still glinted in his eyes when he was aroused.

In twenty-four-year-old Jane he had found his perfect other half. Witty, flirtatious, and impetuous, she was very beautiful, with a petite figure, large lavender eyes, and raven hair that was diligently curled and then combed so that two long dark ringlets were teased forward over her shoulders. There was an ivory fan looped over her wrist and she wore a blue velvet gown, the parted skirt of which was looped back to reveal a primrose satin undergown. A sapphire necklace rested high around her slender throat. She cradled Rowley in her arms. The spaniel was happy to be carried, for to be in Jane's arms was to establish a superiority over Kit, of whom he was intensely jealous.

Surveying the glittering scene, Jane and Kit were reminded of their courtship. In 1714, their respective families, the newly wealthy Courtenays and the old established, exceedingly aristocratic Fitzpaines, had for several years in succession spent the festive season at the residence of their mutual friends, Lord and Lady Mulborough, and it was at just such a ball as this that Cupid's arrow had suddenly found its mark. Jane and Kit had known each other for some time, but were betrothed to others when their hearts were pierced with passion. Of the prior attachments, Jane's was the lesser, for she had an arranged match with a profligate lord whose arrogance was matched by his peacock vanity. He had deigned to enter the contract because he had discovered that her unmarried maternal uncle, a nabob in the East India Company, was considering leaving his vast fortune to Jane's father. This did indeed turn out to be the case, which was why future generations of Courtenays were so very wealthy, but Jane's calculating lord was not to share this largesse.

Kit's marital situation, on the other hand, was no small matter because his intended was cousin to Queen Anne herself. To flout such a match was a recipe for social disaster, not just for him, but for his whole family. Therefore, for him to have commenced a clandestine affair at all was exceedingly reprehensible, but to have then eloped to America, thus risking not only a terrible scandal but also their families' exclusion from court, was heinous beyond belief!

They had not been entirely unmindful of the effect their conduct would have upon others, and had left a letter in which they promised to vanish completely into their new life together. They suggested that no offense would be given to anyone if the truth were suppressed, and it was put out instead that Kit had died in a riding accident and that Jane had succumbed to influenza. The relieved families promptly acted upon the suggestion; there were even false tombs in the churchyard on the southern headland above Mulborough to prove the fabrication. But then came the awful news that on St. Valentine's Day, the very day the runaways were supposed to have been buried at the Mulborough parish church of St. Tydfa's, their ship, the *Wessex*, upon which they'd taken passage all the way from Yorkshire to Boston, Massachusetts, had foundered upon the infamous Goodwin Sands off the coast of Kent, with the loss of all life.

It happened because a French privateer, the *Basilisk*, chanced upon the *Wessex* in the English Channel, and even though there was an armistice between Great Britain and France, the British vessel was forced to flee. She made for the secure anchorage called the Downs, which lay between the natural breakwater of the Goodwins and the well-guarded Kentish port of Deal. The tide was at its lowest, and miles of golden sands were exposed, but the channel believed by the fleeing *Wessex* to be navigable, was in fact blocked just beneath the surface by a fresh spur of sand. As she drove hard upon this lurking hazard and broke her back with a rending and splintering of timbers, the only consolation for those on board was that the *Basilisk* could not avoid the same fate. Survivors from both vessels scrambled onto the iron-hard sands, but then the tide turned. Foaming and crashing, it swept in, changing the hard sands to liquid, and within minutes everything had turned to a heaving maelstrom of conflicting currents and waves. No one survived, and two days later the last trace of the wrecked ships disappeared beneath sands, which more than earned their terrible nickname, the "Ship Swallower."

The runaways' presence on board was never widely known, and as far as society was concerned, the original story of their deaths remained in force. Between their families, however, Jane and Kit had left a legacy of bitter recrimination. The Courtenays privately blamed Kit, the Fitzpaines hotly accused Jane, and neither family deigned to speak to the other again. They still converged upon Mulborough Abbey at Christmas, though, each side fearing that to withdraw would be seized upon by the other as an admission of defeat. These annual visits to Mulborough became a tradition which successive lords of Mulborough bore with resignation, taking comfort in the fact that at least the families' mutual aversion ensured they kept as far apart as possible. It was a feud that ranked alongside that of the Montagues and Capulets.

Now the invisible wraiths of the two people who'd started it all gazed down at an occasion where, as usual, various of their descendants were among the guests. Jane drew a deep breath. "Well, Kit, my dearest, here we are again, and at least this time the snow will remain for long enough to give us a chance of succeeding," she declared.

"A month and a half should indeed be more than sufficient," he agreed, keeping a wary eye on Rowley, whose jealousy often took the form of biting.

Jane held her pet fondly as she looked down at the ball. A *ländler* was just coming to an end, and as the ladies curtsied, her ghostly eyes widened at their daringly décolleté gowns. In her day such revealing fashions would never have been tolerated, except by demireps!

Kit sensed her reaction. "I trust you do not think *I* approve of such wantonness?"

Her eyebrows twitched. "Sirrah, your predilection for feminine charms is too well known to me for me to think otherwise."

He smiled. "Only *your* charms draw me now, my darling," he whispered, drawing her hand to his lips, then quickly releasing it again to avoid the possessive snap of Rowley's jaws. "Dear God, how I wish we didn't have to bring that damned mongrel with us every time!"

"He's not a mongrel; indeed he's very well bred!"

Kit gave the creature a savage look. "That's a matter of opinion," he muttered.

"He's defending my honor," she declared, stroking the dog's head.

"No, he isn't. He's trying to keep you all to himself."

Her glance was teasing. "As you do yourself, sir."

"Maybe so, but I dislike competing for your attention with a mangy canine!"

"He's not mangy either!"

"He's everything dire that a dog can be," Kit replied shortly, deliberately flicking the lace at his cuff so that it flapped in Rowley's face.

"Kit, you can be lamentably childish at times," Jane chided.

"Just make sure you keep a tight hold of him, for I have no desire to have to entice him down from a ceiling as high as this one." Kit glanced up at the lofty hammer beams far above. He and Jane were invisible and inaudible to the living, and were bound by the laws of gravity. Their powers were confined to moving inanimate objects and passing through everything solid. Due to Old Nick's meddling, Rowley was tiresomely different. He could defy gravity by scampering up and down walls, or across ceilings, but he couldn't go *through* anything. For him every door or window had to be open. He could also be heard by those of the living who were psychic. His whines, barks, and pattering paws could cause considerable consternation, especially when coming from the direction of a ceiling, and keeping him quiet at awkward moments could be very wearying indeed. Which, of course, was exactly what the Master of Hades intended.

At that moment a lady and gentleman descended the steps, and as they passed, the lady playfully popped a sugared almond into the gentleman's mouth. Sugared almonds were Rowley's favorite tidbit, and even though he could no longer eat anything at all, he whined.

The lady heard, and looked around in puzzlement. "Did you hear that?" she said to her companion.

"Hear what?"

"A dog."

The gentleman eyed her. "At a ball? I hardly think so, sweeting. More likely it was the ancient catgut of that second violin!"

"But—"

Rowley whined again and was abruptly silenced by a stern tap on the nose.

The lady had heard, however. "Surely you heard *that*?" she protested.

"I heard nothing at all," the gentleman insisted, raising his voice as the master of ceremonies announced a polonaise, and couples flocked onto the floor. "Come, let's dance!"

As the two guests hurried down to join one of the sets, Jane's disapproving gaze raked the lady from head to toe. "I vow it must be the thing to appear a doxy. She looks fit only for the boards at the Haymarket, or possibly even a Covent Garden bagnio! I am more modest even in my stays!" she declared.

"And very fetching stays they are too," Kit replied.

"Fie, sir." Jane chided smilingly.

He smiled too. "Forget the excesses of today's fashions, my dear. We must turn our thoughts to finding two star-crossed lovers from our respective families."

"I'm not exactly optimistic," she replied. "Each time we return, they all seem more entrenched than ever in this wretched feud. Just look at that fellow over there; he's the image of my Uncle Jasper Courtenay, and he's scowling most disagreeably at that lady in green, who just *has* to be a Fitzpaine!" She pointed to a portly red-faced gentleman of about fifty, who was helping himself from a punch bowl. The lady concerned was about forty-five years old, and thin as a stick, with a sour expression suggestive of the presence of a bad smell.

Kit raised an eyebrow. "A descendant of Cousin Wilhelmina, if ever I saw one," he murmured.

"I wish we weren't the cause of this disagreeable quarrel."

"Come now, my love, we can't take the blame entirely. Maybe we were the start of it, but by now I'll warrant neither side can recall the original reason for their falling out! Queen Anne never knew the truth, and as for King George I, well, I doubt if he ever knew we existed. The business with the false tombs was very effective, you know. We really did disappear."

"Once out of sight, one is usually out of mind too, which, I suppose, is what we wanted. Come on, let us circulate and see if any of our reprobate descendants offer us some hope of redemption."

The wraiths descended the staircase. A little knot of guests was gathered at the bottom, and Jane was careful to step around them because of Rowley, but Kit passed right through. One or two people shivered, but no one saw anything at all, nor did the phantoms imagine for a single moment that anyone would. However, on that score they were soon to receive a considerable shock.

Chapter Two

As the specters began to inspect everyone at the ball, Miss Henrietta Courtenay was with Charlotte, Lady Mulborough, who had been her close friend since their school days in Bath. The two young women had decided to sit for a while, because twenty-three-year-old Charlotte was expecting her first child at the beginning of February, and the rigors of the ball were proving quite wearying. She was also seeking the refuge of the red velvet sofa, which stood in a quiet corner and was flanked with ferns, in order to escape her adoring husband, who at sixty was considerably her senior. Russell, Lord Mulborough, had once been a senior secretary at the Treasury, and until he met Charlotte had been renowned for being stuffy, but she had changed all that. He had been her willing slave from the moment they met, and she returned the affection, but, oh, how he did fuss!

Charlotte was dressed in a loose pink silk robe, her shining chestnut hair was worn in a Grecian knot, and her hazel eyes were warm as she smiled at her much loved friend. "Oh, it's good to sit down for a while. The combination of being huge, dancing all night, *and* avoiding the fussing of one's spouse, is really quite tiring. Besides which, we don't seem to have had much opportunity to talk this evening, and I do enjoy a little gossip with you."

Henrietta laughed. She was the same age as Charlotte, and the fact that she was a Courtenay was immediately apparent, for she was Jane all over again, albeit in the flimsy fashions so deplored by that ghostly lady. In Henrietta's case, the offending garment was a white silk gown embroidered with silver rose-buds. There was a diamond-studded comb fixed to her shining dark hair, which had been expertly tended by Charlotte's maid, her own having suddenly left to be married on the eve of the journey to Yorkshire. Her right wrist was securely bandaged, and as she employed her fan with her left hand, a rather cumbersome emerald betrothal ring caught the light.

Charlotte winced suddenly, and Henrietta's lavender eyes expressed concern. "Are you all right?"

"Yes, it was only your godchild kicking a little forcefully."

Henrietta's lips parted with delight. "*My* godchild?"

"I warn you, I will not take no for an answer."

"Of *course* I accept!"

"Good, for you are my dearest friend. You know, it's a most curious thing, Henrietta, but I don't feel as if there are five or more weeks to go; indeed it feels much more imminent than that."

Henrietta was alarmed. "You don't mean you've started your pains?"

"Oh, good Lord, no, it's just an odd feeling I have. I know Dr. Hartley was very precise about my dates, and I'm only about eight months, but nevertheless . . ." Charlotte laughed. "Oh, well, he should know, I suppose. After all, this is my first baby. *He's* delivered them by the score."

"I'm surprised you're being attended by Dr. Hartley. You always swore you'd secure Nurse's services." Henrietta thought of the frail gray-haired woman who lived in the small hamlet of Mulbridge, about half a mile inland over the moors. No one knew quite how old she was, but she had been Russell's nurse and was universally regarded as the local midwife. Her real name was Miss Rose Hinchcliffe, but she was always simply called Nurse, even by those for whom she had never performed such a role.

Charlotte sighed. "Well, that *was* my original intention, but she has at long last decided she is too old to continue, and anyway Russell insists upon Dr. Hartley, who aspires to be something of an *accoucheur*." Charlotte winced once more as the baby moved. "Oh Lord, he or she is very active tonight."

"Would you like me to bring you a glass of water?"

"*Water?* At a New Year's Eve ball? Heaven forfend." Charlotte smiled, and beckoned a footman to bring glasses of champagne.

"Russell's finger will wag if he catches you with champagne."

"Russell is a great trial to me at the moment. Do you know, he even attempted to make me stay in this morning instead of joining everyone for the walk on the cliffs?"

"Well, it *was* rather cold," Henrietta said, putting her fan in her lap in order to take the glass with her left hand.

Charlotte looked anxiously at her bandage. "How is your poor wrist? I do hope it isn't too uncomfortable."

"It will do. I vow your skill with dressings is nothing short of miraculous, and as to the finishing touch of my diamond pin . . ." Henrietta smiled, and raised her wrist so the light caught the little brooch securing the bandage.

Charlotte chuckled. "Miraculous? Oh, I wouldn't go *that* far, but I have to say I'm usually quite good." Her smiled faded. "I still can't really understand how you slipped like that. One moment we were all walking along the top of cliffs, the next you were sprawling on the ground and had almost gone over the edge!"

Henrietta shivered as she recalled those dreadful moments. "There must have been a little patch of ice," she said, although privately she was only too aware that someone in the party had stumbled awkwardly against her. She didn't know who it was, and because she was sure it had been entirely accidental, she didn't intend to cause any distress by mentioning it.

"Ice? Yes, I suppose so. Anyway, you survived the incident. Now I come to think of it, you've been disaster prone ever since you arrived here."

"I wasn't exactly safe and sound in London," Henrietta replied. "My horse bolted in Hyde Park and I almost fell through a trapdoor at a lace warehouse."

Charlotte was horrified. "Oh, Henrietta, how dreadful! Bad

luck certainly seems to dog you at the moment, doesn't it? There was that runaway carriage that almost ran you down while you were traveling here, then the piece of falling masonry on Christmas Eve, to say nothing of the shellfish supper that so disagreed with you and you alone."

"Don't forget the lace snapping on my walking shoe," Henrietta teased.

"Oh, you may think it amusing, but yes, given everything else, the broken lace *should* be included."

Henrietta was patient. "Charlotte, it was only a broken lace. They do break, you know. I even recall it happening to you on occasion."

"I suppose so," Charlotte admitted, then glanced at her again. "Why you and dear Amabel *walked* all the way to St. Tydfa's churchyard when you could easily have ridden, I really don't know."

Henrietta ignored the acid reference to Amabel. "After all the rich Christmas food, we felt in need of the exercise, although, to be truthful, we did misjudge the distance." Henrietta recalled how, after climbing the long flight of steep stone steps from the lych-gate, she and Amabel Renchester had rested in the church porch before commencing the long walk home. The steep churchyard steps were slippery because yew trees shaded the overnight frost from the winter sun. Her lace had suddenly snapped, and she'd fallen very heavily, tumbling down at least ten steps before she managed to halt the fall by grabbing a low-hanging branch. She'd only suffered bruises and the indignity of having to hire a farmer's cob to carry her back to the abbey, but she knew it might have been much more serious.

Charlotte sipped the champagne and decided to say nothing more about Henrietta's mishaps. She looked at the crowded floor. "Well, all the local guests will disperse to their homes at dawn, and everyone who's been staying here since Christmas will depart at various times tomorrow, then there will just be you right up until February, and I'm *so* looking forward to that! Oh, how I wish you weren't to be your cousin's chief brides-maid; otherwise you could stay even longer!" Her smile of anticipation faded then. "Oh, sweet Amabel will be here as well, of course, but with luck she will not join us *all* the time."

Henrietta could no longer let it pass. "*Dear* Amabel, *sweet* Amabel. Oh, how I regret bringing her. It was clearly very foolish to imagine you two could make friends at last."

"Where Amabel Lyons—I mean Renchester—is concerned, old school enemies remain old school enemies. But your motives were laudable, Henrietta, and I do not blame you." Charlotte gave her a sideways grin. "On reflection, yes I do."

"Don't be beastly."

"I'm sorry, but you do rise to the bait."

Henrietta suddenly noticed Russell's distinguished gray-haired figure only ten yards away at the edge of the dance floor. He was standing on tiptoe to scan the sea of dancers, and it was clear he was searching for his wife. Henrietta put a finger to her lips and as one, she and Charlotte leaned back on the sofa, so the flanking ferns hid their faces from view should he glance their way.

By now, the two spectral interlopers had noticed Henrietta, and knew from her startling likeness to Jane that she had to be a Courtenay. Having already determined the uninspiring selection of unattached Fitzpaines, and the apparent absence of any unattached Courtenays at all, they hastened over to examine her more closely. Unobserved and unsensed by either young woman, they took up positions behind the sofa. The discovery that she wore a betrothal ring did not deter them, for of *all* people, they knew that such things could be set aside!

Henrietta and Charlotte continued to watch poor Russell through the fronds of green, and as he at last moved away toward the supper room, they sat forward again. Charlotte took a relieved sip of champagne. "Take my advice, Henrietta, don't marry an overprotective man."

"I doubt if my future husband will ever be accused of *that*," Henrietta replied, looking down at her ring.

Charlotte was immediately remorseful. "Forgive me, I spoke without thinking."

"What is there to forgive? I don't pretend that my match is anything other than a marriage of convenience."

"Convenience? For the sole heiress to the Courtenay fortune? I doubt it. For strutting, financially straitened Lord Sutherton? Yes, definitely!" Charlotte was scathing.

The eavesdropping shades exchanged startled glances, for the gentleman Jane had forsaken for Kit in 1714 had been none other than the then Lord Sutherton! Jane leaned forward to inspect the emerald betrothal ring again. What a deplorably showy bauble it was, she thought disparagingly. It had to be Lord Sutherton's choice, for the phantom instinctively knew that Henrietta would have selected sapphires, or possibly amethysts, to go with her eyes. Jane decided there and then that Henrietta was ideal for guiding toward another. But who? The ghost sighed as she mulled over the woeful selection of Fitzpaines present tonight. What Henrietta needed was another Kit! Oh, yes, that would be perfect, for how could such a combination *fail* to end in marriage?

"We have found our prospective bride, don't you think?" Kit whispered suddenly.

"I agree. However, given the collection of Fitzpaines we've observed thus far, I doubt if there is a prospective groom," she whispered back, even though she was as certain as he that no one could hear them. It was only Rowley who could be heard.

Meanwhile, Charlotte had also glanced at Henrietta's ring. The wedding at St. George's, Hanover Square, would be a social highlight of the season. It was a shame the bridegroom was so unworthy! She fixed Henrietta with a gimlet gaze. "This seems as appropriate a time as any to say my piece. If you bow to your parents' wishes and marry Sutherton, you'll be throwing yourself away on one of England's most cynical, heartless, and *impoverished* creatures. Impoverished by his own incontinence, I might add. He is an incorrigible gambler, and there isn't a gaming hell in London that doesn't have duns on his trail! I'm mightily relieved he did not accompany you here, for to be sure he would have fleeced half my guests by now."

Henrietta flushed. "Please don't say that."

"It's the truth, Henrietta. He's completely the wrong man for you, as I thought you well knew when you turned him down originally. Why you changed your mind and accepted him after all is quite beyond my understanding."

Henrietta looked away. There were things her friend did not know, things *no one* knew. When George first approached her parents, they had been eager to see her married to such an ancient title, but because she shared Charlotte's opinion of him, and because she had foolishly loved another at the time, she had defied them by refusing. Then George had saved her from humiliation and scandal on a scale of which she did not dare to think, and on learning of the parlous state of his finances, she felt she owed it to him to change her mind regarding the match. She toyed with her fan. "Charlotte, I know George has faults, but then so do I."

"*You?* My dearest Henrietta, your only fault is that you are too trusting."

"If you say much more, you and I shall fall out."

An atmosphere had descended over the two young women on the sofa, but then Charlotte gave a quick smile. "Look, ignore my carping; it's probably due entirely to my condition. Being this much with child makes one snappish."

Henrietta raised an eyebrow. "The only person you are snappish with is Amabel."

"Perhaps because I really can't understand why you have suddenly taken up with her again after all this time. It's been *years* since school." There was more than a hint of jealousy in Charlotte's tone.

"Well, we'd encountered each other on several occasions over the years, but then about a month before I left to come here, she called upon me. We got on famously, and when she told me how she longed to be reconciled with you, well, I—I just asked her to join me."

Charlotte's strong feelings on the matter were written large on her face. "Longed to be reconciled? I would as soon trust Beelzebub as that sly *chienne*! She and I have loathed each other since our first meeting at school. In plain language, Amabel Lyons was a spiteful, conniving miss, and Amabel Renchester is now a spiteful, conniving widow!"

"Maybe she *was* a little, er, difficult at school, but she was an orphan, and very much ill at ease," Henrietta reminded her.

"There are orphans and orphans, and Amabel had been taken in by a good, loving émigré family here in England, so didn't want for anything, except manners and amiability. As for her unbelievable airs and graces *now*! To hear her at dinner on Christmas Day was to think she must be the most ardent and noble-minded French royalist in all creation! All that talk of spending her early years at Versailles, and of having poor Queen Marie Antoinette as a godmother! Why have we never heard of it before? I vow there was not a single mention of it at school."

Henrietta shifted uncomfortably. "If I'd known your antagonism toward her went so deep, I would never have brought her with me. But she pleaded and pleaded because she was so very anxious to make up, and you *had* said I could bring a guest, so I really thought all would be well."

"If making up was indeed her real reason for coming here, I'll eat every one of Russell's hats!"

"Why do you *insist* on disliking her? People change, and the Amabel we knew at school is no more. I admit she was a little tedious on Christmas Day, but on the whole she is sweet-natured, witty, and excellent company. And don't forget how much odium she had to endure because of her late husband's treasonous activities in the Peninsula." Henrietta lowered her eyes, for the treachery of Major Renchester had been a terrible scandal. A much decorated hero, it had been discovered that he had been betraying secrets to the French. If he hadn't been found dead in his bed, of shame and fear it was said, he would certainly have been shot for a traitor. Amabel had adored him, even to the extent of accompanying him to Spain. Her shock and distress on learning the truth had been immeasurable.

"Russell knew Major Renchester and still refuses to believe he was guilty as charged. As for Amabel's claims to have been the shocked, grieving widow, I find it strange she discarded black within *days* of returning to London."

"As she said on Christmas Day, she was devastated that he

had secretly supported the French Republic. His treachery destroyed her love."

"Hmm." Charlotte's lips twitched disbelievingly.

"Oh, come now, Charlotte, Amabel isn't a monster! She could not have been more concerned and caring on the cliff this morning when I fell."

"She probably pushed you in the first place."

"Charlotte, you can't say things like that!"

Charlotte became a little contrite. "I know, and I'm sorry. Forgive me. I concede that she *was* admirable this morning."

"Yes, she was. That's what she's like now, Charlotte."

A thousand and one nuances passed over Charlotte's face, but then she shrugged. "You're entitled to your opinion, but as far as I'm concerned, there will always be something nasty about her. A whiff of sulfur, if you like."

A chill sensation passed over the eavesdropping ghosts.

Chapter Three

Henrietta was dismayed. "A whiff of sulfur? Oh, for heaven's sake, Charlotte!"

Charlotte suddenly reacted vehemently. "Henrietta Courtenay, there are times when I could shake you! You are my dearest friend, but I have to say your judgment is hopeless! You cleave to the likes of Sutherton and Amabel Renchester, yet declare yourself full of loathing for poor Marcus, whose only crime is being a Fitzpaine!"

Now it was Henrietta's turn to react hotly, and the wraiths sensed the lightning in her lavender eyes. "*Poor* Marcus?"

Charlotte pursed her lips. "My, my, it would seem even to mention the Marquess of Rothwell inflames your temper."

"He treated me most basely, but then I suppose it's what a Courtenay should expect of a Fitzpaine."

Charlotte groaned. "Oh, spare me the endless feud. Far be it from me to ask, but can anyone actually recall what started it all?"

"The Fitzpaines behaved abominably toward us in the time of Queen Anne," Henrietta replied.

"Which is the same boring stock answer one hears from them, except that they, of course, insist it was the Courtenays who behaved abominably."

"Well, the Fitzpaines would, wouldn't they?"

Charlotte studied her. "What, exactly, did Marcus do that was so heinous? All you've ever said is that his conduct toward you was base. What happened?"

"I—I'd rather not say." Henrietta colored agitatedly.

"Oh, Henrietta, surely after all this time you know you can trust me?"

Henrietta hesitated. She hadn't revealed to a soul the extent of what happened, and it would be so good to unburden it just this once. Especially to Charlotte. "If—if I tell you, you must *promise* faithfully not to divulge a word to anyone, not even Russell."

"I'm not given to spreading other people's secrets, as you well know."

Henrietta smiled apologetically. "Yes, I do know, it's just that my personal conduct was so very remiss, that I could not bear it if anyone found out. It was last year, just after he'd returned from six years in the West Indies. . . ."

"Seven," Charlotte corrected.

"All right, seven. Suffice it that I didn't know who he was, because when he left England, you and I were still at school in Bath. That aside, it was just after I had turned down George's first proposal of marriage. My parents had been called away to my sick aunt, and I attended a masked ball at Devonshire House. I really shouldn't have gone alone, but I've always loved masked balls, and the invitation had been accepted by my parents before my aunt fell ill. Anyway, Marcus singled me out, and was so gallant and attentive that I suppose I was flattered." Henrietta paused, for there was much she still wasn't saying. Her cheeks were very pink and shame shaded her eyes as she went on. "He pressed me to ride in Hyde Park the next day so that we could meet again, and after that to attend the theater in order to see him again. I was foolish enough to agree. I'm afraid I was so completely gulled that—that . . ."

"Yes?" Charlotte waited with bated breath.

Henrietta raised guilty eyes. "I allowed him to kiss me."

"In the middle of Hyde park?" Charlotte's eyes were like saucers, for few places in London were more open to the full gaze of society.

Henrietta blushed with mortification. "Yes, and in the passage behind the boxes at Drury Lane, during the second act of *Romeo and Juliet*."

"Oh, Henrietta! I can't believe you conducted yourself so wantonly!" Charlotte was shocked.

"Hush, for this must remain a secret." Henrietta gazed anxiously toward the crowded floor.

"No one can hear." Charlotte assured her, then drew a long breath. "Henrietta, what on earth possessed you? I've never known you to break a single rule, and now you regale me with a positive catalog of sins!"

"Please don't, for I can hardly believe it myself."

"If you reached the point of a kiss, surely you had by then discovered his identity?"

"He said his name was Mark Paynson."

Charlotte's lips twisted. "Paynson, Fitzpaine. How clever."

"Yes, wasn't it? Anyway, I was so happy for those few days. Indeed I believed I had met my true love, but then I received a visit from George."

Charlotte's eyes cleared. "Ah, I might have guessed Sutherton's cunning shadow would soon fall over things."

"George's motives were noble, Charlotte."

"Hmm."

"They were! He had come direct from White's, where, according to the betting book, a great deal of money hung upon whether or not Marcus could seduce me! I was supposed to meet Marcus again that night at a concert in the Hanover Square Rooms, but instead I sent a footman to inform him I no longer wished to have anything to do with him. That was the last I heard, and I was so grateful to George, that I felt obliged to help him in turn. There, now you have the reason why I'm going to become Lady Sutherton."

For a long moment Charlotte was speechless, but at last she recovered. "Well, I'd never have expected such things of you, Henrietta! Clandestine meetings and stolen kisses? However, such a despicable wager doesn't sound like the Marcus Fitzpaine I know."

"Charlotte, he masqueraded as Mark Paynson!"

Charlotte put out a quick hand. "Even though he flew false colors, you may be sure his heart was genuine. The Marcus I know would soon have revealed the truth about himself, and if he were here at Mulborough right now, I'd confront him in the certain knowledge he would confirm my faith in him. However, the fact that *Sutherton* figures so prominently in the scheme of things makes me very suspicious. He had been pursuing your fortune for some time, but you had turned him down, so he had to resort to foul means. Mark my words. There was never a bet at White's. Somehow dear George found out you were meeting Marcus, and his sole motive was to prevent you—and thus your fortune—from going to another."

"Defend Marcus if you will, but I was humiliated at his hands, and I would have suffered a public shaming if his shabby wager had not been revealed. I tell you this, Charlotte, this year I came to Mulborough in trepidation, because he might be here too. If you only *knew* how relieved I was that he and his wretched schooner are in Scotland."

"The *Avalon* is a sloop, the swiftest quarterdecked ship-sloop in England, to be absolutely accurate," Charlotte said quietly, thinking of the sleek, magnificently ornamented vessel that made the Marquess of Rothwell the envy of Cowes.

"I wish it were a rotten bucket with a hole in the bottom!" Henrietta snapped.

The conversation trailed into a long awkward silence, then Charlotte gave a sheepish smile. "We're on the brink of a horrid quarrel, aren't we?"

Henrietta met her eyes for a moment, and then smiled too. "Not if we speak of something less contentious."

At that moment the lady and gentleman who'd been on the staircase passed by. They were perambulating the entire ballroom, and Rowley, whose yearnings never failed when it came to sugared almonds, whined again. This time the brief sound was lost to the lady amid the noise of the ball, but it carried clearly enough to Henrietta, who turned sharply. Her eyes widened and her unfinished glass of champagne slipped from her fingers as she saw two hazy, transparent figures standing behind her.

Jane and Kit were thunderstruck to realize they were visible to her. It was the first time in their hundred years that such a thing had happened. Jane was thoroughly shaken. "Oh, Kit, she can see us!" she cried.

Kit regained his wits. "Come, Jane!" he cried, snatching her hand with the intention of disappearing through the wall behind the sofa onto the cliff terrace outside. Jane just had time to hastily put Rowley down on the floor, then she and Kit fled through the wall.

Yelping in alarm, the spaniel made for a nearby arched doorway. In his panic he dashed along the ballroom wall, about six feet up from the floor. Henrietta watched until he disappeared from view into the fifteenth-century cloisters, which allowed access to the terrace.

Charlotte, who had heard and seen nothing at all, sat anxiously forward. "Oh, Henrietta, your champagne has splashed your hem! Whatever is wrong? You look as if you've seen a ghost."

Childhood recollections swept headily over Henrietta as she quickly bent to retrieve the fallen glass, which somehow had not shattered. Visions of past ghosts hovered palely before her, wraiths she alone had witnessed. When she'd spoken of them, no one had believed her, and so she had soon learned the wisdom of holding her tongue. Gradually she had seen them no more. Until now. She gave a smile that was meant to reassure Charlotte. "I—I'm quite all right, it was just an accident."

"You don't seem all right to me." Charlotte called a footman. "Bring a towel quickly, for Miss Courtenay's drink has been spilled," she instructed, and as he hurried away, she gave Henrietta a concerned look. "What happened?"

"If I tell you, you will probably think me quite mad."

"I doubt it."

Henrietta met her eyes. "Very well, Charlotte. I really did see a ghost. Three of them to be precise—a lady about my age, a gentleman some ten years older, and a King Charles spaniel. They were indistinct; indeed I could scc right through them to the ferns behind, which is how I know they were ghosts."

Charlotte gave an uneasy laugh. "Henrietta, if this is a jest . . ."

"I'm telling the truth, Charlotte. The spaniel ran that way

along the wall about Russell's height from the floor." Henrietta pointed.

"Oh, Henrietta!" Charlotte laughed incredulously.

"It's the truth. The dog went that way and the lady and gentleman passed right through the wall, out onto the terrace, I suppose. They called each other Jane and Kit, and were dressed in the clothes from the time of Queen Anne." Henrietta toyed with her fan. "Charlotte, the lady looked so like me that it was like seeing myself in fancy dress! And—and the gentleman was the very image of . . ."

"Yes?" Charlotte prompted curiously.

"He was a perfect likeness of Marcus Fitzpaine."

Charlotte's face was a study, then she laughed again. "I think you have sampled too much punch."

"I'm far from being in my cups."

"A little fresh air on the terrace is in order, I think. Ghosts indeed. Whatever next?" The footman returned with the towel, and as Henrietta mopped the splashes of champagne on her skirt, Charlotte instructed him to bring two warm cloaks. As he hurried away again, she eyed Henrietta. "I must say, for someone who has just claimed to see ghosts, you do not seem all that rattled; indeed *I* am more rattled than you, and I didn't see anything."

"Perhaps it's because as a child I saw so many phantoms of one sort or another."

"You did?"

Henrietta nodded. "Yes, but I quickly discovered that if I said anything I could only expect censure, if not downright punishment, so I learned to keep quiet on the subject." She folded the towel slowly. "I confess I thought it was simply a childhood thing, for until tonight I hadn't seen anything since school."

Her matter-of-fact attitude was bewildering to Charlotte, who suddenly realized there was a side of her oldest friend which she had never dreamed existed. She gave an uncomfortable laugh and looked away. For Henrietta, it was a horridly familiar reaction, and she wished she'd had the presence of mind not to respond at all when she'd seen the wraiths. It was too late now, however, so the best she could do was brush the incident aside. "Oh, well, perhaps I *was* a little liberal with the punch, so maybe some fresh air is advisable," she said lightly, although the terrace was precisely where she believed the apparitions to have gone.

That was indeed where the startled ghosts were now to be found. Lanterns cast a soft light over everything, and a fine layer of snow had settled, but for the moment only a few flakes drifted on the motionless air. It was incredibly cold, but they felt nothing as they recovered from the shock of having been seen. Jane glanced back at the wall through which they'd emerged. "That was quite dreadful. I thought we would always be invisible and able to do as we pleased without detection, but she saw and heard us quite clearly!"

"Well, since there *are* truly psychic people, I suppose it was always on the cards that one day something like this would happen."

Jane glanced heavenward. "And since we haven't been immediately returned to limbo until the next suitable winter, I can only presume we haven't fallen foul of the rules," she said.

"I should hope not. After all, it wasn't our fault Henrietta saw us," Kit replied.

Jane sighed. "This makes things very difficult if she is to be one of our lovers, but in the absence of anyone else—"

"It isn't beyond our capabilities to keep out of sight," Kit reminded her. "There is always a convenient wall or cupboard."

"I suppose so." Jane sighed. She became aware of the gentle splash of the waves at the foot of the cliffs. It was a sound that made her put a nervous hand to her throat. "Oh, I do hate the sea, for I cannot forget the Goodwins. . . ."

"Beloved, we are on terra firma now," Kit said reassuringly.

"I know, but I just can't help it."

He kissed her forehead tenderly, and for a moment she pressed lovingly to him, but then she drew back sharply as the sound of a bark carried from the open doorway into the cloisters. "Rowley!" she cried, and turned, expecting to see the spaniel bounding toward her, but he didn't come. "Rowley?" she called. Another bark was the only response.

Kit put a gentle hand on her arm. "Wait here, and I'll go find him."

He strode swiftly across the terrace, leaving no footprints in the thin carpet of snow. The cloisters enclosed a grassy quadrangle which was brightly illuminated by variegated lanterns, but in spite of the light, he couldn't at first see Rowley anywhere. Then he espied the spaniel cowering in a nook of the vaulted ceiling. "Come down, you tiresome cur!" Kit ordered.

Rowley made no move. He'd come face-to-face with a cat, and nothing was going to make him come down. He remembered only too well that cats had sharp claws, and it didn't occur to him that now he was a ghost he would be immune to such things.

Kit heard Henrietta and Charlotte approaching as they left the ball, and he looked urgently at the spaniel. "Rowley, if you don't get down from there this instant, so help me I'll use my sword, and I won't be responsible for where I jab it!"

Seeing the grim determination in Kit's eyes, the little dog leaped down and dashed out onto the terrace. Kit followed at the double, and as Jane scooped her pet into her arms, they fled toward the flight of stone steps that led down to the open cliff top. They were out of sight as Henrietta and Charlotte emerged from the cloisters.

Charlotte immediately stopped when she realized it had been snowing. "Well," she declared, "the local weather sages have all declared the temperature far too *low* for snow, yet here it is!"

"Since we're only wearing satin slippers, perhaps we should go back inside?" Henrietta suggested, glancing around for any sign of the ghosts, but seeing nothing.

"We'll just go to the balustrade and then come back. Come along." Charlotte caught her hand and hurried her out into the night.

Chapter Four

Away from the hothouse temperature of the ballroom, the cold was so intense that as Henrietta and Charlotte crossed the east-facing terrace, they both immediately raised their hoods and pulled their cloaks closer. The lanterned balustrade was right at the edge of the sheer cliff, and the lights of Mulborough shone about a quarter of a mile away to the south. Beyond the little town, which stood where the river Mill spilled into the sea from its steep tree-choked valley, there was another headland, upon which was built St. Tydfa's church. There was no breeze, and the clouds obscured the moon, so the bay was very still and dark. The only sounds were the washing of the waves far below and the music drifting faintly from the ballroom.

Charlotte shivered. "It isn't often that everything is this quiet up here. In fact it was the very opposite one day early last month."

"What do you mean?"

"A notorious French privateer called the *Légère* had the audacity to try to enter Mulborough harbor in broad daylight. All the able-bodied men had gone out with the fishing fleet, so can you imagine the consternation in the town when a black-masted vessel was seen approaching? Only the French paint their masts black, and of all the privateers, the *Légère* is the most feared! She carries so much spar and sail that to see her in full cry is to wonder she does not take to the air. Her captain is rumored to be young and handsome, but he is also completely ruthless, and stories abound that he gives no quarter, not even to women. Anyway, Russell had the presence of mind to order the firing of our poor little cannons." Charlotte pointed along the terrace to the two cannons which had always stood there. "The *Légère* made off, and afterward it was learned that several local pilots had been approached and offered large bribes if they would divulge the new location of the channel."

Peeping onto the terrace, the watching ghosts had heard every word. Mention of a French privateer renewed the echoes of their fate upon the Goodwins, and Jane shrank a little closer to Kit. He slipped a comforting arm around her, and for once Rowley did not snap at him.

"New location of the channel?" Henrietta looked inquiringly at Charlotte, who nodded.

"Yes, it changed last autumn after a particularly savage storm. The *Légère* is a large, deep-drafted vessel, and even with exact knowledge could only negotiate the approach with a foot or so to spare. But there isn't another landing place anywhere along this part of the coast, so she had no choice if she wanted to put men ashore."

Kit's hand crept to the hilt of his sword and his knuckles gleamed white with the force of his anger. "Damned Frenchies!" he said darkly, and Rowley growled, for all the world as if sharing the sentiment.

Henrietta was puzzled about the whole incident. "I can't understand why this is the first I've heard of this."

"We didn't want to alarm our guests, so the servants were instructed not to mention it."

Henrietta detected something odd about the whole business. "Charlotte, I've already confided in you tonight, so now it's your turn. What is the real reason nothing has been said?"

"Well . . . Oh, I suppose it's all right to tell you, but this isn't really my secret; rather is it a national secret, so you must promise not to breathe a single word to anyone else."

Henrietta stared. "A *national* secret?" she repeated.

"Yes, and it has to do with Russell's Treasury connections. It was deemed wise to split the nation's gold into small lots and take it to various hiding places throughout the land, so it couldn't all fall into enemy hands at once. Some of it is here at Mulborough."

Henrietta's eyes widened. "Actually in the abbey?" Her interest was now so thoroughly aroused that she forgot the cold.

"No, in the old icehouse in the woods."

Henrietta blinked. "The *icehouse*? But it's in an advanced state of dilapidation!"

"That's why Russell thought it perfect. All seemed well, and we were confident the gold's presence somewhere near Mulborough was unknown to anyone, but whispers seem to be circulating. Amabel overheard something in the town and asked Russell about it, but he said it was just rumor. Now we have to conclude that somehow the *Légère* has probably gotten wind of it too. What other reason could there be for her to take such a risk?"

"Perhaps it would be prudent to move the gold away from Mulborough," Henrietta suggested.

"Russell has already sent word to London to that effect. We're still awaiting a reply. Oh, Henrietta, I wish it was all over and done with, because something else occurred on Christmas Eve."

"What happened?" Henrietta was mystified, for she'd slept very well that night, and knew nothing.

"It was a very cloudy night, if you remember, and at two in the morning Dr. Hartley was returning from a call at a farm just inland on the moor. He came right past the abbey and saw a signal from a vessel out in the bay. There was an answering signal from St. Tydfa's. It couldn't have been smugglers, because there aren't any at Mulborough now, and anyway he knows enough to realize the signals weren't from local vessels. He felt certain it was to do with the *Légère*, although by the time he reached the town to raise the alarm, the signals had stopped."

Henrietta was dismayed. "Are you saying someone in Mulborough is helping the *Légère*?"

"It seems so."

"One of the pilots?"

"They can all account for themselves. We have no idea who

it was." Charlotte managed a smile. "Maybe it was the Mul-borough bogle," she added lightly.

The eavesdropping ghosts exchanged startled glances. Bogles were Old Nick's creatures—nasty red-faced goblins whose sole purpose was to cause trouble. They were only about twelve inches high and possessed sharp teeth they delighted in using at every opportunity.

Henrietta gave a short laugh. "The Mulborough *bogle*? What on earth is that?"

"Supposedly they are wicked imps who torment mankind, and Mulborough churchyard apparently boasts one. They are said to be particularly active on Christmas Eve, which is why no one from the town would go up to investigate. You see, the doctor wasn't alone in observing the lights, but superstition had the upper hand, and everyone stayed indoors."

Henrietta smiled "I fancy an only too flesh-and-blood hand was sending those signals."

"Russell and I think the same. Distasteful as it is, we have to face the fact that someone in the neighborhood is either a French sympathizer or is simply prepared to help in return for payment." Charlotte sighed. "It's all so frustrating, because Uncle Joseph almost captured the *Légère* when he was in the Caribbean two years ago. Would that he had succeeded! I re-ceived a letter just before Christmas. He's in the Mediterranean now, in command of a ship of the line." Charlotte's voice glowed with pride, for Rear Admiral Sir Joseph Harman was a brilliant naval officer.

Suddenly Henrietta heard a faint rhythmic sound from some-where out on the water. For a moment she couldn't think what it was, but then Charlotte heard too. "Isn't that the sound of oars?" she gasped.

The two women glanced uneasily at each other, then gazed out at the bay again. Gradually they perceived a dark shape about a hundred yards off the harbor mouth. A two-masted sloop was being hauled in by two gigs, each crewed by about half a dozen men.

Kit began to draw his sword in readiness. "Dammee, if I'm

about to let Johnny Frog set foot on English soil!" he declared heroically.

Jane put a hand on his sleeve. "I think you may put your sword away. If the *Légère* had to risk daylight because of the channel, she's hardly likely to come in the dark!"

Charlotte's grip on Henrietta's arm began to relax. "She's much smaller than the *Légère*, and by her white masts I'd say she's British."

Suddenly there was a burst of light as a rocket soared high into the sky. It was followed by another and another, brilliant flashes of red, orange, crimson, and blue that illuminated the hitherto inky night. Charlotte laughed incredulously. "Fireworks! We are being treated to a display of New Year *fireworks*!" More rockets flew skyward, and the ballroom emptied as the guests poured onto the terrace to see what was happening.

The vessel was inched into the safety of the encircling sea walls, and all the time there were fireworks. Girandoles glittered, Chinese fire danced, tourbillions whirled, and pretty golden sparks cascaded like a molten cataract into the water. In the scintillating light, the sloop was revealed as an elegant craft that boasted sumptuous gilding and polished brassware. Also visible was the proud Union Jack on her mainmast.

On the terrace, there were exclamations of delight and ripples of applause as everyone pushed forward to get the best view possible. Henrietta was forced against the balustrade, and her heart began to pound as she glanced over the black precipice. The lapping of the waves far below seemed suddenly louder, and her senses swam unpleasantly as she felt a strange urge to throw herself over the edge.

If she had but known it, the urge was of Old Nick's doing. Hell's dark master was unable to resist the opportunity to destroy the ghosts' plan, but as he concentrated still more, meaning to turn the urge into a compulsion, Henrietta found the strength to pull away from the balustrade. As she did so, someone gave her a harsh shove. She cried out as she lost her balance, and her fan fell into the yawning darkness below, but then two people caught her, Charlotte from the right, and a second or so later Amabel Renchester from the left. They ushered her, trembling and frightened, out of the crush toward a stone bench set against the wall of the abbey.

Old Nick was livid. Henrietta had caught him off guard by displaying the wit to resist, so that she was in the act of stepping backward at the very moment his agent acted. If he'd refrained from interfering, his agent would probably have succeeded. What was more humiliating still was that hell's master had no one but himself to blame for the botch! Well, it was a salutary lesson; in the future he wouldn't intervene on impulse. His only consolation was that St. Peter's back had been turned at the relevant moment. Dark with anger and embarrassment, he retreated to his vile abode.

Sensing nothing of Old Nick's brief intrusion, Jane and Kit emerged hesitantly onto the terrace. They hadn't been able to see or hear what had happened because of the crowd of guests, but were aware that something terrible had almost befallen Henrietta. Jane was particularly concerned; after all, Henrietta was her blood relation, as well as her double! They kept out of sight but within earshot as Henrietta was made to sit down on the bench.

Charlotte sat next to her, with a reassuring arm around her shoulders, and Amabel crouched in front. The widowed Mrs. Renchester was one of the few guests who'd taken the precaution of putting on a warm cloak before venturing out into the cold night, and her hood had been raised, but now it fell back to reveal her heart-shaped face. She was lovely, with rich brown hair and wide green eyes that were large with disquiet. "Oh, Henrietta, are you all right? I saw you suddenly lurch forward! Whatever happened?"

From the moment she spoke, Jane became conscious of a deep unease about her. What had Charlotte said of her earlier? A whiff of sulfur? Yes, that was the perfect phrase for Amabel Renchester, thought the ghost.

Henrietta closed her eyes as her senses reeled again. "Someone pushed into me. It was such a jolt I almost thought it was deliberate. It couldn't have been, of course, but for a moment I was very frightened indeed."

"I'm sure I would have been as well." Amabel squeezed her left hand, then looked down as she felt the heavy betrothal ring. "Poor Lord Sutherton would be most distressed if he knew how in the wars you've been today."

Charlotte didn't approve of her words. "Amabel, Henrietta has almost fallen to her death twice today, on both occasions over high cliffs, so I hardly think *in the wars* is an appropriate phrase, do you?" she said coolly.

Jane's disquiet about Amabel had increased by the second. There was something about her that sent a cold shiver down the ghost's spine. Malice was veiled behind her lovely eyes, and it was directed toward Henrietta.

Amabel released Henrietta's hand. "I—I think I'll go back inside, it's rather too cold for me out here," she said, as she rose to her feet. Her cloak parted slightly so that the spangles on her jonquil satin gown glimmered as another cluster of rockets soared dazzlingly overhead. Her heavy peridot earrings flashed in the moving light. She gave a rather embarrassed smile, then gathered up her cloak to hurry back through the cloisters.

Henrietta's accusing eyes swung to Charlotte. "That wasn't very nice."

"She doesn't make me feel nice."

"Even so—"

"Henrietta, if you wish us to quarrel after all, then do pray continue in your role as defense counsel for Amabel Renchester."

Henrietta said nothing more, and after a moment got up to return to the balustrade. She chose a quiet spot close to one of Russell's cannons, and Charlotte joined her. Lanterns and smoking torches now bobbed along the town quay, and shouts carried audibly on the still night air as the men of Mulborough lit beacon bonfires on the harbor walls. The sloop dropped anchor and was suddenly revealed more clearly by a particularly spectacular burst of fireworks. Charlotte immediately exhaled slowly. "Oh dear, I'm afraid it's the *Avalon*. You're going to have to face Marcus Fitzpaine after all, Henrietta."

Dismayed, Henrietta gazed down at the beautiful sloop.

Yachting was very much the thing in the highest social circles, but few gentlemen possessed vessels of such size and luxury.

Jane and Kit were now hiding behind the cannon, and Jane was suddenly alert. The new vessel belonged to the dastardly Marquess of Rothwell, who had pursued Henrietta in order to win a wager? The ghost's lips pursed pensively. Henrietta had also described Kit as a perfect likeness of the marquess, and Jane was sure that anyone who resembled Kit could not *possibly* be bad! Sensible Charlotte believed Marcus Fitzpaine incapable of ignominy. What if she was right, and the absent Lord Sutherton had lied in order to win Henrietta—or rather, her fortune—for himself? Jane's eyes began to gleam schemingly. "Kit, I do believe our bridegroom may be at hand."

Kit was startled. "The *marquess*? Oh, but surely—"

"Come on, let us visit the harbor and see if he comes ashore. We'll soon be able to make up our minds." Without further ado, and keeping well out of sight of the two young women by the cannon, the ghosts hastened through the gathering of guests and then down the steps to the exposed, grassy cliff top toward the wooded valley where the icehouse stood crumbling among the winter trees.

Behind them on the terrace, Charlotte's husband hurried to where she still stood with Henrietta. He was a generation older than his wife, and of medium height, with a figure that had thickened only a little with the passage of years. His graying hair receded at the temples, and he had gentle brown eyes that never failed to soften with adoration whenever he gazed at his young wife. Like the other gentlemen present, he was dressed in a black evening coat and white breeches. "It's Marcus!" he cried delightedly, then remembered his wife's delicate condition. "My dearest, you shouldn't be out in the cold—" he began.

Charlotte interrupted. "Russell, I'm perfectly all right."

"Yes, but you're only in your satin slippers!"

"I promise to go in right away. Now, look to your duties. Shouldn't you be going down to the quay to meet Marcus?"

"Eh? Oh, yes, I suppose I should. I'll ride and take a second mount with me. I do hope he intends to stay, for he is excellent company."

Chapter Five

It was snowing heavily once more as the ghosts descended Mulborough's steep, winding streets toward the quay, which had changed little since medieval times. They found almost the entire population gathered at the waterside to watch the fireworks from the *Avalon*, whose Union Jack had swiftly allayed any initial fears as to her identity and purpose. The snow obscured a great deal of the show, but enough could be seen for there to be cries of delight, especially from those children fortunate enough to be allowed to leave their beds. Eyes shone with excitement and breath stood out in frozen clouds as the townsfolk enjoyed the unexpected entertainment, but at last the final rocket burst colorfully overhead. Darkness descended, except for a few lanterns and torches, and the dimly visible beacon fires at the harbor mouth.

Most of the crowd began to disperse to their warm homes, but some remained to see if anyone grand came ashore. From the glimpses of gilded paintwork, they did not doubt that the sloop was a very exclusive private yacht, and some even wondered if the Prince Regent himself had arrived in Mulborough in the middle of the night. There were sounds from the sloop, voices, and then once again the rhythmic rumble and splash of oars. Gradually the dim glow of a small lantern appeared through the snow, drawing closer and closer until the ghosts saw it was fixed to the prow of one of the gigs that had hauled the *Avalon* into the harbor. Carrying torches, men from the town hastened down some stone steps set against the quay, and one of them challenged the occupants of the boat to identify themselves. "Who comes ashore?"

A tall cloaked man in the stern of the gig rose to his feet. "I am the Marquess of Rothwell, and a loyal Englishman! Will Mulborough deny me hospitality?"

"You are most welcome, my lord!"

The oars were shipped as the gig came alongside, and Marcus Fitzpaine stepped lightly ashore. Snowflakes swirled around him, clinging to his hat and cloak, but his face remained in shadow in spite of the torches.

For Jane, the closeness of the water was daunting, especially since the steps were the very ones down which she and Kit had hurried to board the *Wessex*, but she bravely pushed Rowley into Kit's unwilling arms, then descended to take a much closer look at the marquess. The first thing of which she approved was his height, for that was what had first drawn her attention to Kit. His breath was silver in the uncertain light as he turned to converse briefly with the pigtailed sailors in the gig, but then he removed his top hat to push his hair back from his face, and she stared in astonishment, for Henrietta was right, he was Kit to a T!

Oh, and how deliciously attractive this twin was, the phantom thought as she inspected him from every angle. His features were strong, yet possessed that faint air of vulnerability that still affected her in Kit. His smiles could break hearts, she thought, and his memorable blue eyes were capable of the sort of subtle warmth that could caress a woman with a glance. He was half Viking, half romantic, and the ghost could see only too well why Henrietta Courtenay had been tempted from the straight and narrow. Marcus Fitzpaine exuded an exhilarating air of danger and forbidden excitement, but was he a heartless rogue? Jane wasn't sure. Kit she could read chapter and verse, but there was part of this man that was closed to her, hidden pages in a totally absorbing volume.

One of the Mulborough men handed him a torch, then they withdrew up the steps and dispersed to their homes. The rowing boat shoved off to return to the *Avalon*, and at the same moment there came the clatter of hoofbeats on the quay as Russell arrived. He tethered his horses to an iron hoop set into the wall of the custom house, then hastened to the steps. He grinned as he saw Marcus at the bottom with the torch. "How now, sir, is it not a little ostentatious to arrive in such a blaze of lights!"

Marcus turned with a grin and the flicker of the flame leaped over his face. "One should always sing for one's supper!"

"And one should usually take the precaution of requesting a pilot. The channel has changed, you know." Russell's long greatcoat brushed the snowy steps as he came down to join him.

"The channel can move wherever it please. At high tide the *Avalon*'s shallow draft will always see her safely into this particular harbor."

Russell removed his glove to shake Marcus warmly by the hand. "It's good to see you, my friend, but why arrive at such an hour?"

"Tides and French privateers allow no quarter."

For Jane his words conjured the groan of breaking timbers, then the thunderous roar of the incoming tide as it sped hungrily across sands that were gray in the fading light of dusk . . .

Russell looked intently at Marcus. "French privateer? The *Légère*, perchance?"

"The amount of sail she carried would suggest so."

"Where was she?"

"Near Hurdle Point an hour before dusk yesterday. She had the weather gauge, and might possibly have overhauled us if we hadn't taken refuge in water too shallow for her." Marcus searched Russell's face in the uncertain light of the torch. "Surely you haven't had dealings with the *Légère*? This must be one of the safest harbors on the entire east coast!"

Russell related what had happened, and when he'd finished, Marcus nodded. "Her captain is audacious, I'll grant him that. I was close enough to see his damned face when I crossed his path in the Caribbean about two years ago. He hoisted a red flag without a second thought, and if Charlotte's uncle hadn't happened along in the nick of time, well, I wouldn't be here to speak of it. Anyway, at the moment the *Légère* is many miles away to the north, so the good people of Mulborough can certainly rest easy in their beds tonight." Marcus's eyes rested shrewdly upon the older man. "What haven't you told me?" he asked.

Russell briefly related the same facts that Charlotte had earlier told Henrietta, and finished. "I've ridden up to St. Tydfa's several times since Christmas Eve, but have seen nothing, not even the Mulborough bogle."

Marcus raised an eyebrow. "Treasury gold, bogles, *and* French spies sending signals? I was expecting my sojourn at Mulborough Abbey to be quiet!" Suddenly he turned sharply toward Jane, as if he knew she was there, but to her relief he clearly saw nothing.

"What is it?" Russell asked uneasily.

"I'm not really sure, I just had the strangest feeling someone was behind me."

"Imagination, dear boy." Russell gave a nervous laugh.

"In abundance, it would seem." Marcus looked at him again. "How is Charlotte taking all this?"

"Stoically."

"I trust she's blossoming well?"

Russell nodded. "She's never looked lovelier, and is becoming impatient for the great day to come. I was about to write to you, actually, for it would please me greatly if you would be a godparent."

Marcus returned the grin. "I'll be honored."

"I trust I'll one day soon be able to return the compliment. By the way, what exactly does bring you here? I was under the impression you were staying on with your Scottish relatives until March."

"I just felt like making my way home to Kent."

Jane could tell this wasn't the truth, and wondered what his real reason could be.

"Surely Bramnells is closed for the winter?" Russell replied, thinking of Marcus's vast ancestral estate high on the cliffs near the town of Deal.

"Closed, but not unaired."

"I trust that doesn't mean your stay with us is only going to be an overnight affair?"

"I thought a week or so, if that's all right?"

"You know it is." Russell hesitated. "Actually, there's one thing you should know. Henrietta Courtenay is here."

"Really?"

To Jane's disappointment, Marcus seemed unmoved. She wanted a reaction, any reaction, just to show he wasn't indifferent.

Russell cleared his throat. "You're bound to see a great deal of her. Everyone else leaves in the morning, but she's staying on until sometime in February, when she has to be in London for her cousin's wedding."

"I'll survive."

"Yes, but will she?"

"That is a question only the future Lady Sutherton can answer, but I doubt my presence will impinge greatly upon her, er, sensitivity."

Russell was curious. "May I be inquisitive?"

"Would it make any difference if I said no?"

"Not really," Russell admitted disarmingly. "It's just that I can't help wondering what happened between you two. I mean, I know this damned foolish family feud has been going for centuries, but even so—"

"Only one century," Marcus corrected him.

"Very well, one century."

"There's nothing between myself and Henrietta Courtenay; indeed I hardly know her."

Jane's hopes were dashed. Had Marcus affected to stifle a yawn, he could not have been more lukewarm.

Russell persisted. "All I know is that Henrietta's opinion of you is apparently most detrimental, not that she has ever elaborated on anything, of course."

"Oh, of course," Marcus murmured dryly.

"Look, Marcus, of all the Courtenays, she is the one I would least expect to form adverse opinions without provocation."

"The implication being that I must have done something heinous?"

Russell was in a cleft stick. "I, er, didn't quite mean that—"

"No? My dear Russell, you may consider her to be eligible

for sanctity, but I certainly do not. There endeth the lesson."
Marcus looked him square in the eyes.

Russell felt a little uncomfortable. "As you wish, but . . ."

"Yes?"

"I would be grateful if you'd forget the damned feud for a
while, and at least be civil to her. Charlotte is already distressed
by all the mishaps that have befallen her since arriving here,
and . . ."

"Mishaps?"

"Yes. Henrietta herself tries to make light of it, but given
Charlotte's present condition, I'm anxious that she should
relax."

"You may rest assured that Charlotte will not suffer any distress because of me." Marcus smiled a little, and then changed
the subject. "Who else is here?"

Russell reeled off a list of names and added at the end, "Oh,
and Amabel Renchester, although I'm not aware if you know
her."

"Oh, yes, we're, er, acquainted. I first met her just before she
and Renchester left for the Peninsula. I'm surprised she's here.
Don't tell me she and Charlotte have settled their differences
after all this time?"

Russell sighed. "Well, the truth is that Charlotte and Amabel
haven't settled anything; indeed we didn't invite her, Henrietta
decided to bring her."

"How very thoughtful." Marcus shivered. "I trust this cold
relents soon, for I vow it's cold enough to freeze the very sea."
A thought struck him. "Has this harbor ever frozen?"

"It has been known, although not in my lifetime. Don't fret,
the *Avalon* is in no danger."

"Good, but right now I'm more concerned about my own
precious hide. Does the hospitality of Mulborough Abbey
await, or are we to stand here all night?"

"You know the abbey is always at your disposal, but what of
your luggage? There is a ball in progress, and—"

"And I am suitably garbed," Marcus interrupted, flicking his
cloak aside to reveal superb evening clothes beneath. "The rest
will be brought ashore in a while."

Russell grinned. "You never fail to amaze me, Marcus. Come on, then." They ascended the steps and crossed the deserted quay to the customs house, where Marcus snuffed the torch against the wall as Russell untethered the waiting horses.

As the two men rode off into the snow, Kit looked at Jane, who had joined him at the top of the steps. "Well? Does my Fitzpaine descendant pass muster as far as you're concerned?"

"I fear not."

Kit was surprised. "But you were quite set on it when we left the abbey."

"The Marquess of Rothwell is a book with some disturbingly secret pages," she replied, taking Rowley from him.

"He and Henrietta appear to offer our only hope this time," he reminded her.

"I know, but he seems completely uninterested in her. I confess I think they are poles apart, and will remain so."

"Poles apart? Dearest, where is your usually infallible perception? Even I could see that he was as sensitive to every mention of her as she was to him! Besides, he is my very twin, even to our shared liking for sailing, so at heart he *must* be a good fellow. There's much to do, I grant you, but I think he and Henrietta Courtenay have definite possibilities."

New hope stirred through Jane. "Oh, Kit, do you really think so?"

"Of course." Kit put an arm around her and pulled her close to kiss her on the lips. At the same time, unseen by Jane, he clamped his other hand firmly around Rowley's muzzle.

Chapter Six

Meanwhile at the abbey, the ball had resumed. A country dance was in progress, and Charlotte and Henrietta stood at the edge of the floor. Henrietta would have preferred to retire to her room now that Marcus was in the offing, but Charlotte was determined that she should remain.

"You have to face him sooner or later, and it might as well be sooner," she declared firmly. "Please steel yourself, because once the first moment is over, the rest will be easier."

"Charlotte, you've never behaved as shockingly as I did, so how can you possibly know? Marcus will no doubt find it amusing to whisper the tale to his relatives, and before long it will be all around the ball!" Henrietta felt sick with trepidation.

"Don't be silly. If he intended to spread the tale, it would have been all over London by the time your parents returned from looking after your aunt. He didn't say a word, did he?"

"Well, not that I know of, but—"

"No buts. He didn't say anything, and that's the end of it."

Henrietta fell silent, and when the country dance came to an end, she was claimed by her uncle, Thomas Courtenay—he of the punch bowl—for the polonaise that followed. If she hoped this would prove a distraction from Marcus Fitzpaine, she was disappointed, for her uncle knew who was responsible for the fireworks. "Another damned Fitzpaine, eh?" he declared as he and his niece came together in the dance.

"It—it would seem so, Uncle Courtenay."

"Damned scoundrels, all of them."

"Yes, Uncle Courtenay."

"Are you acquainted with him?"

She hesitated, then fibbed. "No, Uncle."

"See it remains so."

"I can hardly embarrass Charlotte and Russell by refusing to be introduced," she pointed out.

"Hmph," he grunted disparagingly.

It was as the polonaise came to an end that Russell and Marcus entered the ballroom. Marcus was recognized immediately, and there was rapturous applause, for fireworks were a rare and costly diversion, and everyone appreciated the magnificent display given from the decks of the *Avalon*. The orchestra began to play the minuet from Handel's "Music for the Royal Fireworks," and sets began to quickly form, so that soon the floor was a crush of dancers.

Charlotte hastened to greet her new guest. "Marcus! Oh, Marcus, how good it is to see you again!" she cried, hugging him as best she could now that her shape was so vastly changed.

He smiled and kissed her warmly on the cheek. "Charlotte, my dearest, you are positively aglow! Approaching motherhood suits you!"

"Why, thank you, sir." Charlotte glanced surreptitiously around, hoping to spot Henrietta so that a meeting could be engineered without further ado, but there was no sign of her.

Marcus spoke again. "I've presumed somewhat upon your hospitality, but trust you will endure me for a week or so?"

"You have no need to ask, for Mulborough's doors are always open to you."

He looked at the crowded floor. "Charlotte, will you favor me with this dance?" he asked.

She gave a rueful smile. "I trust you will not be offended if I decline, but I've danced sufficiently tonight to put my ankles in imminent danger of swelling. Such disagreeable things, swollen ankles. Very unfeminine."

Marcus laughed. "Your ankles would remain delightful no matter how swollen they became."

"Your charm never ceases to amaze me, sir. How is it that you have yet to race home in the marriage stakes?"

"My heart has to be engaged, Charlotte, and what other woman is there now you have been claimed?"

"*More* charm? La, sir, my head and ankles are likely to swell simultaneously!"

Marcus spent the next few minutes in conversation with her, and after that with various of his relatives, but then Amabel caught his eye as she quickly threaded through the crush at the edge of the ballroom. He excused himself from his relatives and followed her. Jane and Kit, who had only just returned from Mulborough, followed as well, being careful all the while to look out for Henrietta.

Marcus caught up with Amabel by the archway into the cloisters. "Well, if it isn't Mrs. Renchester. What brings you to Mulborough? I wonder."

She met his eyes, then walked out into the cold of the cloisters, where she turned and waited to face him. He followed, and closed the door behind him, but Jane and Kit managed to slip through in time with Rowley. The noise of the ball immediately became muffled, and the quiet of the cloisters seemed to press close. The glow from the lanterns in the quadrangle showed Amabel quite clearly. As the ghosts came into close proximity with her, Jane was again conscious of the unpleasant atmosphere surrounding her. Charlotte's whiff of sulfur.

Amabel's voice echoed around the stonework. "Well, Lord Rothwell, what an agreeable surprise."

"Is it? I confess I'm astonished you should feel that way. I'm equally surprised you should leave London and all its, er, attractions."

"No matter what you may think, I'm here to make my peace with Charlotte."

"There's more than just snow flying through the air at the moment. In fact I distinctly hear grunting," he remarked dryly.

"You misjudge me, Marcus."

Jane's ears sharpened. Marcus? They were on first-name terms?

Marcus gave a short laugh. "Misjudge you? I think not, Amabel, for how is it possible to misjudge a widow who flaunted bright colors almost the day after her husband's funeral?"

"Would you have me wear black for the passing of a traitor?"

"If traitor he was."

"It was proven."

"So it's said."

Amabel raised her chin. "And what brings you here to Mulborough, sirrah? The society of your dear friends, Lord and Lady Mulborough? Or is it perhaps because of Henrietta Courtenay?"

"Why should my actions have anything to do with her?"

"Because you had a liaison with her, and maybe hope it will resume."

He became very still. "How did you know that?"

"She told me in London just after it happened."

Jane and Kit exchanged glances, for Henrietta insisted to Charlotte that she had never mentioned it to anyone.

Marcus studied Amabel in the lantern light. "Well, Sutherton's timely arrival on the scene is now fully explained. He learned through you."

"Sutherton learned nothing from me; indeed I hardly know him."

"Yet again the sound of grunting rends the night," he replied dryly.

She shrugged. "Believe what you will, I know I'm telling the truth."

"You and the truth don't even share a common language," he answered.

Her eyes flickered. "All I'm concerned about now is that it is definitely over between you and Henrietta."

"Of what possible interest could that be to you?"

"Simply that it means there is hope for me."

He was startled. "Hope?"

"Charlotte is not the only one with whom I wish to make my peace, sir, and your presence here is an opportunity I do not intend to squander," she said softly, stepping closer and putting a soft hand to his cheek.

Jane looked daggers at her, for this wasn't what was wanted at all! Marcus and *Amabel*? Oh, dear me, no!

Amabel smiled, and her rose perfume filled the air as she drew a seductive fingertip across Marcus's lips. "Do you remember what pleasure we once shared?"

Jane's dismay intensified. They'd been lovers in the past? This became worse by the moment!

"How well you play the tempress, Amabel," Marcus said softly.

"Well enough to succeed with you again?" she inquired, reaching up suddenly to link her arms around his neck. She molded her body to his, then she smiled into his eyes. "Oh, sir, how very impressive a figure you have, but then I knew that already, did I not?"

"I do not deny our past encounters, but the key word is past. I cannot gainsay that you are a very beautiful woman, Amabel, but beauty should be more than skin deep, and with you it is most certainly on the surface only. You showed yourself to be spiteful, grasping, callous, and hard. Shall I go on?"

She flushed a little. "Such compliments. Will you also accuse me of lacking passion?"

"If I did, I would be lying."

"Yes, you would." She searched his face and then smiled. "You haven't ceased to desire me, Marcus, I can see it in your eyes. What if I were to say that it is our future encounters that interest me now?" she whispered, putting her lips to his.

For a long moment he resisted, but then his arms moved around her and as he returned the kiss, Jane's chagrin was complete. How could she and Kit hope to pit an innocent like Henrietta against such creature? The dejected wraith acidly surmised that Amabel Renchester was an experienced demimondaine who had probably graced more beds than Rowley had had sugared almonds!

Amabel moved familiarly against Marcus, and he could not help his body's response. She drew away enough to slide a hand over the front of his silk trousers. "Oh, yes," she breathed huskily, "I play the temptress well enough to succeed with you. I will come to you tonight, and you will not turn me away."

Then she left. Light and noise from the ballroom swept briefly over the cloisters before the door closed behind her. Marcus exhaled very slowly, for this was a development he could never have foreseen. Many a thing, but not this.

Kit ran a hot finger around his neckcloth. "God's teeth, that creature knows her business," he muttered, and was rebuked by a swift rap on the arm from Jane's closed fan.

"That's enough of that!" She gave him a furious look.

He cleared his throat apologetically. "Oh, be reasonable, my love, what red-blooded fellow could fail to respond?"

"That is the difference between male and female, sirrah. The male is not ruled by his head or his heart, just by his loins! You included!"

"But once I'd met you, beloved, I neither loved nor lay with any other woman," he reminded her.

"That had better be the case, sirrah, for if I discover you were ever unfaithful, I swear I will—"

"Chop off the relevant member? Yes, I believe you would, but I am safe in the knowledge that I have never betrayed you by so much as a single kiss."

Jane melted a little. "Oh, Kit . . ."

"I will remind you of my ardor at the first opportunity," he said softly, bending his head to kiss her lips. Rowley squirmed jealously, but again his muzzle was firmly held, this time by Jane.

Marcus rejoined the ball, but went through the door so quickly that the shades were caught unprepared, and found themselves shut out.

"Damn!" Kit exclaimed angrily, and gave Rowley a dire look. "Oh, if ever a cur was more trouble than it was worth, this one is!"

"It's not his fault!" Jane cried.

"Maybe not, but he's hampering us, I think you'll agree."

"I'll stay with Rowley. You go into the ball to see what's happening," Jane suggested.

"And will you trust me to correctly interpret what I see and hear?" Kit inquired acidly.

Jane hesitated.

"You see?" Kit irritably drew his sword slightly, then slammed it back into the scabbard.

Jane's eyes filled with sudden tears. "Oh, don't be angry, Kit."

"Look, beloved, surely that pest of a spaniel can be trusted to stay quietly out here on his own?"

Rowley was wily enough to know he was the cause of dissent, and so picked his moment to whine pathetically. It was the last straw for Kit, who snatched him from Jane's arms and placed him firmly on the floor. Then he pointed at the cloister ceiling. "Right, you odious fleabag, you get up there and you *stay* there."

Rowley looked mutinously at him.

Kit drew his sword. "Do as I say!"

Rowley's eyes widened, and without further ado he fled up a column to the ceiling, and retreated into a corner. Kit put his sword away, then eyed the dog. "If you move so much as an inch from where you are now, I swear I will spit you in a most painful way. Am I clear?" Then he offered Jane his arm. "Very well, my dear, let us sally forth and see what goes now."

Jane looked wistfully up at Rowley, but slid her hand over Kit's sleeve. "Very well, my love," she replied, and together they glided through the closed door into the ballroom.

Earlier, when Marcus had first arrived and the orchestra began to play Handel's fireworks music, Henrietta's faltering courage had failed completely. Seeing Charlotte glance around for her, she had withdrawn to the farthest end of the ballroom, rather than risk having to confront Marcus so quickly.

She took refuge in a corner in the small space between the wall and an extravagant arrangement of tall ferns, and from there watched as Marcus conversed first with Charlotte, then with his relatives. Suddenly the prospect of staying beneath the same roof as him was too much to bear. The abbey was simply not big enough! The best thing would be to leave tomorrow with Uncle Courtenay, but what would Charlotte say?

Distracted by her thoughts, Henrietta didn't notice anything else until Amabel, and then a minute or so later Marcus, emerged from the cloisters. The conclusion was there to be drawn, and a jealous pang caught Henrietta unawares as she was confronted by the harsh fact that the Marquess of Rothwell could still breach her defenses. George's kisses didn't turn her blood to fire in her veins as Marcus's had, nor did his caresses stir a desire so powerful that there was no thought of caution, only of ecstasy. Was Amabel now enjoying his embraces? A confusion of emotion engulfed her.

Marcus suddenly looked toward the corner where she was hiding. She released the ferns and drew back in dismay, but the shivering green fronds had revealed someone to be hiding behind them, and he began to walk toward her.

Jane and Kit emerged through the door and looked around for any sign of Marcus. They saw his tall, fair-haired figure heading for the fern-decked corner, and wondered what was of such interest. Reaching the greenery, he parted it and spoke abruptly. "Well, madam, we meet again."

The ghosts were startled to realize he was addressing Henrietta, and they hastily took up positions from where she could not observe them. Then they watched what happened next.

Henrietta looked at Marcus in dismay. "My—my lord?" she stammered, her face aflame with embarrassment.

His gaze swept appraisingly over her. "You're looking remarkably well," he observed, as if commenting upon an elderly aunt who was in better health than expected.

"Your compliments were ever hollow, my lord," she replied, managing to achieve a coolness that matched his, even though her pulse was racing unbearably just to be near him again.

His glance moved to her bandaged right wrist, and she felt it necessary to explain. "I fell while walking on the cliffs."

"Indeed? How very unfortunate." His tone suggested he wished she'd fallen right over the cliffs. Next he glanced at her ring. "So Sutherton and his duns can rest assured of the imminent sharing out of the Courtenay fortune."

The accuracy of the comment made her color still more. "That was uncalled for."

"On the contrary, I think it very pertinent." He caught her left hand suddenly and made a pretense of examining the ring. "A tasteless bauble; just what I would have expected of that cox-comb."

"Are you intending to stay at Mulborough, sir?" she asked, snatching her hand away.

"Why? Do you fear my close proximity?" he asked softly, looking deep into her eyes.

"No, sirrah, I merely shudder at the prospect of having to endure your continuing contempt and rudeness."

"If I am contemptuous and rude, madam, it is no more than you deserve."

Henrietta's breath caught in disbelief. "Than *I* deserve?"

"Naturally." With a cool nod, he turned and walked away.

Jane was so indignant that she almost rushed impulsively after him to hit him soundly on the head with her fan, but Kit put a finger to his lips and pointed warningly at Henrietta, who might hear or see them at any second.

Henrietta's heart pounded uncontrollably. The noise of the ballroom seemed suddenly to echo, and she felt so weak that she had to lean back against the wall. As she closed her eyes, the glint of candlelight on his fair hair remained with her, as did the ice in his frozen gaze, but beyond these there was a sweeter memory, that of stolen kisses, mirrored passion, and tender words . . .

Jane's eyes filled with tears too, for she felt Henrietta's pain as keenly as if it were her own. Shared blood carried shared emotions, and the phantom knew in those wretched seconds that Kit was right, Henrietta was in love with the Marquess of Rothwell. Pray God he was equally right about said marquess's feelings. If so, all that had to be done was show Marcus that Henrietta—not Amabel—was the one for him.

Chapter Seven

The ball was over and the first glint of dawn lightened the eastern sky as the local guests drove home through a white carpet a mere three inches deep. No more snow fell for the moment, and the air was so cold and brittle that it seemed almost to ring. The sea was the color of lead beneath the lowering clouds, and curls of smoke rose from the chimneys of Mulborough as the men prepared to go out on the morning tide. The *Avalon* lay at anchor in the harbor, her gilded paintwork glinting in the changing light. Mulborough Abbey fell silent as everyone, servants included, retired exhaustedly to their beds.

Russell and Marcus didn't feel quite ready to sleep, and so decided to play billiards for a while. It was at this point, with Henrietta already having gone to bed for the night, that Jane and Kit decided to retire for a while as well, for even ghosts need their rest. As they found an unoccupied bedchamber and settled down on the comfortable feather bed, Rowley went wandering around the abbey, leaving Kit to draw a more than compliant Jane into his arms.

Rowley's nighttime ambles had but one purpose—to find sugared almonds. Old habits die hard, and the spaniel had been such an incorrigible sweetmeat thief when alive, that he couldn't help going through the same motions now. His ghostly paws pattered along the deserted passageway toward the staircase, and then down to the ground floor, where a distant burst of male laughter caught his attention. He set off toward the sound.

The billiard table stood in the conservatory across the cloisters from the ballroom, and looked out onto the terrace, where the lanterns were now muted by the strange half light of snow and dawn. Inside, Russell bent at the green baize table to play the opening shot of their second game. As the ivory balls knocked pleasantly together, he leaned on his cue with a satisfied grin. "Your defeat is imminent, I fancy," he said to Marcus.

"Overconfidence ever was your failing," came the murmured reply as Marcus prepared to play.

Russell watched ball after ball slip obligingly into the pockets, and then he sighed. "I fancy Lady Luck is with you tonight," he said at last.

Marcus paused a moment. "To briefly change the subject, have you ever considered placing a boom across the mouth of the harbor?"

"A boom? Well, no . . ." Russell became thoughtful. "That's not a bad idea," he said then.

"Even the simplest device can play havoc with any unwanted visitor, and will certainly hamper them long enough for you to use your cannon here. It is simply opened to let any friend in."

Russell nodded. "I'll give it some thought."

As play resumed, Rowley ambled into the conservatory, sniffing here and there at various interesting scents. Slowly he made his way to the table, walked up one of the ornately carved legs, and then sat on the cushioned rim to see what the two men were doing. A red ball rolled gently down the table, and halted right in front of him. Concentrating a little more than was his custom, the ghostly spaniel patted it with his paw. The ball rolled a few inches.

Marcus's lips parted in astonishment. "Did I imagine that?"

"If you did, so did I," Russell replied. Then he shook his head dismissively. "It must have been a trick of the light. Play on."

But Rowley had warmed to the trick, and patted the ball again. Amazed, the two men watched its uneven progress along the cushion, then Marcus stepped forward to pick it up. Rowley scowled invisibly at him, and then jumped down from the table to wander off again on his briefly interrupted search for sugared almonds.

Marcus examined the ball closely. "I see nothing untoward.

It's just an ivory billiard ball," he declared at last, handing it to Russell.

Russell inspected it as well, and then replaced it on the green baize. "Perhaps we both had one brandy too many," he said at last.

"Speak for yourself. I've only had two!"

"Two very large ones," Russell reminded him. "Oh, let's continue our play. If it happens again, we'll call it a day and sleep it off."

"Agreed."

They played steadily for about a quarter of an hour, and then Russell asked Marcus if he had encountered Henrietta at the ball.

"Yes, I came face-to-face with the future Lady Sutherton. There was no bloodshed, so you may rest easy."

"I think it's a damned shame she's marrying that maggot Sutherton."

"Like cleaves to like."

Russell was taken aback. "I say, that's a little strong, isn't it?"

"No."

Russell put down his cue. "I think it's about time you came clean on this. What exactly happened between you two?"

Marcus hesitated and then placed his cue on the table as well. "I met her at a masked ball at Devonshire House last summer. I'd managed to ascertain who she was, but because she was a Courtenay I fear I introduced myself under a false name. Look, I really don't want to talk about it. Suffice it that the whole sorry business is over now."

"How much of a sorry business was it?"

"That is none of your business," Marcus replied with a disarming smile.

"I have no doubt she's confided in Charlotte," Russell suggested, hoping to prompt an explanation after all.

"If she has, you may be sure it won't be the truth. Henrietta Courtenay is not at all likely to confess how entirely without merit her conduct was. As far as I am concerned, she and Sutherton richly deserve each other. Now then, is it my turn?"

Russell yawned and stretched. "I have no idea. To be truthful, I'm tired at last."

As they left the billiard room, Henrietta was asleep in her room at the end of the second floor on the north wing. It wasn't the most sumptuous guest apartment in the abbey, but it was her favorite because it had a view inland over the formal gardens toward the high moors. Firelight danced gently over the pink silk walls and caught the shadows in the exposed stonework around the arched door. The hangings of the four-poster bed were silver brocade, fringed and tasseled in gold, and the scent of roses hung in the air from the opened potpourri in the hearth.

After the upset of Marcus's arrival, she hadn't expected to sleep at all, but her head had hardly touched the pillow before she was lost in troubled dreams filled with threats from Marcus that he would tell the world how loose her conduct had been in London. She tossed as she slept, but didn't hear the door softly open. A shadowy figure crept in. Cloaked and hooded, it moved stealthily to the dressing table, where Henrietta's jewelry box stood among the clutter of ribbon stands, brushes, combs, scent bottles, and pin bowls. The figure reached out to the box, then paused as Henrietta turned restlessly in the bed.

In the meantime Rowley's hunt for sugared almonds had led him to the passage to Henrietta's room. He ambled along the ceiling, saw the cloaked figure, and followed. Suspended from the ceiling close to the silver brocade bed, the spaniel cocked his head curiously to one side as he watched the intruder open Henrietta's jewelry box and remove her betrothal ring. Rowley knew something was very wrong, and gave a concerned whine, which the intruder didn't hear, but Henrietta certainly did. Her eyes flew open, and without realizing there was anyone else in the room, she looked directly up at the ghostly dog on the ceiling. She stared at him in the moving light from the fire. The King Charles spaniel she'd seen in the ballroom! Was he really a ghost? Or was she still asleep and dreaming?

The cloaked intruder turned to leave and Henrietta saw the stealthy movement. She sat up with a cry of alarm, and the figure froze momentarily before dashing from the room. Rowley followed in hot pursuit, barking at the top of his lungs. Seeing her open jewelry box, and fearing everything had been stolen,

Henrietta gave chase as well. Common sense had no place in her actions; she was intent only on apprehending the thief.

The night light in the passage swayed in the draft from the intruder's cloak as he turned the corner at the far end, toward the main staircase. Rowley's claws slithered on the ceiling and his barking rang loudly through the house, disturbing those guests who had psychic inclinations, but most of all alerting Jane and Kit to the fact that something was wrong. The ghosts left their bed and Kit hastily donned his sword as they rushed through the closed door into the passage, which was at the opposite end of the abbey.

Henrietta's thoughts were in confusion as she ran after the thief. Perhaps this was all a dream, and she was really still in her bed! But as she turned the corner, she knew it was no dream, for the intruder was standing there, his identity still concealed by his hooded cloak. She had no time to protect herself as he struck her on the side of the head with a candlestick. Pain flashed vividly through her eyes, and she felt herself falling to the cold stone floor. She heard the clatter of the candlestick as it was dropped nearby. The last thing to penetrate her fading consciousness was Rowley's hysterical barking from the ceiling.

Old Nick had happened to observe events, and was delighted, but as he began to rub his hands together gleefully, he realized Rowley's barking might bring timely help. He raised a hand to dash the spaniel into oblivion, but for once St. Peter was alert. A bolt of lightning flashed down from heaven, singeing Old Nick's fingers so badly that he gave a howl of pain and drew back down into his realm. He wished he'd remembered what happened when he'd interfered on the terrace. He really wasn't very successful when it came to acting on the spur of the moment, and the sooner he remembered that disagreeable fact, the better.

Rowley, who knew nothing, continued to bark for all he was worth.

Chapter Eight

The thief ran on toward the staircase landing, from where he could go up or down, or even take one of the three other passages that led off it. Rowley dashed in his wake. The spaniel was beside himself with fury and indignation, and redoubled his noise as at last he saw Jane and Kit hastening from the passage opposite.

Russell and Marcus were just approaching the staircase on the ground floor when Marcus halted in puzzlement. "Can you hear a dog barking?"

"A what?"

"A dog, a small one."

"There aren't any small dogs here," Russell reminded him.

"That's what I thought, yet I can definitely hear one. It's somewhere on the floor above."

As they both looked up the staircase, the cloaked figure fled across the landing, then disappeared again into the passage opposite. The two men were so startled that for a second or so they didn't react, but then Russell shouted and they both ran up the staircase. Rowley's almost hysterical barking was still audible to Marcus, and to the various guests whose sleep was disturbed by the noise. The intruder was running directly toward Jane and Kit, but saw nothing. Kit drew his sword and blocked the way, but, of course, the thief ran through him unhindered. Furious to be so helpless, Kit gave a shout of rage, and chased him.

Rowley had slithered to a halt on seeing Jane and Kit. Still barking, he scampered back the way he'd come, followed by

Jane, who realized he was trying to tell her something. She was horrified to find Henrietta lying unconscious. Rowley, who knew he'd done well, jumped down into his mistress's arms, his plumy tail wagging. Jane cuddled her beloved pet close as she cast distractedly around for a way to help Henrietta. Then, just as Russell and Marcus ran shouting on to the landing behind her, the specter saw the discarded candlestick lying nearby. Closing her eyes tightly, she concentrated hard upon making it move. It rocked to-and-fro, then rose abruptly into the air and dashed itself noisily against the flagged floor.

Marcus had begun to follow Russell after the cloaked figure, and because Rowley was quiet now, the clatter of the candlestick carried very clearly. He halted and looked back in puzzlement. What in God's name was going on tonight? Intruders, self-propelling billiard balls, invisible dogs, and now . . . Now what? He strained to see along the other passage, where the night light was very dim. He saw the candlestick and knew that was what he'd heard; then he made out something small and white just visible on the floor around the corner. A bandaged wrist! Henrietta!

Jane hovered anxiously nearby as he crouched concernedly by the motionless figure. "Oh, dear God," he breathed on seeing the bloodstain on Henrietta's forehead. Then he felt the pulse at her throat. She was still alive! He could see an open door farther along the passage, and guessed it must be her room, so he gathered her carefully into his arms to carry her there. Jane followed as he laid Henrietta on the bed. Then he dampened a handkerchief in the water jug on the washstand, and returned to examine the bloodstain more closely. By now the castle was in an uproar, but because the room was at the end of the wing, no one passed the open door. Jane leaned intently over Marcus as he gently wiped the blood from Henrietta's hair. He saw immediately that her loose hair had almost certainly saved her from much worse, possibly even fatal injury, and he recalled what Russell had said to him on the quay about a series of mishaps having befallen Henrietta. This was certainly no mishap, for she had been deliberately struck with the candlestick.

He sat on the edge of the bed, taking in the rich tangle of her raven hair, the thickness of her long dark lashes, and the pale perfection of her complexion. His glance lingered too on the gentle curve of her breasts beneath the soft stuff of her nightgown. There had been a time when he'd caressed and stroked her until she arched against him with pleasure. A heady time. But so brief . . .

Jane observed him shrewdly. His unguarded expression reflected feelings he would otherwise have kept hidden, and which he would certainly have striven at all costs to conceal from Henrietta herself! Kit was right, the wraith thought, the handsome marquess was no more exempt from emotion than Henrietta herself. There was hope!

Old Nick chose that moment to glance up from the depths of Hades to see how things were progressing, and was appalled by what he saw. Things were going far too well for the ghosts, and the end of his hundred years of amusement suddenly seemed in sight. This time he wisely resisted the temptation to do something precipitate, and instead retreated thoughtfully into his fiery abode to ponder the situation.

Marcus spoke to Henrietta. "Henrietta? Can you hear me?"

She didn't respond.

He took her left hand in his and began to rub and pat it persistently. "Henrietta? Can you hear me? Henrietta?"

As she began to stir a little, Jane carried Rowley swiftly behind the lacquered Chinese screen that shielded the washstand and adjoining dressing room from view.

Marcus spoke again. "Wake up, Henrietta. Please open your eyes!"

Her eyelids fluttered, and she smiled. "Marcus?" she whispered drowsily.

"Yes, it's me. Wake up now."

"Is it time to go?"

He gazed at her. "No, sweeting, it's just time to wake up," he said softly.

Her eyes opened and she smiled again. "Oh, it's so good to be with you like this . . ." The words trailed away on an uncertain note as she began to recall.

"It's all right, don't be afraid," he said quickly. "I found you lying in the passage. You'd been hit with a candlestick. Do you remember anything?"

"There was a dog, a King Charles spaniel . . ." Her glance went to the ceiling, and she bit back any further explanation.

Marcus's eyes cleared. There *had* been a dog, and if it didn't belong at the abbey, then clearly it must belong to the intruder. He was still puzzled, though. Why had *he* been able to hear it when Russell couldn't?

Henrietta struggled to sit up. "Someone was here, a—a cloaked man!"

Marcus put reassuring hands on her arms. "I know, but you're all right now."

"My jewelry box . . . ! It's open now, but I *know* I closed it. Was everything stolen?"

He went to the dressing table and returned with the box. "It seems full enough to me, so I guess you interrupted him in time."

But she saw immediately what was missing. "He took my betrothal ring," she said.

Marcus raised an eyebrow. "Evidently a thief of little taste," he observed beneath his breath.

She ignored him as she closed the box. "I wonder why he only took that? I was so convinced everything had gone that I could only think of getting it back. So I chased him."

"That wasn't wise."

"Well, I'm not wise, am I? That's something we both know." There was an edge in her voice.

He met her eyes. "Now is not the time for raking over dead embers."

She drew back. "Embers I wish had never been kindled," she whispered.

He got up once more. "That sentiment is mutual, I promise you. Now then, it's hardly proper for me to remain here with you like this. As you can hear, there's a hue and cry for your intruder, so I doubt if Charlotte can possibly still be asleep. I'll go and find her, and bring her to look after you."

"I'm quite all right now, so there's no need—"

"There's every need," he interrupted, then sketched a bow and left the room, but in the passage he paused. The bleakness of the Yorkshire dawn fled, and for a moment it was a warm evening in a summerhouse in a Grosvenor Square garden. Henrietta was in his arms, pressing to him as they kissed. He should have taken her then, for it was no more than she would have deserved. No more at all . . .

When Marcus found them, Charlotte and Russell were endeavoring to calm the gaggle of guests who'd been aroused by all the noise. On hearing what had befallen Henrietta, Charlotte and the ladies immediately hastened alarmedly to attend her, leaving the gentlemen to hear about Russell's unsuccessful pursuit of the intruder.

He told them he had had the miscreant in full view, when Henrietta's uncle, awakened by the shouts and Rowley's racket, suddenly emerged from his room. A collision had been unavoidable, and when Russell regained his balance, the cloaked figure had vanished.

Kit had fared no better in the chase. He'd dropped his sword and bent to retrieve it at the very moment Russell and Jasper Courtenay collided, with the result that the intruder eluded him as well. Russell had given up the chase, because the abbey was vast and contained so many doors, but Kit had searched on. He had moved diligently in and out of all the nearby rooms, but he only found sleepy guests, some sitting up nervously in bed, some pulling on their dressing gowns to see what was going on.

In Marcus's room, which the ghost expected to find empty, there was something that stopped him in his spectral tracks. The dawn light was silver upon Amabel's naked body as she combed her rich brown hair. Her carnation perfume filled the fire-warmed air, but the touch of sulfur was still there. Oh, yes, it was there, Kit thought as he drew back against the wall to study her. His gaze moved shrewdly over her face and slender figure. Her dark eyes were too knowing, and her lips were rouged just a little too much. If this wanton was going to grace Marcus Fitzpaine's bed tonight, the marquess wasn't about to have much sleep!

Amabel donned Marcus's gray paisley dressing gown, then went to the window and flung open the casement. The new day lightened by the minute against the eastern horizon, but the sky was still leaden. A few stray snowflakes drifted in, catching in her hair as she leaned out to look down at the sea far below, for this wing of the abbey stretched right to the very edge of the cliff's sheer drop. After a moment she drew back in again and closed the window.

Her lips were now curved in a smile that Kit found deeply disturbing. He moved closer and shivered a little as she brushed briefly through him on her way to an armchair in the corner. To his surprise she pulled the chair aside and then bent to retrieve her clothes, which must have slipped down when she draped them there after undressing. She arranged them very carefully over the back of the chair, and then went to the fireplace, where she sat on the rug and held out her hands to the heat. The flames danced in her eyes as she waited for Marcus to come, Kit waited too, for if Marcus was as enthralled by Amabel as he appeared, there seemed little point in trying to pair him off with Henrietta. The shade needed to be certain.

It was another half an hour and almost completely light when Marcus came. He'd lingered to consult with Russell about the attack upon Henrietta and the theft of her ring. The implications were plain; the thief was probably a guest or one of the servants, the only other explanation being that someone had come up from Mulborough. The latter possibility had been discounted when a brief examination of the grounds revealed that apart from the footprints of the man sent to bring Dr. Hartley, the only other tracks belonged to the sailors who'd brought Marcus's luggage from the *Avalon*. These men had come and gone while it was still snowing, and their footprints were partially filled. Therefore the only conclusion to be drawn was that the intruder was still in the abbey.

Amabel rose from the rug as Marcus entered. "I've been waiting an age for you," she murmured.

He whirled about at the sudden sound of her voice. "Amabel!"

"I told you I'd come to you tonight. Or is it morning now?"

He recovered a little. "I'm flattered, but think it would be better if you returned to your own room," he said.

"You don't mean that," she said, untying the dressing gown and allowing it to slip to the floor. Then she went to him and linked her arms around his neck.

"Please, Amabel, I really don't want . . ."

"Oh, yes, you do," she whispered, stretching up to put her parted lips to his.

He was betrayed by his body, and by the fierce anger revived because of Henrietta. Once again the cold Yorkshire dawn retreated, and it was a summer evening, this time in Hyde Park. Amabel wasn't the woman in his arms, it was Henrietta, and he wasn't going to repeat the mistake of letting the moment slip! He lifted Amabel roughly into his arms and carried her to the bed. Kit did not linger to see any more, but with a heavy heart melted through the wall into the passage. He didn't relish having to tell Jane that Marcus Fitzpaine wasn't suitable after all.

Because of Rowley, Jane had found it difficult to escape from Henrietta's room without being seen. But for the spaniel, she could have passed through the wall behind the screen and that would have been that, but with him, she had to wait for the door to be opened *and* for Henrietta's attention to be diverted. It was most vexing. Holding the spaniel in her arms, with her fingers firmly around his muzzle to be sure of his silence, the shade was forced to remain behind the screen until an opportunity presented itself. At last Henrietta's bed was completely encircled by Charlotte and the other ladies, and the door was briefly left open. Jane waited no more and glided briskly out to return to the room she and Kit had selected for themselves. There she settled on the bed, and as she waited for Kit, she stroked and praised Rowley, who had done so much to save Henrietta tonight. The spaniel basked in her undivided attention.

At last Kit stepped through the wall, and Jane sat up expectantly. "Did you catch up with the intruder?"

"I fear not," he replied, taking off his sword and then joining her on the bed. He was dismayed when Jane related the attack upon Henrietta, and the theft of her ring. "Damn it all, if only I hadn't dropped my fool sword, we'd know who perpetrated such vile deeds!" he fumed.

"Well, it cannot be helped."

"And as if that were not bad enough, I have something to tell you about Marcus and Amabel Renchester. He may be our choice for Henrietta, but I fear that at this very moment he is between the sheets with Amabel. And they are not reading bed-time stories," he added dryly.

Jane stared at him, and then shook her head. "No, I don't believe it! I saw him with Henrietta, and I would *swear* she is the one in his thoughts."

"In his thoughts, maybe, but certainly not in his bed. If you don't believe me, go see for yourself. They're in the room directly above the cliff edge."

Jane began to get up, but then sat back again. "No, if you say that's what's happening, then clearly it is. But I tell you this, it isn't because he loves Amabel, for I would stake my eternity that he loves Henrietta."

"He didn't put up much resistance," Kit replied.

"Men don't as a rule," Jane observed. "They are poor creatures who are ruled by the contents of their breeches."

Kit smiled. "Speaking of which . . ." he murmured, putting a hand to her cheek.

Rowley growled and bared his teeth.

"Kit, we can't. There's so much we should be attending to," Jane murmured a little guiltily.

"And we have weeks of snow in which to accomplish it, so why should we not pleasure ourselves a little in the meantime?" he replied, taking Rowley from her arms and placing him at the foot of the bed.

Rowley growled again, but Jane ignored him as she succumbed to Kit's caresses. Disgruntled, the spaniel jumped down from the bed and left the room.

Chapter Nine

Sunlight broke through the clouds as Dr. Hartley arrived on his sturdy cob. The rays touched the southern headland first, causing the shadow of St. Tydfa's church to creep across the tombs and ancient yew trees in the churchyard as if searching for the legendary bogle. Everything was white with snow and possessed a cold clarity that made the events of the night seem like a dream. Mulborough town was well awake, and the fishing fleet had already set sail, although it would not venture far because of the ever present threat of the *Légère*. The *Avalon* lay peacefully at anchor, her speed on the open sea evident in her lean gilded beauty.

At the abbey, such was the disquiet caused by the night's incident, that few guests had felt able to return to their beds. All were eager to depart without delay, and made arrangements accordingly. This included Henrietta's uncle, who was anxious to return south for an important sale at Tattersall's. Racehorses were his passion and there was a splendid colt about to be sold, but he knew he could not leave until his niece had been pronounced safe.

There was much bustle in the stables as the doctor dismounted and hastened into the house to attend Henrietta. She had awoken with the worst headache of her life. The side of her head was bruised and swollen, and she had never felt more fragile or weak. Dr. Hartley, who was a disagreeably pompous man, prescribed laudanum and instructed her to remain in bed for at least three days. He administered the first dose immediately, then at Russell's request, took himself off to examine Charlotte. Henrietta's uncle waylaid him on the landing, and after extracting a reassurance that Henrietta was in no danger, scuttled away to finalize his departure. Within ten minutes, Thomas Courtenay's carriage was bowling along the drive away from the abbey.

Rowley was sulkily wandering the abbey. The spoiled spaniel hated it when Jane ignored him in favor of Kit, and was determined to stay away as long as possible because he knew it would worry her. He rambled along the ceilings, and at length found himself in the passage that led to Marcus's room. Seeing a dead end ahead, he was about to retrace his steps when he was intrigued by a glint of gold on top of the window pelmet close to Marcus's door. A closer examination soon revealed that it was Henrietta's stolen ring. As he went to sniff it, an interesting scent pricked his nostrils; it was the scent of the intruder.

At that moment Kit appeared at the end of the passage, having been dispatched by Jane to find the dog. "Ah, there you are, Rowley. Come here this instant."

The spaniel wagged his tail and whined.

Kit frowned. "Don't just hang there like that! Come here!"

Rowley remained stubbornly where he was.

Muttering dire threats beneath his breath, Kit strode purposefully toward him, but to his astonishment, instead of backing away, Rowley seemed pleased! Tail wagging nineteen to the dozen, the spaniel patted the ring with his paw. It fell to the floor with a bell-like tinkle.

Kit stared at it, and then at Marcus's door. Was it coincidence that the ring was here? Marcus couldn't have stolen it and placed it there, because he'd been coming upstairs with Russell at the time the intruder fled, but someone else had been here last night who *could* have taken it. Amabel Renchester. She of the whiff of sulfur. The ghost's mind raced back to the previous night. Amabel said she'd been waiting in Marcus's room for "an age," but she might have just arrived. Her clothes had fallen behind the chair, but she could have just flung them there in haste as she took them off. Then, when she was undressed and knew there was time, she retrieved them and put them neatly over the chair. But what of the cloak, which would have told the truth if she was the intruder? Kit's brow creased thoughtfully, then he remembered how Amabel had opened the window and looked down the sheer drop of the cliff to the rocks below. Had she thrown the cloak out? Yes, of course she had, and by now the tide would have washed it away.

He glanced down at the ring, wanting to take it to Jane, who must be told what he'd discovered about Amabel—or, at least, what he *guessed* about her. Closing his eyes in concentration, he made the ring lift into the air. Once it was weightless, he opened his eyes again and the ring followed obediently as he and Rowley went down to the breakfast room, where Jane was closely observing Marcus, Russell, and Amabel, who were the only three at the table.

Conversation was noticeably absent. Russell toyed endlessly with the sugar tongs. He wore a sage-green coat and gray-and-black striped neckcloth. His breakfast of deviled kidneys were untouched. He was tired from the night's events, and anxious because Charlotte was upset by it all, so his temper was far from equable. Amabel was very dainty and fresh in yellow-and-white checkered wool, and there was a secretive smile on her lips as she daintily ate a delicious local kipper. Jane didn't like that smile, for it signified the successful seduction of Marcus Fitzpaine.

However, if Amabel was satisfied with the way things had gone, Marcus gave no similar sign. He had been the very last one to arrive for breakfast, and could have sat next to her; instead he sat opposite, and a little way down the table. He wore a dark gray coat and cream trousers, and there was a blue silk neckcloth at his throat. His fair hair was tousled and his eyes thoughtful as he poured himself some of the excellent Turkish coffee that was always served at the abbey. He didn't studiously avoid Amabel's eyes, but neither did he go out of his way to look at her, and when the occasion arose, he was polite and conversational. That was all. Jane was puzzled. Was it an act to preserve appearances? If so, there seemed little point, for they were both free to do as they pleased.

Kit waited a moment or so to gain Jane's attention, but as she continued to watch the table, he impatiently directed the ring right in front of her nose. "Behold, the missing item," he whispered.

Jane stared at it, then turned inquiringly to him. "How——?"

"Rowley found it on the pelmet opposite Marcus's door. I think Mrs. Brimstone was the intruder. I don't know what her motive was, but she certainly had the opportunity."

"Amabel, of *course*!" Jane's gaze swung back to the woman at the table. So the whiff of sulfur had been more than mere imagination; the Renchester woman *was* wicked.

Kit explained how he'd deduced Amabel's guilt, and then added, "Come to think of it, she didn't ask Marcus what all the disturbance was, which I'm sure she would have done if she had indeed been in the room for that long. I suspect she didn't ask because she already knew!"

Jane's mind raced. "What motive do you think she has?"

"I don't know." Kit met her eyes. "You're not just thinking about last night, are you? You think she is behind everything that's befallen Henrietta."

"It's hard *not* to think it." Jane glanced at the breakfast table again. "Enough of this for the moment. I've thought of a way we can force Marcus and Henrietta into each other's company again."

"To what purpose? He spent last night with Amabel, remember? Jane, my beloved, I think we have to abandon this whole business."

At that moment Rowley associated Amabel's scent with that on the ring, and he growled.

Marcus turned sharply. "I hear that dog again!"

Russell frowned tetchily. "Oh, for heaven's sake! I told you last night, there *is* no dog!"

Amabel glanced around. "I didn't hear anything," she said.

Russell pushed the sugar bowl away. "That's because there's nothing to hear."

Marcus looked at him. "May I remind you that I wasn't the only one to notice it last night?"

"It was my shouting that aroused everyone," Russell insisted. Nothing was said for a moment or so, then he glanced at Marcus again. "I've been thinking about that boom idea. It would work very well here, so I've decided to put it to those who matter in the town."

"I'll come with you, if you like."

"I'd appreciate that."

Amabel sat forward interestedly. "What are you talking about?"

Russell explained. "Marcus thinks a boom should be put across the channel into Mulborough harbor."

She looked inquiringly at Marcus. "To keep the *Légère* out, I suppose?"

"That's the general idea," he answered.

"How very clever. Will it work?"

"Oh, yes. With luck both she and her damned crew could be captured."

Russell got up. "I'll speak to you about it later, Marcus. In the meantime, I think I'll go to see Charlotte." He went to the door and then paused. "I, er, apologize for my lack of grace this morning."

"Think nothing of it," Marcus replied.

As the door closed, Amabel pursed her lips. "How distant you are now, Marcus" she murmured.

"No more distant than I was an hour or so ago, if you recall," he replied quietly.

Specks of color touched her cheeks. "Maybe you didn't finally succumb this time, but you will soon."

"I regret giving in to the extent I did, but I will show you the door if you try to do anything like that again."

Jane's face lit up. The stiltedness at the breakfast table was explained. He'd resisted!

Amabel's dark eyes were unfathomable. "I want you, Marcus."

He smiled. "I doubt it. You always have an ulterior motive, and in this instance I fancy I know his name."

Jane could have stamped her foot in frustration. *His?* Whose?

Amabel's gaze was all hurt innocence. "He never meant anything to me. Why do you refuse to believe me?"

"Only a fool would believe you, Amabel," he said softly.

"What if I tell Henrietta how odiously you've used me?"

At that he got up and leaned his knuckles on the table to hold her gaze. "Henrietta means nothing to me, but my reputation certainly does. If you breathe a word to my detriment, you can be certain that *I* will do some talking of my own when I get back to town, and by the time I've finished, you will be the laughingstock of society." He inclined his head, then departed from the room.

Amabel's lips pressed thinly together; her fists were clenched. "No one threatens me and gets away with it, Marcus Fitzpaine," she breathed.

Jane recoiled from the evil glittering in Amabel's eyes, but then remembered her own plans. She caught Kit's arm. "Quick, we must see that Marcus goes to Henrietta now."

"Now? But—"

"Just come with me!"

Seizing control of the ring, Jane hastened away after Marcus, who had just reached the second-floor landing. He halted in startlement as she caused the ring to fall right at his feet. "What the—?"

Jane eyed him determinedly. "Take it to Henrietta, you dunderhead!" she willed.

Marcus recognized the ring as he picked it up. He glanced around, perplexed. How in God's name had it just appeared like that? It was almost as if someone had thrown it, yet there was no one around. His fingers closed over it, and to Jane's relief he turned toward Henrietta's room.

The ghosts gathered at his shoulder as he knocked at the door. "Henrietta? It's Marcus. May I come in?"

Chapter Ten

When Henrietta didn't reply to Marcus's knock, Jane quickly put Rowley down, then caught Kit's hand to lead him through the wall into the adjoining room, and then through a second wall behind the screen which offered concealment. The ghosts peered cautiously around it, and were startled to find Henrietta not only out of bed, but dressed, and about to commence packing her things. She swayed just a little, because the first dose of laudanum was beginning to take effect, although she did not realize it.

She had donned a warm rose mohair gown. There was a thick knitted shawl around her shoulders and her hair had been pinned up rather untidily because her bandaged wrist made her awkward. Her traveling cloak was draped in readiness over the fireside chair and her gloves and ankle boots were warming in the hearth. She had just lifted a portmanteau onto the bed, and was looking uneasily toward the door, clearly hoping Marcus would think she was asleep.

He knocked again. "Henrietta, I've found your ring."

Surprise caught her off guard. "My ring?"

He heard. "May I come in?" he asked again.

She put the portmanteau and cloak on the floor as quickly as she could with only the full use of her left hand, then pushed them beneath the bed with her foot, but as she sat in the fireside chair and put her shawl over her knees, she forgot the gloves and boots in the hearth. "Yes, please come in," she called.

The door opened and Marcus entered. He was taken aback to

see her sitting by the fire. "I was under the impression the doctor prescribed laudanum and a few days in bed," he said, his shrewd glance taking in the traveling accessories warming in the hearth. He glanced back to the bed again and saw the handle of the portmanteau and the hem of the crumpled cloak peeping out beneath the counterpane

"I feel quiet well," she replied lightly, trying not to wince as a shaft of pain jabbed behind her eyes. "You, er, said you've found the ring?" she prompted.

"Yes." He handed it to her.

He described what had happened. "And before you ask, I can offer no explanation. It hadn't been lying there unnoticed all along, for I heard it fall. It came literally out of thin air," he finished.

"Well, whatever the circumstances, I'm grateful to you for finding it."

"Grateful? Believe me, you were better off without it, and if you had any sense left, you'd be rid of Sutherton as well."

"I think you should leave now," she replied coolly.

He smiled. "I rather thought *you* were the one intending to leave," he said, pushing one of her gloves with his foot.

"I don't know what you mean."

"Oh, yes, you do. Don't take me for a fool, Henrietta. The evidence is in the hearth and beneath the bed. You mean to quit Mulborough, don't you?"

She didn't deny it. "I think it best if I do."

"Best?"

"Yes. I thought I could manage being under the same roof as you, but I can't. I can leave with Uncle Courtenay, and that will be that. I'm sure Charlotte will understand."

"I fear you're too late. After satisfying himself that you were not at death's door, your uncle left a little earlier. The call of Tattersall's is evidently greater than the ties of family. Which is just as well, because in your present state, an arduous journey is out of the question."

Henrietta rose to her feet in dismay. "Remaining here with you is equally out of the question."

"I'm sure we can get along within the bounds of politeness."

She turned her face away as tears stung her eyes. "I'll warrant you haven't told Russell how abominably you behaved in London, for you know you would sink in his estimation if he knew," she said.

"Maybe, but for the same reason I'd hazard a guess you haven't fully confided in Charlotte either."

She didn't reply.

"I thought not," he murmured.

A blush sprang to Henrietta's cheeks, but not just from embarrassment. She had begun to feel very hot and weak, and too late realized the laudanum was taking a grip upon her. The room began to spin, gathering speed until she felt herself swaying. Marcus saw she was on the edge of fainting and quickly caught her. "*Now* will you accept that you can't possibly travel?" he said, and for the second time since arriving he lifted her into his arms.

"I hate you," she whispered, the words running drowsily together.

He gave a thin smile. "Do you? Well, let us test that claim," he murmured, and put his lips to hers, toying with her mouth in a way he only ever had with her. For a moment she was alive to him, returning the kiss with the passion that had sparked between them at the outset, but then her lips softened into stillness as she drifted further toward unconsciousness.

Behind the screen, Jane caught Kit's hand excitedly. "The odds begin to turn in our favor!"

"You may be right, sweeting, but these two are very stubborn, so it's far from done," he warned.

After placing Henrietta gently in the bed, Marcus drew the bedclothes snugly over her, then went to find a maid to sit with her. But as he left the room, Jane and Kit were dismayed to see Rowley begin to follow him. They knew Marcus was psychic enough to hear the spaniel, so they hastened through the wall and then back into the passage, intent upon catching Rowley before his invisible presence was detected. But as Jane gathered her wayward pet close once more, Rowley gave a little whine. Marcus turned, only to see nothing. He listened curiously. Damn it, he *knew* there was a dog here somewhere! But where?

Was there a secret passage? Mulborough Abbey was just the sort of place that might possess such a thing! He went to the rich oak paneling lining the landing wall, but although he tapped it in various places, the dull sounds produced seemed only too solid. After a while he drew a mystified breath and told himself he must be imagining it all. Putting the strange business determinedly from his mind, he went downstairs to find a maid for Henrietta, and to tell Charlotte and Russell about the reappearance of the ring.

The maid sat by the fire in Henrietta's room with some darning, and she hummed to herself as she stitched. Henrietta felt warm and drowsy, and at last the pain in her head was deadened. If only the pain in her heart were deadened too, but it was as fresh as ever. The maid's humming became mixed up with her thoughts, and the present blended with the past, bringing memories of things more shockingly improper than anything she'd told Charlotte.

She was in the garden of her parents' house in Grosvenor Square, and she was both wildly happy and stricken with guilt. She knew her reputation would have counted for nothing at all if her recent behavior became known, but for days now she had walked on air, and she hummed to herself as she gathered a basketful of the fragrant white roses that climbed all over the little summerhouse.

The displeased Edinburgh tones of the butler, Hanson, spoke suddenly behind her. "Begging your pardon, Miss Courtenay, but a Mr. Mark Paynson has called. He has found a riding glove in Hyde Park and believes it belongs to you. I told him he could leave it, but he insists upon speaking with you."

The thrill of helpless excitement that tingled through her was touched with unease as she turned, for suddenly the consequences of her misconduct were painted a little too clearly upon the hitherto rather hazy canvas of her foolishness. The butler was a spruce, rather bony man of about forty-five, with pale eyes that were set above a large hooked nose. He wore a plain brown coat and fawn breeches, and his receding red hair was hidden beneath a simple bag wig. A stickler for all the rules, he frowned upon a gentleman calling when she was alone, and everything in his manner was calculated to prompt her into merely sending a polite message of thanks, so that the unwanted male caller could be sent on his way. But in spite of her fears, she could not bring herself to allow Mark to be sent on his way.

"Please show him out here, Hanson," she instructed.

His eyes widened. "Out here, Miss Courtenay? That is most irregular."

"If Mr. Paynson has taken the trouble to bring my glove, then the least I can do is take the same trouble to thank him in person," she said.

"As you wish, Miss Courtenay."

As he stalked disapprovingly away, she put the basket of roses down on the bench in the summerhouse, and then smoothed the sprigged muslin folds of her pink gown. Did she look well enough? Her hair . . . ! She patted the dark curls that were piled up on top of her head, and her fingers shook as she removed a pin in order to push it in more firmly. Then she drew a long breath to steady herself. Hanson was right to disapprove, but she hadn't been able to think clearly since that heartstopping moment at the masked ball when her eyes had met Mark's behind their masks. From that second onward, common sense had taken flight with the four winds.

The French doors leading to the terrace were opened and closed, and then he was conducted toward her. How handsome he was in his claret coat and cream trousers, and how wonderfully the sun shone on his blond hair.

Hanson paused. "Mr. Paynson," he announced stiffly.

Mark bowed to her. "Your servant, Miss Courtenay," he murmured, his eyes caressing her with one brief glance. The smile on his lips was warm with the secret knowledge of their acquaintance.

"Thank you, Hanson, that will be all," she said, marveling that her voice sounded so natural.

Almost on the point of stating his disfavor, Hanson drew himself up, but then turned and walked away. He was still within hearing when Mark spoke to her. "I trust you will forgive my impudence in asking to speak with you, Miss Courtenay, but I confess to . . ."

Her heart lurched, and her anxious gaze swung after the butler, whose steps faltered noticeably.

Mark went on. ". . . an intense interest in the horse you were riding today."

Hanson walked on, and her heart ceased to lurch. "M-my horse?"

"I have been seeking just such a mount for my sister, and I wondered if you would be prepared to sell?" The French doors closed, and Mark smiled. "There, that was not so difficult, was it?"

She gazed at him. "Maybe not, but you should not call here like this."

"I know it, but I could not stay away." He came closer and made to put his hand to her cheek.

She moved back as if his touch would burn. "Please . . ."

"Would you have me deny what I feel? What we *both* feel?"

"No, it's just . . ."

"Just?"

"What price my good name if this should get out? I should not have done any of the things I've done since meeting you."

"We are both free to do as we please."

"You may be, but I have my parents to consider. You know as well as I that no young lady of good family can abandon propriety and expect to survive with her good name intact."

"That is to assume that something will get out, or indeed that my intentions are anything but honorable."

She lowered her eyes. "It could be argued that an honorable gentleman would not have persuaded me into folly."

"Does the fact of your folly make you any less a creature than you were before? Are you now wicked, when previously you were good? Have your stolen moments with me led to the forfeit of your worth, principles, kindness, and charm?"

She colored. "My principles have indeed been forfeit," she murmured.

"Why? Because of a kiss?"

She looked away. "Perhaps."

He stepped closer suddenly and drew her into the sun-dappled shadows of the summerhouse. Then he made her face him and tilted her chin so that her eyes could only look directly into his. "My intentions toward you *are* honorable, Henrietta. Indeed if you only knew how much I love you, you would trust me implicitly." For a moment it seemed his eyes were shadowed, but then he continued. "My thoughts are only of you, and of the happiness we could know together. I know that my approach has been unconventional, and that the pace I force is perhaps too swift, but when the heart dictates as it does now, what else can I do but strive with all my might to be with you. Do you honestly imagine I want anything less than to have you as my wife?"

"But, I know nothing of you, nor you of me!"

"What else is there to know, except this . . . ?" He bent his head to kiss her, drawing her seductively close, and slipping an arm around her waist in order to hold her body to his. His breath was fresh and intoxicating, as if it were he who filled her with life, and his contours cleaved to hers in a way that made her feel she had been created just for him. Her lips softened and parted, and she felt the gentle caress of his tongue against hers. Her breasts tightened with desire and she put her arms around his neck as she returned the kiss. A wanton passion surged irresistibly through her and her breath caught as his hand moved to tentatively cup her left breast. Wonderful sensations washed over her, and all the time his lips moved yearningly against hers. Oh, the pleasure, the sweet, sweet pleasure. *Marcus, I love you in spite of your cruelty. I will always love you. . . .*

A sob escaped, and the maid came quickly to see that all was well. She saw cheeks that were wet with tears. "Miss Courtenay?"

But Henrietta did not hear, because at last the laudanum enveloped her completely.

Chapter Eleven

For Henrietta, the next two days passed in a haze. The laudanum forced her to rest, and as a result she felt much better on the third morning. Sunlight streamed through a crack in the drawn curtains, and the clock on the mantelpiece read just past ten o'clock. For some reason she found herself recalling the fall she had had in St. Tydfa's churchyard. In particular she remembered a rather ornate gravestone next to where the fall had halted. Richly carved, it's inscription read *Anno 1714. Here resteth Jane Courtenay. Buried this sad St. Valentine's Day. May she rest in peace.*

Jane Courtenay? 1714? The significance rang through Henrietta like a bell. Jane had been the name of the ghost at the ball, and she had been dressed in the fashion of Queen Anne, whose reign ended in 1714. On top of that, if ever one Courtenay had recognized another, it had been at the ball! Surely the phantom and the woman buried at St. Tydfa's had to be one and the same!

Someone tapped at the door. "Henrietta? It's me, Charlotte, are you awake?"

"Yes. Oh, do come in." Henrietta sat up, and as she did she realized how much improved her wrist was; indeed it felt strong again.

Charlotte entered. She wore a loose peach velvet robe, and her chestnut hair was intricately pinned beneath a lacy day cap, but her face was drawn, and there were shadows beneath her eyes that gave the lie to the bright smile she gave Henrietta. "How are you this morning?"

"Much better, I fancy, and that goes for my wrist as well."

"Rest is a sovereign remedy."

"Will you remove the bandage for me?"

"Of course." Charlotte sat on the edge of the bed, removed the little diamond brooch and placed it on the table beside the bed, then began to unwind the bandage.

Henrietta studied her. "You don't look well, Charlotte."

"What nonsense," was the brisk reply.

"You don't fool me."

Charlotte sighed and then smiled a little ruefully. "I never could pull the wool over your eyes, could I, not even at school."

"What's the matter?"

"Oh, just reaction to what happened to you. I worked myself into such a pother that Dr. Hartley insisted on bleeding me."

Henrietta was dismayed. "I wish I could feel confident that bleeding is always beneficial."

"It certainly calmed me down," Charlotte said, neatly rolling the removed bandage. "I fear that two weeks of a full house proved rather too much this year."

"Amabel and I will leave directly, and leave you to rest properly," Henrietta said firmly.

"I will not hear of it. Besides, would you really leave me without female company?" Charlotte smiled and placed the bandage on the table beside the brooch. "You wouldn't believe how amiable Amabel has been the past few days. Maybe I was wrong about her after all."

"You have indeed been wrong."

"Anyway, I'm happy for you both to stay; indeed I wish you to." Charlotte got up and went to draw the curtains back.

The morning sun swept dazzlingly in, made more bright than ever by the crisp layer of snow that still covered the countryside because each night the clear skies brought a raw frost. The sky was a flawless blue and the high moors seemed to float against the heavens as Henrietta sat up in bed to look out. "How lovely it is out there," she murmured.

"Yes, it is, and so clear I can actually see the smoke from the chimneys in Nurse's hamlet." Charlotte pointed toward Mulbridge, which lay just out of sight in a fold of the moor.

Henrietta smiled. "Just how old is she? If she was Russell's nurse . . ."

"Well, Russell is sixty, and she was about seventeen when she was hired to take care of him. So I suppose she's in her late seventies. Something of the sort, anyway."

"I'd like to see her again before I leave," Henrietta said.

"And so you shall. We will ride over soon."

Henrietta was appalled. "*Ride?* With you barely a month from your confinement? Certainly not."

"Very well, we'll drive then." Charlotte moved to the fire, which a maid had tended while Henrietta still slept.

Jane glided through the wall behind the screen. She was alone because Kit had taken Rowley for a walk along the cliffs, well out of sight of this particular room. Wondering how to proceed next with Henrietta and Marcus, the shade settled to eavesdrop.

Henrietta chose that moment to recall her thoughts on awakening. "Charlotte, there's a tomb in St. Tydfa's churchyard that belongs to a Jane Courtenay. She was buried on February 14th, 1714. Do you know anything about her?"

Jane sat forward alertly.

Charlotte's brows drew together pensively. "I believe there is something about her in Lady Chloe's journal."

"Lady who?"

"Chloe. She was Lady Mulborough at the turn of the eighteenth century, and very diligently kept a journal. It's rather difficult to read, but quite interesting."

Jane's lips twitched. Lady Chloe Mulborough had been a superior, interfering old busybody!

Charlotte looked at Henrietta. "Why do you ask about Jane Courtenay?"

"Oh, I just remembered the grave, that's all." On no account was Henrietta going to mention ghosts!

But Charlotte made the association anyway. "Are you also thinking about what happened at the ball? You said the lady was called Jane and looked exactly like you."

"Yes." Henrietta avoided her eyes.

Charlotte cleared her throat a little awkwardly. "Well, I'm sure the journal mentions a Jane Courtenay. I can't be sure, but she was rumored to be at the heart of a scandal, an elopement, I think." Something struck her, and her lips parted on a half gasp. "Actually, now I come to think of it . . ."

"Yes?"

"You said the gentleman you saw at the ball was called Kit, and was an excellent likeness of Marcus. Well, I've just remembered that Lady Chloe named Jane's lover as Lord Christopher Fitzpaine. Kit is short for Christopher, isn't it?"

"Yes, it is."

Jane was impressed. Full marks, Charlotte.

Charlotte shivered and then drew herself together. "A cold finger just went down my spine. Anyway, I can't recall the details, but I know a good many feathers were ruffled by the elopement. Indeed, it may even have been the start of the infamous feud."

Jane sighed. How right you are, my dear, she thought.

Henrietta was intrigued. "Could I read the journal?"

Charlotte nodded. "Yes, of course. It's in the library. I'll have a maid bring it with your breakfast."

"I'd appreciate that."

The clock on the mantelpiece chimed half past ten, and Charlotte turned to leave. "It's time for the midmorning rest Russell has decreed for me, but first I must discuss tonight's dinner with the cook."

"I trust you will include me at table tonight?" Henrietta said quickly.

Charlotte hesitated. "Are you sure? I mean, you may feel very strong right now, but this evening is a long way away."

"I'll be all right."

"Then yes, of course I will gladly include you."

"Don't forget the journal."

"I won't." Charlotte went out, and closed the door softly behind her.

Jane was still behind the screen when the breakfast tray was brought, together with the journal. The wraith regretted Henrietta's ability to see and hear the supernatural, for it meant having to stay out of sight instead of standing at the bedside reading the journal as well.

Unaware of the ghostly presence only a few feet away, Henrietta began to examine the journal. Lady Chloe's writing was difficult to decipher, but at the pages concerning the beginning of 1714, she soon found mention of Jane and Kit, who were among the seasonal guests who even then gathered at Mulborough Abbey. The first reference, concerning Jane's betrothal to the then Lord Sutherton, sent a shiver through Henrietta, whose breakfast began to go cold as she read on.

Lady Chloe clearly thought Jane had done unexpectedly well for herself, for Sutherton was wealthy and very well connected indeed, whereas the Courtenays were parvenus who were only tolerated at the abbey because Jane's mother was Lady Chloe's cousin and because of the family nabob's expected intentions. The first reference to Kit concerned his contract with a member of the royal family. The lady had only her portion of royal blood to commend her in the marriage stakes, whereas Kit was heir to a rich marquessate, but in Lady Chloe's lofty opinion he had the better part of the deal. Oh, what hypocrisy, Henrietta thought, outraged at the insults heaped upon her unfortunate ancestor by the writer of the journal.

Lady Chloe soon perceived that there was something reprehensible afoot between Jane and Kit. Then, on February 12, she entered: "It has happened as I feared. Foolish Kit has been quite led astray by the scheming Courtenay minx. They have run away together to America, leaving dire social consequences behind them. The merchantman *Wessex* sailed on this morning's tide, and was long gone before their flight was realized. Now we must face a scandal that involves the royal family itself. My sympathies lie entirely with the Fitzpaines, for the Courtenays are no better than they should be."

The breakfast tray was totally forgotten as Henrietta read quickly on. She expected to find much more, but the next entry wasn't until two days later, on February 14, St. Valentine's Day. "I have not been able to bring myself to write more about what has happened, for it is too delicate. However, the truth is contained, and a solution found. Today, with full panoply, we laid them both to rest at St. Tydfa's. Kit has gone in a riding accident, the Courtenay coquette of influenza. May God forgive such profanity, but what else were we to do? Mulborough and I are relieved it is resolved, because we greatly feared being condemned at court if it should have been discovered that such a deplorable liaison took place here at the abbey."

Henrietta read the entry again. Influenza and a riding accident? How could that possibly be? Kit and Jane had run away to America on February 12, so how could they be buried at St. Tydfa's on the fourteenth? And why use a word like profanity? She read the rest of the St. Valentine's Day entry. "That is the end of it, never again will their names be mentioned. As for the Courtenays and Fitzpaines, each clan blames the other, and I believe that from now on they will be enemies forever."

So Charlotte was right, the elopement *was* the origin of the feud! Henrietta leafed through the following pages, and on February 26 found one last entry. "Shocking intelligence has just reached us in the *Gentleman's Magazine*, that on St. Valentine's Day, pursued by the dishonorable French privateer, the *Basilisk*, the *Wessex* was lost upon the Goodwin Sands near Deal, within sight of Kit's estate, Bramnells. All lives were lost. What a double irony that he and his siren should have perished on that of all days, but better empty tombs with false inscriptions than the calamity of social disgrace for all concerned."

Henrietta's breakfast was quite congealed as she stared in dismay at these few uncompromising sentences. Tears shone in her eyes. On the day of the so-called burials at St. Tydfa's, Jane and Kit had actually perished some two hundred miles away on the terrible Goodwins. The two families, as well as Lady Chloe and her husband, had colluded in lies to avoid falling from favor at court! *That* was what was profane.

There was a tap at the door, and she closed the journal. "Yes?"

"It's Amabel. I've come to see how you are."

"Come in."

The door opened and Amabel slipped inside with a rustle of sage taffeta. There was a warm cashmere shawl around her shoulders, and her rich brown hair was pinned up daintily on her head. Her green eyes were sympathetic as she came to the bedside. "Charlotte says you're feeling much better."

"Yes, I am. See, even my wrist has decided to get well." Henrietta raised her right hand.

"I'm so glad." Amabel bent to kiss her cheek, but it was the scent of roses that drifted on the air, not sulfur.

Jane's lips pressed together disapprovingly. Mrs. Brimstone was the very opposite of a friend, and the shade wished that Henrietta could see it. Don't trust her, Henrietta. I do not know what reason she has, but she means you great harm! Smell the sulfur when she draws near! She stole your ring and assaulted you with a candlestick, yet pretends concern! Heaven knows what else she has tried to do to you, so have a care. Have a care!

As Amabel sat on the bed, she noticed the untouched tray. "You haven't eaten. Are you feeling unwell again?"

"Oh, no. Actually, I feel so well that I intend to go for a ride to St. Tydfa's." Until the words were said, Henrietta hadn't even realized her decision.

Amabel was taken aback. "You're what? Oh, I don't think Charlotte will permit that, Henrietta."

"That's why Charlotte isn't going to know. She's resting now, and I can slip out the back way through the buttery and laundry."

"Why are you so intent upon riding to St. Tydfa's?"

"Oh, just for the ride. I'm so weary of being cooped up inside. Why don't you join me? I know how much you enjoy riding."

For a split second Amabel seemed about to accept, but then shook her head. "I'm about to go to my room to lie down. I have a dreadful headache, and wish to be rid of it for dinner."

Jane's sixth sense stirred. Headache? Mrs. Brimstone didn't have any such thing. She was up to something!

Henrietta touched Amabel's wrist concernedly. "You go to your room immediately. I will not hear of anything else."

"You're so very kind and thoughtful," Amabel murmured,

bending forward to put cool lips to the bruise on Henrietta's forehead.

"Promise you won't tell Charlotte or Russell of my ride?"

"My lips are sealed." With another rustle of sage taffeta, Amabel left the room.

Instinct bade Jane follow, and in a moment she was right behind Amabel, whose steps had quickened so that she almost ran to her own room. There the ghost watched her arrange pillows beneath the counterpane so it appeared someone was in the bed. Next Amabel took a blue woolen riding habit and thick gray cloak from the wardrobe, then began to unbutton her gown. Jane's eyes widened with dismay. Far from taking to her bed with a headache, Mrs. Brimstone was about to go riding! And where else would she be going, but St. Tydfa's? Henrietta was in danger! The ghost fled from the abbey to find Kit and Rowley on the cliffs.

Chapter Twelve

Raising the fur-trimmed hood of her crimson cloak, Henrietta slipped quietly down the back staircase, past the kitchens, and then out through the kitchen gardens. The sun was dazzling upon the snow and the air was bitterly cold as she crossed the stable yard to the empty stall where she knew the grooms and stable boys congregated at quiet moments. No one questioned her as she asked for a horse to be saddled.

A few minutes earlier, while she was still dressing, Marcus had been reading a newspaper in the conservatory. He wore a wine-red coat and gray trousers, and his unstarched muslin neckcloth was tied in a casual morning knot. His hair was very golden in the sunlight that streamed unhindered through the surrounding windows, and the only sound was the rustle of a page being turned. He was just reading a report concerning a recent attack by the *Légère* upon an unescorted East Indiaman in the North Sea, when he heard the mysterious dog again. This time it whined from somewhere close to the billiard table. With a start, he jumped to his feet.

After a very hasty consultation, Jane and Kit had decided to use the spaniel to lure him to a window from where he could see Henrietta riding out of the stable yard. Rowley was only too willing to oblige. He barked and then pattered noisily toward the door from the cloisters. Marcus flung the newspaper down in exasperation. "Devil take it, show yourself!" Nothing happened, but he could still hear the creature. It was leaving the conservatory via the ceiling, if he wasn't mistaken! Damn it,

this foolishness had to be solved once and for all! Pressing his
lips determinedly together, he followed the sounds.

Encouraged by Jane and Kit, Rowley lured him up to a
second-floor bedroom that was seldom used because it faced
rather uninterestingly over the kitchen garden and stables. By
the window the delighted spaniel was permitted to bark to his
heart's content.

Then he was silenced, and the sudden quiet made Marcus
shiver. He glanced around, his natural cynicism insisting he had
imagined it all. There was no such thing as the supernatural!
Suddenly his attention was drawn out of the window to a movement of crimson in the stable yard. He recognized Henrietta in
a moment. Was she completely mad? She shouldn't be outside
because she hadn't had time to fully recover! What point was
there in Charlotte sending for the doctor, worrying over her, instructing maids to sit with her, and so on, if the future Lady
Sutherton was going to undo all the good by rushing out into
the bitter cold? Damn it all, Henrietta Courtenay needed a lec-
ture, and right now he was just the man to deliver it! Ghostly
dogs forgotten, he turned on his heel, and strode from the room.

Jane breathed out with relief. "We've succeeded, Kit. He's
going after her."

"To give her the wigging of her life, if I'm not mistaken," Kit
replied.

"Better that than the forfeit of said life," Jane pointed out
sagely. "Come on, let's see what happens."

Marcus paused only to don his greatcoat, gloves, and top hat,
then in a minute or so he hastened to the stable yard. He and his
invisible companions were just in time to hear the hooves of
Henrietta's horse echoing beneath the clock-tower entrance as
she set off on her ride. He shouted her name, but to the ghosts'
frustration she didn't hear because of the clatter of her chestnut
mare upon the cleared cobbles. Then she turned onto the undis-
turbed snow of the open cliff top, and rode swiftly away. Marcus called a groom. "A horse, if you please! And quickly!" he
instructed.

Clutching Rowley close, Jane looked urgently at Kit. "I'll
stay with Marcus; you go after Henrietta, you're quicker than I

am. But for heaven's sake, remember she can hear and see you. And be vigilant for a whiff of sulfur!"

As Kit nodded and sped away in Henrietta's wake, Marcus assisted the groom with a large bay thoroughbred. "Did Miss Courtenay say where she was going?" he asked, swinging the heavy saddle onto the horse while the groom attended to the bridle.

"No, my lord, just that she felt like going for a ride."

At last the horse was ready, and Marcus mounted. "On no account are you to let Miss Courtenay ride again unless Lord Mulborough expressly says so, is that clear?"

The groom touched his hat. "It is, my lord."

With Jane and Rowley at his heels, Marcus urged the bay in Henrietta's wake, following the tracks her horse had left in the snow. They led him into the woods in the Mull valley, and past the old icehouse, which resembled little more than a tree-covered mound. Its entrance was choked with brushwood and fallen branches, placed there by those who'd hidden the Treasury gold, and to all intents and purposes it was as if no one had been inside for many a year.

The gold hardly crossed Jane's mind, or Marcus's as he rode on toward Mulborough. He reached the only road, which crossed the Mull on a fine stone bridge. Here he lost the tracks on the hard-packed snow. He rode on, and for a while thought he had found them again by the livery stable on the outskirts of the town, but soon he had to concede that he had lost the trail completely. There was nothing for it but to start questioning anyone he encountered, for someone would have seen a lady in a crimson cloak mounted on a chestnut mare. The first person he asked, an old fisherman returning to his cottage with a folded net over his shoulder, shook his head. A lady in crimson? No, he hadn't seen her. And so it was to go on. No matter who Marcus asked, no one had seen Henrietta. It was as if she had vanished into thin air.

Realizing he was on the point of giving up the chase, Jane knew she had to do something to point him toward St. Tydfa's. She didn't really want to resort to supernatural means out here in the open, but all she could think of was drafting Rowley into action again. The spaniel was pleased to do as he was bade, and gave another ghostly whine. Marcus turned sharply in the saddle, hoping that this time it would prove to be an only too real town dog. But there was nothing. Groaning inwardly, he prepared to follow the sounds, for by now he knew what was expected of him.

The reason Henrietta had eluded Marcus was simply that she hadn't ridden right into the town, but had instead taken a narrow back lane that afforded a shortcut to the church. She was only acquainted with it because the farmer who'd taken her safely home to the abbey after her fall on the church steps, had brought her that way on his sturdy cob.

With Kit following at a safe distance, Henrietta reached the junction of the lane with the road to the church, and she reined in as a woman with a donkey heavily laden with brushwood went down toward the town. The woman was singing "Greensleeves," and the melody carried Henrietta back to the masked ball at Devonshire House. She and Marcus had come anonymously together during a cotillion being danced to the very same melody. Cotillions demanded forfeits, on this occasion a kiss. Their lips had brushed like the touch of gossamer on an autumn morning, but warm and trembling. Lip to lip, flesh to flesh, like the rediscovery of a long lost portion of both their souls. Was that too fanciful a way to describe her feelings in that heartstopping moment? Maybe, but it was how it had been. That, and so very much more. She had known even then that he was her fate and her folly, but not that he was also her foe. *That* bitter realization had come later.

The woman's singing still echoed in the lane as Henrietta rode up the steep gradient toward the southern headland, where St. Tydfa's soared against the immaculate blue sky. By now she was finding the effort of riding rather exhausting. The vitality she'd enjoyed on waking had dwindled considerably, and she wished she hadn't been quite so impulsive. But, having come this far, she intended to look at Jane Courtenay's "grave." And Kit Fitzpaine's too, since it appeared he was also falsely supposed to have been interred at Mulborough. Henrietta shivered, both because of the cold and the horrid thought that the tragic runaways had really died on the dreaded Goodwins.

The headland was exposed and a bitter breeze came in off the sea. The snow was bright and ivy leaves rustled against the high churchyard wall as she dismounted and tethered her horse to one of the iron loops sunk into the stonework. Beyond the lych-gate, the yew trees overhanging the steps shivered and swayed as the draft of frozen air passed through them. At the very edge of the cliff precipice she saw where the donkey woman had gathered her brushwood. Some thick bushes had been cleared and left there, and Henrietta was surprised to find they'd been concealing a path that zigzagged dangerously down between boulders and wiry sea-blown shrubs to a narrow inlet where a flat rock formed a natural landing place. It was an old smuggler's way, long since discarded in favor of somewhere less hazardous several miles to the south. Kit had followed her all the way from the abbey and concealed himself farther along the cliff edge among the dense fringe of bushes yet to be cleared. He peered out through the crowding twigs, hoping to glimpse Amabel, but instead saw a boy of about eleven hiding among the branches of the first yew tree in the churchyard. What was the little tyke up to? He was dressed snugly in a heavy brown coat that was several sizes too big for him, and there was a bright green-and-yellow knitted scarf wrapped around his neck. His spiky brown hair jutted beneath an adult's hat that was now rather battered, and his bright eyes had followed Henrietta's every move since she arrived.

Forgetting the smuggler's path, Henrietta gazed at the panorama of Mulborough, the bay, and the surrounding moors. The snow-covered land was dazzling and the sea sparkled in the winter sun. About two miles away to the north was the magnificent clifftop medieval splendor of the abbey, and in between the two headlands was Mulborough, with smoke rising from its clustered chimneys. At the town quay where various vessels were moored, lay the weekly packet, awaiting the arrival of its naval frigate escort. But the finest craft by far was Marcus's *Avalon*. The richly ornamented sloop, with her white masts and decks, and gilt-medallioned stripes of red and blue along the waterline, was a brave sight. Tiny figures were visible descending the steps set against her hull, to a gig that was about to come ashore.

As Henrietta watched, the sloop suddenly seemed to become blurred, and turned to silver. Somehow the two masts became three, and the lean hull assumed the larger, more rounded proportions of an old merchantman. Henrietta squeezed her eyes tightly, then looked once more. To her relief, the *Avalon* was herself again, but the occurrence was unsettling. What did it mean? That it was supernatural, and not imagination, she did not doubt.

Truth to tell, the glow of silver had been the first sign of Old Nick's new plan. After a great deal of thought, the Master of Hades had lighted on a new weapon with which to defeat the struggling ghosts. It was something of which St. Peter guessed nothing, for after being uncharacteristically vigilant with the bolt of lightning, the good saint had been rather resting on his laurels.

All this was unknown to Henrietta as she went through the gate, and then passed right beneath the boy in the tree as she began to climb the steps toward the church. At last she reached Jane's elaborate gravestone. The inscription was exactly as she remembered. *Anno 1714. Here resteth Jane Courtenay. Buried this sad Valentine's Day. May she rest in peace.* Henrietta stared at the weatherworn stone. Jane didn't rest here at all; she'd gone to a tragic grave off the coast of Kent. Turning, she thought how very blue and innocent the sea was today, as if it would never contain anything as treacherous and terrible as the Goodwin Sands. Pushing such things from her mind, she turned to go in search of Kit's memorial inside the church.

Just then the boy dropped suddenly from the tree, and she whirled about with a startled gasp. He pointed out to sea. "It *is* 'er, isn't it, miss?"

"Who?"

"The *Légère*, miss."

Still hiding behind the bushes, Kit shaded his eyes against the sun. He saw nothing, not so much as the tip of a sail. Henrietta looked where the boy pointed, but the sea seemed empty.

"I can't see anything. Are you sure you didn't see the frigate coming for the packet?"

"The Frenchie's the only one with that much rig, and she's there now, I'm certain sure of it."

"Then, shouldn't you warn the town?" Henrietta suggested hesitantly, knowing how justifiably afraid the local people were of the privateer's return.

"Well, I would, 'cept I'm not sure, and I'll get a beating if I raise the alarm and it ain't 'er after all. I was 'oping you'd see her as well. I'll shout loud as anything if someone backs me up."

Henrietta studied the horizon again. The sea and sky seemed to shimmer together, but still she saw nothing.

"Maybe if you was to climb the tower and look from the belfry?" The boy nodded at the church behind her.

Henrietta turned and her mouth went dry at the way the tower seemed to move against the sky. The belfry was open to the elements and she could see the bells inside. Climb all the way up there? "Oh, I don't know about that . . ." she began.

Kit looked suspiciously at the boy. Something was very wrong here . . .

The boy pleaded. "Please, miss, it's important."

"Why don't *you* go?" Henrietta suggested.

He shook his head. "Mam says I'm not to go in the church lessen it's in my Sunday best," he said. "Anyway, *I* already reckon I've seen the Frenchie. It's *you* as needs to see 'er too. Just so I'm not the only one that says she's there."

The point was valid, so Henrietta reluctantly decided to do as he asked. Besides, it was her duty to ascertain whether or not the *Légère* was in the vicinity. She gathered her cloak and cumbersome riding skirt, and continued up the steep steps toward the church porch at the top.

The moment Henrietta disappeared into the church, the boy grinned and tossed a gleaming coin before running off down toward the town. Kit rose to his feet. No doubt that was the easiest money the little tyke had ever made! Who crossed his grubby palm? Amabel? Yes, of course, for who else would want foolish Henrietta to climb to an exposed and exceedingly dangerous belfry? Alarmed, the wraith sped up the graveyard toward the porch.

Chapter Thirteen

St. Tydfa's was shadowy inside, with little daylight penetrating the stained glass window above the altar. The cold air smelled of candles and ancient stone, and Henrietta's footsteps echoed on the uneven stone flags as she walked slowly toward the archway through which she could see the bell ropes hanging from the belfry far above. Her heartbeats had quickened unpleasantly, and she trembled a little as she brushed past them to the narrow door that opened onto the winding steps leading to the tower. There was nothing to hold onto, and over the centuries the steps had been worn away in the middle, so that they sloped unevenly. Going up wouldn't be so bad, but coming down would be very difficult and unpleasant indeed. Slowly she began the climb.

Behind her, Kit swiftly examined the nave, vestry, and side chapel for any sign of Amabel, but he found nothing. The church seemed absolutely empty. Were he and Jane wrong after all to think she had come here? Then he remembered not seeing her horse anywhere either, and he relaxed a little. Maybe the boy was just a prankster, and the coin he'd tossed had nothing to do with Mrs. Brimstone.

Deciding that this must indeed be the case, Kit began to follow Henrietta up to the belfry. If he'd remained in the nave just a little longer, he would have seen the wooden lid of a medieval cope store being raised. Amabel climbed out, and knowing nothing of a ghostly presence, hastened to the foot of the tower, from where she gazed up past the ropes. She was waiting until

Henrietta stepped onto the wooden gallery surrounding the bells.

Henrietta had never cared for heights, and her recent misadventures on the Yorkshire cliffs made the fear even worse. Her whole body shook as at last she reached the gallery and stood beside the bells. There was a sheer fall on either side—to the left a headlong plunge to the churchyard, to the right straight down to the stone floor at the bottom of the tower. The stonework wasn't in good repair and the air moaned softly between the bells, making them seem to hum softly. Her legs trembled and her palms felt damp and cold inside her gloves as she leaned nervously forward sufficiently to look across the bay toward the horizon.

Kit hovered anxiously at the last curve of the steps, ready to pull back out of sight if she happened to turn. Now that he was up here, his suspicions of Amabel returned. Jane had warned him to be on his guard for a whiff of sulfur, and by Gad, his nostrils were suddenly filled with the stuff. His every instinct screamed out that this was a trap! A trap!

Amabel tugged upon the rope, and the bell began to move. Henrietta's back was turned, and she sensed nothing, but Kit saw what was happening. Horrified, he pitted his will against the bell, and it became still again, albeit at an angle that defied gravity. He grimaced with effort as Amabel pulled again and again with all her might. Marcus had followed Rowley's whines and barks to the lych-gate, where he tethered his horse next to Henrietta's. He'd passed the boy running down the lane, but neither gave the other a second glance. With Jane close upon his heels, he began to hurry up the steep steps, calling Henrietta as he went.

She saw him from the belfry and drew back in dismay just as Kit's power failed and Amabel succeeded in swinging the bell. It swept across the very spot where Henrietta had been standing a heartbeat before, ringing with a force that made the whole tower vibrate. Henrietta screamed and fell back against the wall as the noise reverberated through her body. She slumped at the very top of the steps, and saw Kit in a blur just before she fainted.

Amabel had heard Marcus shout and now dashed back into the nave. Knowing she couldn't leave the church without being seen, she returned to her hiding place in the cope store. As the lid closed, Kit ran furiously from the tower, and once again found nothing at all.

Marcus dashed into the church, his fearful gaze drawn instantly to the foot of the tower, where one of the ropes was still moving. He'd heard Henrietta scream and expected to see her lifeless body, but to his relief there was no sign of her. "Henrietta? Are you all right?" he shouted. A tearful voice answered from the belfry, and he tossed his top hat and gloves to the floor and ran toward the steps.

Jane, pale faced and apprehensive, hurried in with Rowley. "Kit! What's happened? Is Henrietta all right?"

"Yes, but it was a close thing."

"Have you seen Amabel?"

"No."

"You're quite sure she didn't come out?"

"Well, I didn't have my eyes on the porch every second, so I suppose she could have slipped out and gone around to the back of the church—"

"We'll look, or rather, Rowley will."

They went outside again and Jane put the spaniel down. "Find Amabel, Rowley," she instructed.

The spaniel's nose twitched. Amabel? Whatever for? There was a *much* more interesting odor to investigate! Nose to the ground, Rowley set off toward the rear of the church. Jane and Kit followed, thinking he'd picked up Amabel's scent. But the foolish spaniel had detected something else entirely, something he was very soon to wish he hadn't found at all.

Amabel peeped from the cope store and saw Marcus's hat and gloves lying on the floor. Hearing him ascending the steps, she clambered out to make good her escape. She paused at the porch, but on seeing no one in the churchyard, she hurried down the steps to the lane and then around the upper corner of the churchyard wall, where she'd hidden her horse. It's hooves clattered noisily upon the hard snow in the lane as she urged it away.

Hearing the horse, Jane and Kit whirled about, but at the same moment Rowley discovered the source of the smell he'd been following. It was beneath a heap of old leaves and other rotting vegetation, and with a volley of excited barks, the spaniel pounced. Supernatural pandemonium immediately broke out as the Mulborough bogle took to its heels. It was a horrid little red-faced manikin, about twelve inches high, dressed in scruffy sacking. It's ratlike face had eyes as black as coal, set above a long pointed nose, and it had whiskers and sharp teeth. Rowley would have done better to remember that bogles were not defenseless, and that if there was one thing they resented above all else, it was being flushed from their smelly hiding places, but the reckless spaniel gave chase, ignoring Jane's cries of warning. "No, Rowley! No!"

Suddenly the bogle turned and Rowley was caught unawares as in a flash the vile manikin jumped on his back and sank its needlelike teeth into his neck. The spaniel yelped with pain and fled, with the bogle kicking its bony heels into his flanks.

Jane and Kit were rooted with shock, but then recovered to cause stones to strike the bogle. But they only succeeded in hitting poor Rowley too, so the dismayed ghosts stopped. The spaniel leaped in terror over the churchyard wall into the lane and set off toward the town, with the bogle still kicking and biting for all it was worth.

As silence returned, Jane pressed trembling hands to her mouth. "Oh, Rowley," she whispered, her eyes filling with tears. Then she gathered her skirts. "We must follow!"

Kit accompanied her as she hastened toward the lych-gate, but he knew that few bogle-ridden spirits were ever seen again, let alone rescued.

Chapter Fourteen

Knowing nothing of the ghostly mayhem in the churchyard, Marcus had reached Henrietta. He glanced down as he heard Amabel's departing horse, but the yew trees obscured his view and he didn't see the rider. His attention returned to Henrietta, who was clinging to the stonework. "Are you all right?" he asked gently, taking one of her hands and pulling her safely into his strong arms.

Hot tears blurred her eyes. "Don't let me go, please," she whispered.

"I have you safely now." He tightened his grip reassuringly.

"S-someone rang the bell. If you hadn't arrived when you did . . ." She looked at him in puzzlement. "Why are you here?"

"I could ask the same of you. I'm here because I saw you leaving the abbey, and I followed intending to give you the grandfather of all wiggings." He prudently omitted the invisible dog; it was too fantasic. "Do you think you can manage the steps?"

"No!"

He put his hand to her chin and forced her to look at him. "You have me now, and I'll help you."

She swallowed. "I'm too afraid. . . ."

"I know, but I won't let anything happen. Come." He untwined her arms, then took one of her hands firmly and stood. "I'll go first, and we'll take it very carefully."

She stared at him. "Please don't make me, Marcus."

"Do as you're told," he instructed quietly, drawing her to her feet and turning to go down the first step. Slowly and tortuously they descended, but at the foot of the tower, her legs, already trembling, collapsed beneath her. She had to be helped to the nearest pew, where Marcus sat with her, still holding her hand. "There, that was not so bad, was it?"

"It was terrifying. I—I'm shaking all over . . ." she whispered. The brief glimpse she'd had of Kit flashed before her, but she knew the ghost had been there to protect, not harm her.

Marcus looked at her. "Can you tell me what happened? What were you doing in the belfry?"

"The boy thought he'd seen the *Légère*, and I climbed the tower to see if I could confirm it. Didn't you see him by the lych-gate?"

"If I'm not mistaken, we passed in the lane."

A thought occurred to her. "Maybe the boy rang the bell. Perhaps he thought it was a joke!"

"Knocking someone from the top of a church tower is a *joke*? A rather strange sense of humor, don't you think? Besides, he must have been virtually in the town by the time the bell was rung; in fact, I believe the real culprit rode away when I was with you in the tower."

"Whoever it was can't have known I was there."

"You surely don't imagine that it was an accident? For heaven's sake, what will it take to convince you you're in danger? Think about everything that's happened to you since you came here."

A sliver of deep unease slid through her. "I—I know I was *deliberately* struck with the candlestick, but are you suggesting that the other things weren't accidents at all? Someone is trying to harm me?" The ghosts came to mind again, but every instinct told her they were benevolent.

"After today, I'd say something more final than mere harm was intended."

She didn't want to consider such a thought. "Oh, what nonsense! Who on earth would wish to do that?"

Amabel's name entered his mind, but he had no proof, only a deeply suspicious intuition where the lady was concerned, so he didn't mention her. "Don't dismiss it as nonsense, Henrietta.

I believe someone wishes to be rid of you. I don't know who, or why, but I am convinced it is so, and if I hadn't come here when I did today, they would probably have succeeded."

She lowered her eyes. "I would prefer not to alarm Charlotte with this. I will tell her I came here to the church, but that is all."

"As you wish. By the way, we've established the reason for my presence, but what of you? You aren't fit enough to leave the abbey at all, let alone ride this distance."

Glad to be temporarily diverted from talk of murderous intentions, she told him the tragic love story she'd read in Lady Chloe's journal. "That's why I came here today. I had just found Jane Courtenay's grave and was about to come in here to look for Kit Fitzpaine's, when the boy jumped down from the tree. The rest you know."

Marcus's eyes moved to the wall behind her. "Well, if you wish to see Lord Christopher Fitzpaine's tomb, you need do no more than turn around."

There it was, flanked by marble angels, wreaths, and various other funereal symbols. The contrast with Jane's simple resting place could not have been greater, but then Kit had been of noble birth; Jane had not.

Marcus got up to examine it more closely. "Are you saying this is pretense, and he isn't buried here at all?"

"Nor is Jane out in the churchyard. On the day they were supposedly laid to rest here, they actually died on the Goodwins. Within sight of Bramnells, apparently."

"The Goodwins? A far from pleasant fate," he murmured, knowing the murderous sands only too well.

She watched as he continued to examine the tomb. "It's good to be able to speak to you without rancor."

The words touched a nerve and he turned sharply. "Rancor that was entirely due to your actions."

Her eyes cooled. "You were at fault, not me."

"You discarded me in favor of Sutherton."

"Discarded? I was *saved* from you." She got up unsteadily. "I should have known it was foolish to think we could be

friends again. There is no need for you to linger here now, for I
can manage by myself."

"And have you say I deserted you? Oh, no. I'll ride back to
the abbey with you."

"I wouldn't say any such thing."

"No? Madam, denigrating my good name appears to be your
favorite pastime, so I trust you will forgive me if I take your reassurance with a considerable pinch of salt."

"Escort me if you wish, but I think it would be better if we
omitted any attempt at polite conversation, don't you?"

"That will suit me admirably," he replied coldly. "One thing
more . . ."

"Yes?"

"The acrimony between us may be great, but I still want your
promise to be more cautious after what happened here today.
Dropping the subject has not made it go away. It is plain you
have a very deadly enemy, and you would be advised to be very
much on your guard from now on. Don't trust anyone." Especially Amabel, he added silently.

"The point is taken. Now, may we please go?"

He inclined his head, and after he'd collected his hat and
gloves, they walked from the church, emerging into a sunlit
graveyard that was now devoid of supernatural activity. Marcus
paused for a moment, shading his eyes against the sun to look
down at the *Avalon*. The gig that had come ashore earlier was
now returning, and figures on the sloop were preparing to un-
load the provisions she brought. He watched for a moment,
trusting that his boatswain, Mr. Pascoe, had properly attended
to the minor storm damage suffered to the hull. Marcus smiled
then. Of *course* Mr. Pascoe had done his job, for there wasn't a
finer boatswain on the seas. Tapping his top hat on more firmly,
he followed Henrietta down the steps. She had also looked
briefly at the sloop, recalling the strange moment when it had
seemed to turn silver and change shape. This time the *Avalon*
did not alter at all.

The return ride to the abbey was accomplished in a silence
that was broken only when they entered the house. Henrietta
paused by the long table that ranged across the hall, and took

off her gloves. Her ring caught a shaft of sunlight from a nearby window, and she glanced down at it.

Marcus noticed, and was goaded anew. "Sutherton won't even be out of his damned bed yet!" he observed scathingly. "If he is, I'll warrant he reeks of the maraschino shared with Prinny last night! And he'll be wearing fine new clothes purchased on account of *your* fortune."

She turned angrily. "How *dare* you say such things!"

"I dare because it's the truth. I thought you were intelligent, Henrietta Courtenay. Instead I find that you are the latest great fool in Christendom!"

After all that had happened, it was the last straw. She struck him as hard as she could, leaving angry marks upon his cheek. She would have struck him again had he not caught her wrist. "Once is more than enough, madam," he breathed.

"It barely touches the surface of my loathing for you!" she cried.

"Loathing? I recall that it was not always so, madam!" He gazed bitterly into her eyes, then suddenly bent to put his lips to hers. It was a brief, savage kiss, filled with rage and other emotions that he himself hardly recognized. Then he released her wrist contemptuously and strode away toward the cloisters.

As he disappeared, Amabel spoke from the staircase, where she had observed everything. "My, my, how strangely the snow affects some people." She came down, looking very becoming in a primrose woolen gown, with matching satin ribbons in her rich brown hair.

"I—I wish you would forget anything you just heard or saw," Henrietta said awkwardly.

"What you and Marcus get up to is nothing to do with me, although I daresay Sutherton might have an interest."

Henrietta removed her gloves. "Marcus and I didn't *get up* to anything, and what you just witnessed was simply Marcus being his most overbearing and disagreeable."

Amabel glanced at the betrothal ring. "So it was nothing over which Sutherton should lose any sleep?"

"Nothing at all, and if one word of it reaches him, I shall know who to blame!"

An odd shadow passed through Amabel's green eyes. Then she said. "He won't hear from me."

Henrietta relaxed a little. "How is your headache? Are you feeling better now?"

"It is quite gone."

"I'm glad. Is Charlotte still resting?"

Amabel shook her head. "No, she and Russell are in the conservatory. Shall we join them?"

Suspecting that to be Marcus's destination, Henrietta declined. "I, er, think not. But you join them, by all means. I'll just go up to change." Gathering her skirts, she hurried toward the stairs.

Amabel watched her. The smile on her lips was fixed, and her eyes were cold. *You escaped again this time, Henrietta, but next time I'll make sure of you. The ring you wear should grace my finger, not yours! George Sutherton belongs to me, and no other woman is ever going to become his wife!*

Everyone gathered in the conservatory that evening, and while Marcus and Russell amused themselves with another game of billiards, Henrietta, Charlotte, and Amabel sat in conversation. The night-darkened windows soared above them and the surrounding foliage shone in the lamplight as the women enjoyed cups of sweet chocolate thickened with cream. Henrietta wore a gown of a particularly becoming shade of figured rose velour, and her hair had been intricately dressed by Charlotte's maid. She was still shaken by events at the church, although her pallor was concealed by a touch of rouge.

Charlotte eyed her. "I think you were quite mad to go out today."

"I'm afraid I was overeager to see the tombs."

"Which have been there for a hundred years. Another day or so wouldn't have made any difference." Charlotte smoothed her russet brocade robe a little impatiently.

"I know."

"Anything might have happened. You could have collapsed and lain undiscovered until it was too late because of the cold."

Henrietta fell silent.

Charlotte raised her cup suddenly. "I fear I have been a neglectful niece. It is my uncle Joseph's birthday today, and I quite forgot to drink his health at dinner. Now it will have to be with chocolate. A toast, ladies. To Rear Admiral Sir Joseph Harman."

They raised their cups and drank, then Amabel sat forward, her blue velvet gown tinged with purple in the candlelight. "I understand he almost caught the *Légère*?"

Charlotte nodded. "Would that he'd succeeded."

"Amen to that," murmured Amabel.

"Speaking of relatives, you have a brother, don't you, Amabel? I recall his name is Charles."

Amabel hesitated. "Er, yes."

Charlotte was curious. "Where is he now?"

"We've lost touch. I haven't seen him since we were children at Versailles."

"Ah, yes, Versailles. I was quite forgetting that Queen Marie Antoinette was your godmother. It must be difficult for you sometimes."

"Difficult?"

"To know whether your loyalties are with Britain or France."

Henrietta was appalled. "Oh, Charlotte, how could you?"

Amabel thrust her chocolate aside and leaped to her feet. "That is a monstrous thing to say, Charlotte! I find Republican France totally abhorrent, and so, I'm sure, does Charles! As Queen Marie Antoinette's godchildren, how could it be otherwise?"

Russell and Marcus looked up in consternation from their play, but Charlotte hastened to smooth the brief contretemps. "Good Lord, Amabel, there is no need for your feathers to fly! All I meant was that as someone who clearly must have fond memories of France, you must find this endless war particularly hard sometimes. So please stop being so sensitive."

Amabel hesitated, but resumed her seat. "I—I'm sorry I jumped to conclusions, Charlotte, but you did sound as if you were questioning my allegiance."

"Well, I wasn't."

The ensuing silence was broken by the chink of the billiard

balls as the men took up their play again. After a moment Amabel returned to the subject of the *Légère*. "Charlotte, I know Russell said it was only a rumor, but I keep hearing the whisper about gold being hidden here, and I can't help wondering if it's based on fact of some sort."

"Believe me, there's no gold." Charlotte's glance slid fleetingly toward Henrietta, then she gave a tinkling laugh. "Gold or not, it's as well the *Légère* doesn't know about the old smugglers' path, or she might try again."

Amabel's lips parted. "Old smugglers' path?" she repeated.

"Yes, down the cliff opposite the lych-gate at St. Tydfa's. Everyone had forgotten about it until the bushes were cleared recently, and it was discovered again. It's a very hazardous descent, but strings of packhorses used to negotiate it quite well. Or so I gather."

Amabel finished her chocolate and then stood. "I feel rather tired, so if you will forgive me, I'll retire now."

When she'd gone. Charlotte poured herself another cup. "Oh, how wonderful a drink this is, but far too wicked for the figure. Still, in my condition it hardly makes any difference, for I can't possibly get much bigger with only a month to go!"

"You do resemble a Montgolfier balloon," Henrietta said teasingly.

"Thank you very much. Anyway, if I last until February, I will be amazed. I feel as if I'm about to explode!"

"Please don't do that."

"I will endeavor not to." Charlotte smiled.

That night, as Jane wept herself to sleep in Kit's arms, and Henrietta and Marcus lay wide awake with their respective thoughts, Rowley was sitting dolefully on the ceiling of a very dark, windowless place, where there was a constant lapping of water. He didn't know where he was; indeed the only thing he knew for certain was that he'd at last tossed the bogle from his back and then hidden under a large heap of crumpled canvas on the quay. The canvas had suddenly been rolled up around him, and when he'd eventually dared to emerge, he'd found himself in this horrid place. He didn't know where the bogle had gone, just that it was no longer with him—for which mercy he was exceeding thankful!

A bell sounded every few hours, and earlier he had heard boots hurrying upon wood, but now there was just a man singing to the squeak of a fiddle, and the endless lap of water. Rowley was more dejected and frightened than he'd ever been before. He'd howled and howled in the hope that someone psychic would hear, but no one came near.

He got up to pace unhappily to-and-fro. How long would he be trapped like this? Giving another loud howl, he cocked an ear hopefully. The fiddle continued to scrape and the song didn't falter. Rowley's tail drooped. Jane or Kit had *always* heard him in the past; why didn't they come now? He paced and howled a little more, then came to a startled halt as everything was suddenly lit by a strange silver glow. Sound echoed very oddly and he saw a simple staircase, little more than a ladder, descending where there had been nothing a moment before.

Trembling with fear, the spaniel pressed back in a corner, and gradually things returned to what amounted to normal in this dreadful place. With a huge sigh, Rowley threw his head back to proclaim his misery anew, but the only response was the jangle of the bell.

Chapter Fifteen

A meeting about a boom across the harbor mouth had been arranged in the town the following morning. It was another bitterly cold but beautiful day, and as Russell and Marcus prepared to ride down after breakfast, they were surprised that Amabel appeared in her riding habit to accompany them. They argued in vain that she would find the meeting very dull, but in the end she had her way.

Charlotte had woken up in an oddly restless mood. She could not sit still and insisted upon a brisk walk along the cliffs with Henrietta, after which she decided to make the promised visit to Nurse. She wanted Russell to come too, but he had a prior luncheon engagement with the local magistrates, and Marcus and Amabel returned from Mulborough alone. Amabel had no desire to accompany the others to see Nurse, whom she did not know, and announced instead that she would attend to some long neglected correspondence. Marcus would not hear of Henrietta and Charlotte going alone to the hamlet of Mulbridge, even though it was only half a mile away. He insisted upon driving them in Russell's curricle, which could easily accommodate three, and so, with the winter sun at its highest, they set off.

Henrietta and Charlotte sat on either side of him. They were well wrapped against the cold, in fur-lined cloaks and matching muffs, and their feet rested on warmed bricks. The team of matching bays was kept at a gentle trot, and the two-wheeled vehicle hardly slid at all on the icy, hard-packed surface of the road.

Henrietta glanced back at the abbey, which stood out magnificently against the sparkling water of the bay. Her breath caught as at one of the windows she saw Jane weeping in Kit's arms. There was such an air of sadness about them, that Henrietta could almost have forgotten they were ghosts and begged Marcus to turn around immediately. She gazed back at them until they were too far away for her to see anymore, and as she faced the front again, she wondered why they were so sad. It was almost as if they were grief stricken.

Jane and Kit watched the curricle drive away. Jane was so brokenhearted about Rowley that she would have agreed to an eternity of haunting if only her beloved spaniel were to return. As Kit rested his cheek against her hair, he had to concede that he too missed Rowley. Tiresome as the little cur was, his disappearance left a void that could never be filled.

Mulbridge was little more than a few stone cottages nestling in a narrow valley where a moorland creek emptied into the Mull. The sound of rushing water echoed and rooks wheeled noisily above the trees as Marcus drove the curricle smartly over the bridge and brought it to a standstill beside Miss Rose Hinchcliffe's green-painted gate.

Frail now, but still active and alert, she was delighted to welcome her unexpected visitors. She was small and resembled a gray sparrow, with bright little eyes and a beak of a nose. Her hair was completely hidden beneath a crisply starched day bonnet, and she wore a comfortable gray woolen gown. Seeing how pink their cheeks were after the cold drive over the moor, she ushered them into her warm parlor. Cups of hot spiced caudle were pressed upon them as they sat on the settles that flanked the hearth. Nurse cast an experienced eye over Charlotte, then promptly declared that things were certainly more advanced than eight months. "Oh, indeed, yes. My lifetime of experience tells me for certain that you are due at any moment, my lady."

"Dr. Hartley saw me only a few days ago, and insists the original date is correct," Charlotte replied, recalling how she herself had questioned the point. He had been so offended that she doubted his word, that she'd felt obliged to apologize.

"That fool of a doctor gives himself airs and graces, but isn't capable of much more than prescribing laudanum. It's his cure-all!" Nurse did not care for the doctor, and the dislike was mutual.

Henrietta smiled. "I can vouch for that, for he dosed me well and truly."

Conversation drifted to other things, but Charlotte's odd restlessness soon got the better of her again. She got up to wander around the room, admiring the various little ornaments that were the nurse's pride and joy. Henrietta began to worry about her, and at last felt obliged to confide her concern to Marcus.

He was startled. "She seems all right to me," he whispered back, watching as Nurse took down yet another porcelain Staffordshire shepherdess to show to Charlotte.

"She seems incapable of sitting still more than a minute."

"What are you saying?"

"That I think Nurse is right. Charlotte is further than eight months. Last year I was at a house when a lady commenced her pains. She'd been behaving in exactly the same way."

Charlotte glanced toward them. "What are you two whispering about?"

Marcus cleared his throat. "We, er, were just agreeing that it would be better to leave soon because of the snow."

"*Leave?* But we've only just arrived!"

"Nevertheless, the afternoons are very short, and if something were to happen, it wouldn't do to be stranded on the moor."

"How very disagreeably cautious you are. I vow you are becoming a second Russell." Charlotte laughed, but then her breath caught and she put her hands to her stomach. "Oh . . . !"

Henrietta leaped to her feet. "Charlotte?"

"It's nothing, I'm sure." Charlotte smiled, but then gasped again. "What a kick my little monster has today!"

Nurse ushered her back to the settle. "My dear, I don't think the babe is just kicking. I'm afraid you won't be driving back to the abbey just yet; indeed you won't be leaving here until your churching in a month's time."

Charlotte was dismayed. "But I *must* go home!" Then she gasped as another pain gripped her.

Nurse spoke gently but firmly. "My dear, your little one is very impatient to arrive."

"Nurse is right, Charlotte," Henrietta said, putting a hand on her friend's shoulder.

Charlotte winced as another pain shot through her. "Well, I— I suppose you and Marcus are to be godparents a little earlier than anticipated," she gasped.

Henrietta and Marcus looked at each other in surprise, for they hadn't realized they had both been asked.

Nurse spoke again to Charlotte. "You'd best come upstairs, my dear, for there's no time to waste."

"It—it will be all right, won't it?" Charlotte asked, fear beginning to wash over her after the initial shock.

"Of course it will. I may be old now, but I'm still the finest midwife in all Yorkshire."

Displaying all the usual male signs of wishing to be anywhere but where he was, Marcus got up quickly. "Er, perhaps I should bring the doctor?" he ventured.

It was the wrong thing to say. Nurse was outraged. "I will not have that peacock in my house! This is women's work, and with Miss Henrietta's assistance, I'm more than able to do what's necessary."

"Then I will at least bring Russell."

Nurse sniffed. "Well, I suppose that must be done, but he's not coming within an inch of the poor dear until the babe is born. The last thing any woman wants at such a time is to look at the fellow who got her in this painful state in the first place! Before you go, you can make yourself useful by undoing all locks and knots in the house," she ordered, with scant respect for his rank. Marquess or mail coachman, the opposite sex were all the same to her when it came to the priorities of childbirth!

Marcus blinked. "Undo all the—? What on earth for?"

"To facilitate the birth, of course. Surely you know *that*?"

"I can't say I do, but if that is what you wish, then of course I will attend to it."

Nurse led Charlotte to the parlor door and then paused to look back at Henrietta. "Come, my dear, we'll look after her together."

Henrietta followed them out, but with considerable trepidation, for she had never before been present at a confinement.

The following hours were very fraught with tension, for although Charlotte's labor was short for a first child, it did not go easily. But at last, in the early moments of the new day, when dawn was still to come and the sky was bright with stars, Charlotte's daughter was born. She was a bonny baby with lusty lungs, and announced her arrival with yells that were clearly audible to Russell and Marcus waiting down in the parlor.

Her trials over, Charlotte's hair was brushed, and she lay back on rosemary-scented pillows. As she tenderly cradled her little girl, there was a soft glow about her that was quite the most beautiful thing Henrietta had ever seen.

Nurse clucked approvingly. "There now, my dear, wasn't that little angel worth it all?"

Charlotte gazed at her new daughter. "Oh, yes!"

"With that fool Hartley dancing around, you'd still be only halfway through because he'd have quietened you with laudanum."

"I hate to even think of it."

"Well, the babe confounded male schemes, did she not?" Nurse smiled fondly at the tiny being wrapped in a crocheted shawl. Then she looked at Charlotte again. "You know you must not leave here for at least a month now, don't you? This is the north of England, where old habits die hard. It would be considered an open invitation to terrible bad luck if you were to neglect the time-honored ways. You must stay inside for the cycle of the moon, and then leave only to go to church. If that is done, all will be well for you and for the babe."

Charlotte smiled. "I will do what is expected, Nurse." She glanced at Henrietta. "Will you keep me company here? I know it's an imposition because staying on will interfere with your plans, but you'll still be in good time for your cousin's wedding. Please say you will."

"Of course I'll stay."

"I'm fortunate to have such a good friend."

"I, er, don't know what Amabel will do, however. She might leave as planned in a week's time, or she could decide to stay on."

"Provided she doesn't come here to Mulbridge I really don't care what she does," Charlotte replied, then looked swiftly at Nurse. "If a Mrs. Renchester comes here and wishes to stay, please promise me you'll tell her you have no room."

"If that is your wish, my dear," Nurse answered.

Charlotte's thoughts moved on. "We'll have to arrange the christening. Nurse, would it be possible to arrange it for the same day as my churching? Or would that be frowned upon?"

"Churchings and christening can be on the same day, my dear."

"Excellent."

"Now then, I have been instructing a young girl by the name of Mary Gilthwaite in all my arts, and very capable she is too. She will be as fine a nurse to your babe as I was to His Lordship." Not for a moment did Nurse expect this presumption to be questioned, nor was it. She patted her starched bonnet and smoothed her fresh apron. "I suppose it is time to permit His Lordship to see his new daughter," she added as an afterthought, and went out.

Footsteps soon rang on the staircase and Russell hastened in, followed by Marcus. Russell was quite overcome, with tears on his cheeks as he first kissed Charlotte's forehead, then gazed down at his daughter.

Henrietta felt her own eyes fill with tears and withdrew from the room to the coolness of the landing, which was only lit by the faint light from the hall below. Minutes passed as she stood by a window, gazing at the dawn sky, then she heard the door open and close behind her.

It was Marcus. "How does it feel to be an apprentice midwife?" he asked, coming to stand next to her.

"Exhausting," she admitted.

"I gather Charlotte has asked you to stay here until she's able to return to the abbey?"

"Yes."

"I will be staying on as well. It would hardly be practical to leave, only to return within the month. However, you will have your wish."

"Wish?"

"Not to be under the same roof as me."

She felt suddenly awkward. "I, er, think I'll go down and see if any of that caudle remains. . . ."

As she turned to go, he caught her arm. "Don't marry Sutherton, Henrietta. He's only interested in your fortune."

"I'm only too well aware of his reasons, sir, and do not need your advice."

"On the contrary, I think you are very much in need of advice."

"Your view of Lord Sutherton has already been established, Marcus, and I really don't want to hear it again. Besides, it really isn't any of your business."

"It's very much my business. You turned me down in his favor, so I think I have a right to express an opinion."

Her eyes flashed in the shadowy light. "And why, pray, did you ask me in the first place? Let us hear the real reason, sirrah!"

"The *real* reason? What do you mean?" He looked at her in puzzlement.

Her gaze was scornful. "How well you ape innocence, my lord. One could almost be taken in by your performance as Sir Galahad reborn! But we both know that you aren't Sir Galahad, don't we? You are the vilest yet of all the Fitzpaines, and I despise everything about you!"

"Damn you for that, madam!" he breathed.

"And damn you too, sirrah." she replied softly, but with immeasurable feeling.

Suddenly he pushed her against the wall and held her there. "You would try even Sir Galahad's patience, Henrietta Courtenay! So I am the vilest yet of all the Fitzpaines, am I?"

"Yes!" she retorted, but her heart was pounding and his touch seared her.

"Then a kiss—for old time's sake—would be meaningless?"

"Totally meaningless."

"Let us test the truth of that."

"No!"

"Oh, yes, madam," he whispered, and bent his head to put his lips to hers.

He pressed her to the wall, his body to hers, and his lips were ruthless. It was a kiss that tore her heart with its wild passion. There was nothing of the drawing room about him now. Instead he was the savage Viking, raiding her soul as well as her flesh.

His hands moved over her, caressing the remembered contours of her waist and breasts. She felt the tip of his tongue against hers; the sensation was arousing for them both. His maleness strained toward her, hard and urgent, and she wanted to remain indifferent, but the blood was coursing through her veins. A treacherous warmth beguiled her. She hated him, *hated* him! But she wanted him too. . . .

Her arms slid unwillingly around him, and she began to return the kiss as hungrily as it was given. Desire swept her up in its net, and she sank against him, her lips as imperative as his own. It was a release of emotion such as she had never known before. Everything about him was vital to her very existence— his touch, his taste, his breath . . .

But at the very moment she acknowledged the truth in her heart and body, he drew scornfully away. His eyes were cold in the darkness as he took her chin roughly between his fingers. "Meaningless? I fancy not!" he breathed, then released her and walked away. His shadow leaped against the wall as he descended the stairs, then his boots rang in the hall before the parlor door closed behind him, and there was silence.

The spell shattered, and the heat on her skin chilled to ice. She had been made a fool of again. She closed her eyes as tears welled. "Oh, Henrietta Courtenay, will you never learn where he is concerned . . . ?" she whispered.

The past swam bitterly before her. It was London, and she was running tearfully down the garden in the rain. As she reached the summerhouse where she had known such joy in Marcus's arms, George's words still rang in her head. "I vow I find this task most distressing, Miss Courtenay, but there is no easy way of telling you. I feel you should know that the Marquess of Rothwell has a wager upon your surrender. It is in the betting book at White's." *In the betting book at White's . . . in the betting book at White's . . .*

Chapter Sixteen

It was February 11, the day of Charlotte's churching and Eleanor's christening, for such the baby was to be named. Henrietta's prolonged stay in Yorkshire was almost at an end, and the next day she and Amabel were due to set off on their long journey south to London. But a question mark now hung over their departure, because the past weeks had seen very heavy snow across the entire kingdom. Many country roads were impassable, and Mulbridge hamlet would have been completely cut off had not the local men labored hard and long clearing a way so that the celebration of Eleanor's birth could proceed as planned. Now the carriage had arrived from the abbey and waited at Nurse's gate.

Henrietta tried not to think of Marcus. On several occasions over the past month he had endeavored to speak to her, but she had successfully managed to avoid him. She wouldn't be able to avoid him today, however, for they would be together at the church and again at the abbey. Oh, how she prayed the roads would be pronounced fit for the journey south, because she did not think she could endure being close to him again for very long. She was dressed in a sapphire-blue woolen gown and a matching pelisse trimmed with gray fur. There was a gray fur hat on her dark hair, and she looked very stylish indeed. Stylish was the last thing she felt however, for that morning at Nurse's breakfast table something had happened that had stabbed her like a dagger.

Russell had arrived in the carriage and had joined the others in the cramped little dining room. "Isn't anyone going to ask me why Marcus and Amabel are driving to the church from the abbey, instead of leaving from here with us? After all, he *is* one of the godfathers," he said suddenly.

Charlotte glanced across at him. She was rocking the Mulborough family cradle, which had been transported from the abbey. She wore peach velvet, and was aglow with health and vitality. "Well, no doubt you are going to tell us."

He nodded. "It seems Amabel has a tendresse for him, and after much flirting, has finally succeeded. I'm convinced that she will soon be the Marchioness of Rothwell."

Henrietta didn't glance up, but her hand shook so much as she poured another cup of tea, that the teapot rattled against the blue-and-white china.

Charlotte stared at her husband. "And what, pray, leads you to such an unlikely conclusion?"

"The evidence of my own eyes. She has been quite shameless, and at first he did his utmost to avoid her, but then he began to change. This morning I saw her creeping from his room."

The teapot slipped from Henrietta's fingers and would have spilled had she not caught it quickly. "F-forgive me," she murmured apologetically to Nurse, whose best crockery it was.

"That's all right, my dear," the old woman replied, looking shrewdly at her.

Charlotte spoke again. "Russell, are you saying you actually saw Amabel leaving Marcus's room?"

"That's exactly what I'm saying."

Charlotte got up. "I can't believe Amabel appeals to Marcus in the slightest."

"Well, I know what I saw. Anyway, if it comes to that, I thought she had other fish to fry," Russell replied casually, then glanced at Henrietta and fell abruptly silent.

Henrietta looked up. "Other fish? What do you mean, Russell?"

Charlotte shot her husband a warning look, and he cleared his throat awkwardly. "Er, nothing. It's just an expression."

Nurse's quick gaze moved from one to the other, but Henrietta detected nothing. She got up. "If you will excuse me, I've left my gloves in my room . . ."

Oh, the agony of despair that had engulfed her as she hurried up to the little bedroom that had been hers for the past weeks. Hot, stinging tears could not be halted, and she'd flung herself on the patchwork counterpane, weeping in silent wretchedness.

It hadn't been easy to mend the damage to her face, and the Chinese box had been much resorted to before she at last considered her tearstains to be satisfactorily concealed. Now she was ready to leave with the others, but she really didn't know how she was going to cope with seeing Marcus and Amabel together.

Charlotte's voice carried from the hall. "We're ready to leave, Henrietta!"

"I'm coming." Taking a final look at herself in the little wall mirror, she pulled on her gloves and left the room.

It was sunny but still cold outside, and as Charlotte emerged with Eleanor in her arms, there were cheers from the inhabitants of Mulbridge, who were to follow in their pony traps to attend the double ceremony. Deep snow lay everywhere, mostly smooth and untouched, but in great heaps beside the road where the men had cleared the way. The creek was frozen, and the Mull itself had a crust of ice. Icicles hung from everything and curls of smoke rose lazily from cottage chimneys into motionless air. The rooks rose in a noisy flock as the carriage set off, followed by its procession of traps.

Half an hour later, the convoy entered Mulborough, where the townsfolk cheered and waved. The atmosphere was joyous, not only because of the new baby, but because the boom was almost finished and everyone felt safe from the *Légère*. Out in the harbor the *Avalon* fired her cannons in salute, and was answered by those on the abbey terrace. Crowds followed as the procession made its way up the steep hill to the church, and as the carriage halted at the lych-gate, Henrietta saw Russell's empty curricle. Amabel's handkerchief lay upon the seat, dropped when Marcus had assisted her to alight.

Composing herself, Henrietta forced a smile to her lips. Russell and Charlotte ascended the steps first, then came Mary

Gilthwaite with the baby. Henrietta followed at a distance, assisting Nurse, who found the climb difficult. The old woman paused to smile at the cheering people thronging the churchyard. "Well, Miss Henrietta, it would seem the Mulborough bogle is far from thought today."

"Indeed so."

"I'll warrant there wouldn't be a soul here if it were midnight." Nurse touched Henrietta suddenly. "Look, the marquess is at the church porch with that Mrs. Renchester."

Henrietta glanced up reluctantly. Marcus looked very elegant in a dark brown coat and fawn trousers, with a brown top hat and cream silk waistcoat. Amabel wore ice green; the white plumes on her wide-brimmed hat fluttered, and as if sensing Henrietta's gaze, she turned suddenly. For the space of a heartbeat she made no acknowledgment, but then smiled and raised a hand in greeting.

As Henrietta returned the salute, Nurse briefly touched her sleeve. "You're doing very well, Miss Henrietta. The marquess won't know a thing." She smiled as Henrietta's eyes flew to her. "You can't hide it from me, my dear, I know you love him."

Henrietta looked away in confusion. "I—I don't know what you mean."

"Deny it if you will, but I know better. Forget him, my dear, for he's a breaker of hearts. Come to that, *all* men are, and many women too, especially the likes of that Renchester woman." Nurse didn't care for Amabel, who had ridden over to Mulbridge only once to see Charlotte and Eleanor. She'd come with Marcus, and on leaving hadn't properly controlled her rather capricious horse, which had started forward, almost pinning Henrietta against the gate. Things might have been very hazardous if Marcus hadn't had the presence of mind to pull her to safety. Amabel had been all tearful apologies, but to Nurse her words somehow hadn't rung true.

"Please don't say that, for Amabel is my friend—" Henrietta began.

"Friend? After what she's done? My dear, she is a serpent."

Henrietta began to sense there was something she should know. "What exactly are you talking about, Nurse?"

The old woman realized she'd said too much, and fell into an embarrassed silence.

"Nurse?"

"It's of no consequence, my dear."

"On the contrary. I think it is of considerable consequence. Please tell me."

"It's not my place, Miss Henrietta."

Henrietta was determined. "You've gone this far, you may as well tell me. I won't let the matter lie, of that you may be sure."

Nurse became quite flustered. "Oh dear, I—I really don't think—"

"Tell me."

"Oh, me and my rattle tongue. I—I don't *know* anything, my dear, I've simply put two and two together from what was said at the breakfast table today. I'm probably wrong anyway."

"Wrong about what? *Please* tell me!"

Nurse drew a long breath. "Well, I guessed from what was said this morning that Mrs. Renchester had been more than she should to the gentleman you are to marry."

Henrietta stared.

"As I say, it's only a guess, and I'm probably entirely wrong."

Amabel and George? And Charlotte and Russell *knew*? Henrietta was shaken. With hindsight it had been clear from the moment Amabel arrived at the abbey that Charlotte's dislike for her moved on more levels than just old school rivalry. Henrietta closed her eyes. To her shame she knew she could cope with the thought of Amabel and George, but Amabel and *Marcus*? Oh, that was pain of the deepest kind.

Nurse put an uneasy hand on her arm. "My dear, please forget all about it. It's clearly long since over, and the marquess is receiving her favors now. Soon you will be Lady Sutherton."

Henrietta made no response. The future suddenly stretched before her with an awful clarity it never had before, and she knew she couldn't marry George. It had nothing to do with his infidelity, but was simply the realization that gratitude was no foundation for marriage. She felt nothing for him, and he felt nothing for her. His warning about Marcus had been delivered

solely with an eye to her fortune, not out of consideration for
her feelings. Henrietta opened her eyes again. Her decision was
final, although she wouldn't say anything to anyone else until
she'd had a chance to tell George face-to-face.

Nurse looked anxiously at her. "Are you all right, my dear?"

Henrietta smiled. "Yes, Nurse. Please don't worry, for
you've done no harm."

"Oh, I'm so relieved."

At that moment the cheering died away and Henrietta saw
that the crowd was moving toward the church. The main party
had already proceeded inside, except for Marcus, who was descending the steps. She steeled herself for a moment she had
been dreading.

He sketched a bow to them both and she inclined her head
stiffly. "My lord."

The formality of the response was not lost upon him. "It's
time to go into the church, but you've been talking down here
for some time. Is something wrong?"

"Nothing at all," she replied, glancing at the porch, where
Amabel had been.

Nurse continued up the steps, but Marcus prevented Henrietta from accompanying her. "We really should talk privately."

"About what?"

"That must be obvious."

"No, sir, it isn't, for in my opinion we have nothing whatsoever to discuss. Let us simply endure the remaining hours we
must be beneath the same roof, and in the morning I will gladly
depart." Henrietta pulled away from him, but then halted as she
saw Jane and Kit moving among the gravestones. The ghosts
were calling a name—Rowley—and she knew they were
searching for the spaniel. She glanced around, half expecting to
see the little dog gamboling toward them, but there was no sign
of it.

Marcus followed her gaze, but saw only the now empty
churchyard. "What are you looking at?" he asked.

"Nothing," Henrietta murmured, watching as the ghosts suddenly saw her looking and hastened away into the lane.

                    *   *   *

While Jane and Kit searched in vain for him, Rowley was still imprisoned in the dark. A little earlier, the whole world seemed to reverberate with thunder. Everything trembled and boomed, and he'd huddled even farther into his corner. There was more thunder, and then came a voice from beyond the door. "We're to celebrate too, lads! Orders are to break out some good rum!"

Suddenly a man came in with a lantern. He wore a thick blue woolen jersey and wide white nankeen trousers, and his long hair was pulled back and waxed into a pigtail. The swaying light revealed a storeroom containing, among other things, casks, barrels of gunpowder, ropes, and rolls of heavy canvas. But just as the overjoyed spaniel prepared to make a dash for it, something else crept in behind the man. It was the bogle, which was only too visible to Rowley, but could only be seen by humans if it chose to appear. The horrid manikin retreated into the shadows by a heap of sandbags, then the man went out with a cask on his shoulder and closed the door again.

Darkness returned, and the bogle sniggered. "I'm after you, dog, and I'll get you. No one disturbs *my* sleep and goes unpunished!"

Chapter Seventeen

Coming face-to-face with Henrietta in the churchyard had delivered a timely reminder to Jane and Kit that they had things to do if they wished to pass through the gates of heaven. They were only too aware that they'd allowed their grief over Rowley to take precedence over all else, and now their time had almost run out. When Henrietta left the abbey in the morning, their chance would be lost until the next time it snowed on New Year's Day. The hapless wraiths had not given up entirely, however, and that night halfheartedly reembarked upon their task.

It was late evening when they went in search of Henrietta, and found her in the grand saloon. From a dark corner, the ghosts watched the suppressed emotion on her face and wondered what she was thinking. She was the only person there. Marcus and Russell had already gone to their rooms. Charlotte was in the nursery with baby Eleanor, and for some time Amabel had been in the library writing a letter of instructions for the housekeeper at Renchester Park, the Wiltshire estate left to her by her late husband.

Henrietta wore a spangled cranberry silk gown and a simple gold necklace. A fringed gold-and-white cashmere shawl rested around her shoulders. Her face was pale and strained because she had endured an unutterably wretched evening. She was angry with Charlotte and Russell for not telling her about Amabel and George, and angry with Amabel for her treachery. But worse than that by far was having to watch Amabel fawning over Marcus, who made no move to discourage the attentions.

The secret pain was acute. Whatever may or may not have happened with George in the past, it was clearly Marcus now. Henrietta's feelings were in turmoil and she wanted to strike out at them all. She had been betrayed on all sides, and the hurt was immense.

In the library, Amabel wasn't writing. Instead she sat by the light of a single candle, mulling over the options that remained for ridding herself of the woman George Sutherton intended to make his bride. Henrietta appeared to possess nine lives, and time was now running out. There only remained tonight and the return journey south in which to succeed; after that the tiresome creature would be at her cousin's estate, and out of reach for heaven alone knew how long. Something had to be done, something utterly final which would dispose of her once and for all. The means was at hand, and she had shrunk from using it until now because there was a risk that its use might arouse suspicions in others.

Might. What a teasing word that was. Just how great *was* the likelihood? Enormous? Moderate? Infinitesimal? Amabel's fingers drummed pensively upon the writing desk, where her reticule lay beside the untouched sheet of vellum before her. A cold smile played briefly upon her lips. Infinitesimal was the word she preferred, and if she was very, very careful, infinitesimal the risk would be. She got up, extinguished the candle, and left the library.

At that moment Henrietta's hurt resentment boiled over. She *had* to confront someone, and Charlotte was the chosen target. Jane and Kit followed. They were still at a loss as to why she was clearly so angry, and also at a loss to know how to make use of this last night. Inspiration failed them, and all they could think of was following her. She picked up a lighted candle from the table at the foot of the stairs, and made her way up to the nursery.

As she went up the staircase, the ghosts were startled to realize they were not alone in following her, for a familiar whiff of sulfur made them turn to see Amabel, a silent shadow in moss-green silk gown. They still did not know why she hated Henrietta sufficiently to try to kill her. They only knew that she was very dangerous indeed, so they lingered until she'd passed, then they followed her as she in turn followed Henrietta. It was a stealthy procession that made its way toward the nursery, where Charlotte cradled Eleanor in her arms and made foolish cooing noises, as new mothers are wont to do. Amabel waited until Henrietta had entered, then tiptoed to press her ear to the door. The ghosts watched uneasily, for they could feel her new resolve and knew that tonight Henrietta was in more peril than she had ever been before.

Firelight flickered in the nursery as Charlotte sat in a hearthside chair, gazing adoringly at her sleeping daughter. The nurse, Mary Gilthwaite, had withdrawn discreetly into the adjoining room to sort through some of Eleanor's tiny clothes. Henrietta did not know she was there as she spoke.

"I must talk with you, Charlotte."

Charlotte's diamond earrings sparkled as she looked up swiftly. She smiled. "You gave me quite a start. I didn't hear you come in. If you've come to dandle your goddaughter upon your knee, I fear I'm too selfish to part with her."

"That isn't why I've come."

Charlotte detected an odd tone in Henrietta's voice. "Is something wrong?"

"Yes, I fear there is. Charlotte do you recall saying no one could have a better friend than me?" Henrietta asked quietly, placing the lighted candlestick on a table.

"What a strange question. Yes, of course I remember."

"Then is it not a pity that I can no longer pay you the same compliment?"

Charlotte's smile faded. "What do you mean?"

"That you have let me down."

Charlotte got up, her dismay visible in the dancing light from the hearth. She went to lay the baby gently in the cradle, then came over to Henrietta. "What is it? What has happened?"

"Why didn't you tell me about George and Amabel?"

At the door, Amabel's lips parted, and Jane and Kit looked at each other in astonishment. So *jealousy* was what lay behind it all! Amabel was intent upon preventing another woman from becoming Sutherton's wife. Suddenly they understood the conversation in the cloisters on the night of the ball. Amabel was aware that Marcus knew of her affair with Sutherton, and she had been at pains to convince him he was wrong.

Charlotte exhaled slowly. "How did you find out?"

"Nurse correctly interpreted what happened at breakfast this morning, and was unguarded enough to let something drop to me. I made her tell me."

Charlotte put a quick finger to her lips. Her gray velvet evening gown whispered as she went to the adjoining room. "That will be all for tonight, Mary. You may retire."

"Very well, my lady." Mary bobbed a hasty curtsy, then went through into the room beyond, which was her little bedroom. Charlotte saw that both doors were firmly closed, then came back to Henrietta. "Please believe me when I say it was not easy to discover what we did, and then say nothing to you. You are going to marry that mongrel Sutherton, and you *insist* upon regarding Amabel as a dear friend, so how could Russell and I tell you they were possibly conducting a liaison behind your back?"

"Possibly?"

"The only proof we have is something Russell was told the last time he was in White's. It was rumor, no more, but it seemed very firmly founded."

"The gist being that George and Amabel are lovers?"

"Yes. Henrietta, if there is any truth in all this, *they* are the ones you should confront, not me."

Henrietta thought for a moment, and then exhaled slowly. "I know. I suppose I'm taking the coward's way out by picking on you instead."

"Henrietta, now you've found out about Amabel and George, I don't understand how you haven't scratched out her eyes."

Henrietta glanced away. She cared very much that Amabel was now with Marcus, but she didn't care at all if Amabel had been between the sheets with George. The marriage wasn't going to take place anymore, and that was that. She'd felt angry and betrayed by the secrecy, not by any involvement of the heart. It was Marcus who had her heart . . . She thrust the train of thought aside. "Charlotte, what exactly did Russell hear in London?"

"Only what I've already said. He made a few inquiries, but could dig no deeper. And please spare me a heated defense of Amabel's virtues, for I believe that deep down you *know* she is a devious, designing *chienne*. She and Sutherton are well matched."

Henrietta moved away to the fireplace, where the spangles on her gown caught the light almost as brightly as Charlotte's diamonds. For a long moment she stood looking thoughtfully down at the flames, then she glanced back over her shoulder. "You're quite right, I *do* know that Amabel isn't an angel."

"Well, at least you admit it at last. Anyway, whatever may or may not have gone on with Sutherton in the past, it must be over now, for Marcus appears to be the latest apple of her designing eye."

At the door, Jane and Kit shook their heads. Oh, no, the affair with Sutherton certainly wasn't over, nor was there now a liaison of any kind with Marcus, just some artful deception on Amabel's part. She had to stay close to Henrietta if she was to succeed in her murderous plans, and an unwelcome denouement might result in untimely expulsion from the abbey. She was therefore intent upon fooling not only Marcus, but also Charlotte and Russell. Fearing the former might tell, and not realizing the latter already knew but had decided not to speak of it, she set out to cast doubt on any unwelcome revelations by pretending to leave Marcus's room that morning at a time when she knew Russell would see her. The puzzled ghosts had seen her just standing there with a hand on Marcus's door, as if she had just emerged, and hadn't understood. Now all was clear.

In the nursery, Henrietta kept a brave face. "Until today, I had no idea Amabel felt anything for Marcus."

There was a faint noise at the door, and Charlotte turned sharply. "What was that?"

"I didn't hear anything."

Charlotte hurried to fling the door open. There was no one there, but the candles just along the passage toward the staircase fluttered as if someone had just hastened past. Charlotte shivered, but then told herself that the flames were only moving because of the many drafts that crept through the abbey. Turning, she closed the door and came back into the nursery. "Where were we?"

"I'd just said I had no idea Amabel felt anything for Marcus." Henrietta swallowed. "Charlotte, I still have feelings for him too. In fact, I'm still hopelessly in love with him," she confessed quietly.

"Oh, good Lord." Charlotte was so shaken she had to sit down.

Henrietta continued. "I've loved him all along, and I think I always will."

"And you *still* intend to marry Sutherton?"

Henrietta hesitated, and then shook her head. "No, I've decided I can't. When Nurse told me what she'd guessed about Amabel and him, I realized I couldn't go through with it. I was suddenly faced with exactly how little regard he had for me. I wasn't going to say anything until I'd had a chance to speak to him, but since you ask me a direct question . . ."

Charlotte breathed out with relief. "Oh, thank goodness, for I vow that if you'd proceeded, you would have been the most wretched bride on earth. But Henrietta, if Marcus is the one you love, you mustn't give up without a fight!"

"He's with Amabel now," Henrietta reminded her. "Besides, mine is not only an unrequited love, it's also a very ill-advised one. I told you why he pursued me in the first place, so I know his ardency was false."

"I still cannot believe he would do such a thing. Not Marcus, and not for a wager."

"Well, he did." Henrietta gave a sad smile, then picked up the candlestick once more and left the nursery.

Chapter Eighteen

The trembling of the candles Charlotte had seen in the passage had been caused when Amabel ran to the nearest passage to hide. It was the passage that led to Marcus's room, and as the nursery door was flung open, she'd just drawn back out of sight in a cold window embrasure behind some heavy arras curtains. The window happened to be the very one where, on the night of the ball, she had hidden Henrietta's betrothal ring on the pelmet. Kit slipped through the curtains to stand with her, but Jane had remained to eavesdrop upon Henrietta and Charlotte. After a few moments the nursery door closed again, and Kit watched as Amabel exhaled with relief. He wished he could read her mind. Whatever it was, the insidious odor of sulfur was all around.

Amabel leaned her head back against the cold glass. She was still shaken to realize that Charlotte and Russell had known all along about her affair with George, and upset too that Henrietta had now found out. Everyone knew, but only Marcus had ever mentioned it. Not that he was sure of his facts anymore. Amabel smiled a little, but then the smile faded. Henrietta's discovery did not seem to have made any difference, for she hadn't indicated any intention to withdraw from the match. Which meant that nothing had changed; tonight the future Lady Sutherton had to breathe her last.

Amabel opened her reticule, which was looped over her wrist. From it she took a tiny blue glass vial. Even behind the curtain there was sufficient light from the passage for Kit to

read the single word written upon it in gold. Curare. Amabel
gazed at the vial for a moment and then replaced it in the reticule. The blood coursed wildly through her veins, and myriad
expressions made her face ugly. A plan had begun to form, and
she parted the curtains to glance toward Marcus's door, beneath
which shone a thin line of light. She stepped from hiding and
hurried to the main passage to get one of the lighted candle-
sticks, then she returned to the embrasure and listened for the
soft sound of the nursery door opening again.

The cold air from the window made her shiver, and she
glanced out. It was the first cloudy night in nearly a month, and
the bay was dark. At two o'clock the *Légère* would lie offshore,
watching for the signal from St. Tydfa's. Amabel smiled as she
recalled how laboriously she had gathered information about
the channel and the boom, only to find there was no longer any
need to even be concerned about such obstacles. Now the
smugglers' path offered a much safer landing! She also had information to divulge about the precise whereabouts of the Treasury gold. In vain had Charlotte denied its existence, for
diligent inquiries among the abbey servants had finally revealed the truth. No doubt Russell thought the old icehouse a
clever ruse, but such a deserted, unprotected place, with the livery stable conveniently on the edge of the town, was heaven-
sent to the *Légère*. A string of horses could soon carry the gold
from the icehouse, down the cliff path to a waiting boat, and the
good citizens of Mulborough would not even realize what was
happening. Before dawn broke, a portion of England's gold
would be on its way to France! Amabel glanced at her little fob
watch. In less than three hours she would start signaling from
the churchyard.

Kit's unease intensified. The creature had more in mind than
just Henrietta's demise; he knew from the way she glanced outside and at her watch. The phantom glanced at the window as
well, but all he saw was the dark, starless sky. His thoughts
broke off as Jane suddenly fled toward him along the passage,
having realized that Henrietta was about to leave the nursery.

"Kit, where are you?" she whispered urgently.

"Here!" He beckoned her behind the curtain. He had no fear

that Amabel would hear or see anything, because he was certain she wasn't in the least psychic. As the nursery door opened again and Henrietta emerged, Kit whispered briefly what he'd witnessed.

Amabel heard the nursery door as well, and stiffened expectantly. Shielding the candle with her hand, she slipped out of hiding to Marcus's door and there took up a position with one hand on the knob, as if she had but that moment come out. She was careful not to make any sound that Marcus might hear.

As Henrietta's footsteps neared the corner, Amabel shook the candle so the flame danced in the otherwise shadowy passage. Henrietta turned and Amabel put a finger to her lips before hurrying to her, whispering excitedly. "Oh, Henrietta, I'm so happy that I feel I will burst. I have long loved Marcus, and he has just confessed he loves me too!"

Henrietta's glance moved toward the light beneath Marcus's door. "I—I'm very glad for you, Amabel."

Amabel linked her arm and accompanied her toward the landing. "I confess I was dismayed when I saw him kissing you in the entrance hall that time, but you said it meant nothing, and he said the same."

Henrietta didn't comment.

Amabel's green eyes shone in the candlelight, and she squeezed Henrietta's arm. "I can't believe he's mine at last. And to think I have Sutherton to thank."

"George?"

"Yes." Amabel gave a rueful smile. "To be truthful, he and I are quite good friends, although we haven't told you for fear you would misunderstand. Others have misinterpreted, you see, and we didn't want you to do the same. There has never been anything between us—we just get on. There, it is off my conscience at last. If you only *knew* how I've worried over it. Anyway, I confided in George how I felt about Marcus and he told me to show my hand. So that is what I did. When you and Charlotte were at Mulbridge, I was quite shameless. I wonder Russell didn't tell you, for I vow he must have seen me leaving Marcus's room on more than one occasion. He certainly saw this morning. Oh dear"—Amabel halted, and bit her lip ashamedly. "How totally without principle you must think me."

Henrietta managed a smile. "Amabel, you and Marcus are at liberty to do as you please."

"How dear a friend you are, indeed. After Marcus, I vow I love you most in all the world. If I can ever, *ever* be as good a friend to you, I will be content." Amabel kissed her cheek, then squeezed her arm again. "I have a fancy for a cup of chocolate, and I'm sure I can persuade the cook to make some specially. Will you join me?"

"Er, no, it's very late, and I'd rather go to bed."

"Then let me bring some chocolate to you."

"I have a headache, and merely require a little sleep."

"Then I *insist* you take some chocolate, for I find it a sovereign remedy for headaches. *Please* let me show my concern and friendship," Amabel urged persuasively. "You go to your bed, I won't be long."

"Oh, very well."

Amabel smiled, then hurried away, her candle shadow looming over the walls, then gradually diminishing down the staircase Henrietta sighed. She didn't want a drink of anything, she simply wanted to be left alone. But Amabel meant well . . . She walked on.

The ghosts peered around the corner, then emerged into the main passage. Jane looked at Kit in dismay. "That—that Renchester creature is going to put curare in the chocolate, isn't she?"

"I would lay odds upon it," he replied.

"We have to stop her!"

"And so we will, but she must not know it."

"What do you mean?"

He told her about Amabel's glance outside and then at the fob watch. "Jane, I can feel in my bones that Mrs. Brimstone is up to far more than just her campaign against Henrietta, and I feel it's vital we find out what it is."

"But what do you imagine she could be doing?"

"I don't know, damn it, but the suspicion is very strong. It's obvious that we must not let Henrietta drink the chocolate, but at the same time we want to find out more about Mrs. Brimstone."

Jane searched his face in the darkness. "Your intuition is very reliable, Kit, so I will not argue. But Henrietta must not come to harm."

"She won't, I promise."

Her fingers closed briefly over his. "What do you want to do?"

"Well, because curare works so very quickly, I think we have to take Henrietta into our confidence, so she can pretend to drink and succumb."

Jane stared at him. "*Tell* her? Are you mad? We are strictly forbidden to communicate with our subjects! It's bad enough that Henrietta has seen and heard us accidentally, but at least that isn't our fault."

"I know, but I called out a warning in the church tower, remember? I feel it didn't result in our recall because I didn't do it to further our cause, but to save her life. We will be saving her life this time, too."

"I don't like it, Kit. Can't we just make the drink spill?"

"Amabel will only insist upon preparing another. No, my dear, we have to involve Henrietta. There is no other way. Besides, I'm sure I'm right. Ghosts are permitted to appear in order to save lives."

Jane looked at him for a long moment, and then nodded. "Very well, we will do as you feel right." She smiled bravely as tears welled in her eyes. "I wish . . ."

"Yes?"

"I wish Rowley were here," she whispered.

Chapter Nineteen

Henrietta had undressed and was seated in her wrap at her dressing table, brushing her hair. She paused, half shocked, half accepting, as she saw Jane and Kit's semitransparent reflections in the mirror. Slowly, and with a trembling hand, she put down the brush. "What do you want of me? Why am I the only one who can see you?"

Kit explained. "Because you have more pyschic power than anyone else. In fact, in all our hundred years you are the *only* person who has been able to see, hear, and speak to us."

"You *are* Kit Fitzpaine and Jane Courtenay, aren't you?"

They nodded.

"I heard you speak to each other at the ball, then I read Lady Chloe's journal."

"We know, we watched you. We hid behind the screen in case you saw us," Jane replied, nodding toward the screen in question.

"But why can I suddenly see you? I've been here at the abbey on numerous occasions without realizing you were here."

Kit smiled. "That's because this is the first time you've been here when it has snowed on New Year's Day."

"Is that what governs you?"

"Yes, we have to have snow. "He told her about St. Peter's error, but not about the mission that would secure redemption.

Henrietta looked from one to the other. "And why have you decided to speak to me tonight?" she asked quietly.

Jane stepped forward. "Because we have to warn you

about—" she began, but then turned in dismay as Amabel's footsteps were heard approaching. Kit immediately fixed his attention upon the door, to keep it firmly closed.

Amabel rattled the handle. "Have you locked the door, Henrietta?"

Jane put a ghostly hand on Henrietta's shoulder, although her touch could not be felt. "Trust us, Henrietta, for we are your friends! Amabel means you ultimate harm, so you must not drink the chocolate. It's poisoned with curare, do you understand?"

Henrietta's eyes widened. *"Curare?* But—"

"We will explain, and we will be with you while she is here, but she cannot see or hear us." Jane nodded at Kit, who immediately permitted the door to open.

Amabel almost stumbled in, and had to steady both the cup of chocolate and her candlestick, which dripped specks of wax on the floor. "Good heavens, what a very stiff door! I was certain you must have locked it, but suddenly the handle just turned!"

"Yes, it does that sometimes," Henrietta answered.

Amabel put the chocolate on the dressing table before her. "If you wonder how I was able to make it so swiftly, I have to confess I caught the servants just about to sit down to some they'd made just for themselves. *And* they had a Madeira cake to enjoy with it! I vow Charlotte should be told they eat and drink more grandly than she realizes!" She laughed lightly, and put the candlestick down as well.

Jane warned Henrietta again. "She is all smiles, but remember not to trust her at all!"

A cold shiver ran through Henrietta as she gazed at the cup, but she managed to speak. "It's very kind of you to bring it to me, Amabel."

"Kind? Oh, what nonsense. Now then, you must drink every drop."

Jane fixed Henrietta with a look. "We must make her turn her back for a moment. Ask her to get you something from the dressing room," she ordered.

Henrietta thought quickly. "Oh, I vow it's colder tonight than

I realized. Amabel, would you be an angel and bring my shawl?
It's in the top drawer behind the screen."

"Yes, of course."

The moment Amabel stepped behind the screen, Kit caused
the chocolate cup to rise in the air and float to the fireplace,
where it tipped its contents into the fire with a hiss that was lost
as the logs shifted. Then the empty cup floated back to the
saucer on the dressing table.

Amabel returned, placed the shawl gently around Henrietta's
shoulders, and then stared at the cup. "Good heavens, have you
drunk it all already?"

"Yes, and it was delicious."

Kit caught Henrietta's eye. "Curare kills by slowing the heart
until it stops altogether, so pretend to be suddenly very, very
tired," he instructed.

Henrietta dutifully stretched and yawned. "Oh, I can hardly
keep my eyes open," she murmured sleepily.

Amabel smiled and hastened to the bed to turn back the cov-
erlet. "Come, I'll even tuck you in," she said.

"Sway a little," Kit said as Henrietta got up.

She did as she was told, and was solicitously helped to the
bed. The moment she was lying down, she pretended to fall
asleep. Amabel waited, and Henrietta began to breathe very
deeply, as if succumbing to the curare.

"Sleep forever, Henrietta, dear." Amabel murmured, then
glanced down at Henrietta's left hand. The emeralds on the betrothal ring caught the candlelight, and after a moment Amabel
removed it and placed it on her own finger. "I regard this as
mine, Henrietta dear. When George bade me choose a betrothal
ring, I believed it was for me, but instead he gave it to you."
She looked down at Henrietta again. "You'll be found cold in
your bed come the morning, and no one will know what happened, just as no one knew why Renchester died." She turned
as the clock on the mantelpiece chimed midnight. "Soon it will
be two o'clock, and all will be well," she murmured, then
picked up the empty cup and the lighted candlestick, and went
out.

As the door closed softly, Henrietta immediately sat up

again. Her face was ashen, for there was no doubt that Amabel was confident of having murdered her as anonymously as she had the unfortunate Captain Renchester. She looked up at the wraiths. "Why has she done this to me? Is it simply because of George Sutherton?"

Jane nodded. "We believe she has been behind every mishap that's befallen you, both here and in London. It will all have dated from the moment she learned Sutherton had decided to marry you."

"To marry my fortune, you mean," Henrietta corrected wryly.

Jane went on. "With time running out, Amabel decided to act once and for all. If it were not for Kit and me, you would now be dying. Jealousy is a terrible emotion, Henrietta, and Amabel is soured to the very core that Sutherton wants you as his wife. It doesn't matter to her that there is no love involved, just that you will have the life she craves with all her wicked heart. Kit and I call her Mrs. Brimstone, for where she is, there also is a whiff of sulfur. She's destined for Old Nick, make no mistake of that."

Something occurred to Henrietta, and she looked up with sudden hope. "Does this mean she isn't in love with Marcus?"

Jane laughed. "Nor he with her. He doesn't even realize how much she has been pretending. More than once Kit and I have seen her *seem* to be leaving his room, but never once has she actually been inside with him. Well, maybe once, on the night of the ball, but even then nothing, er, ultimate took place." Jane colored a little, and then went on. "Her interest in him is an act designed to allay suspicion—his, Charlotte and Russell's, and finally tonight, yours."

Henrietta looked away. "She need not have feared Marcus would trouble to warn me. His opinion of me is very low." She pushed the bedclothes aside and got up. "I fear I am a hopeless judge of men. I still love him and find it hard to accept that he was prepared to lay odds upon my chastity. Still, he is a Fitzpaine and I am a Courtenay, so I suppose I should know how low he would stoop." She remembered then, and turned with a quick blush. "Oh, forgive me, Kit, I—I . . ."

Kit held up a hand. "Do not apologize, Henrietta, for the Fitzpaines have much to answer for."

Jane nodded her agreement. "And so do the Courtenays. Both families are as bad as each other, and it's all my fault and Kit's. If we hadn't eloped as we did, the Fitzpaines and Courtenays would no doubt still be the best of friends."

Henrietta smiled. "You fell in love, that is all."

"Oh, yes, we fell in love," Jane murmured, looking mistily at Kit.

Henrietta smiled. "Jane, looking at you is like looking in a mirror. You and I might be sisters, not two people separated by over a century. And Kit, you look exactly so like Marcus, it's quite uncanny."

"Vikings both, for I too enjoy the noble pastime of sailing," Kit murmured, sketching a bow.

Henrietta remembered something. "Jane, what happened to your little dog? Rowley, isn't that his name? I saw you searching for him in the churchyard. Have you lost him?"

Jane's eyes filled with tears and Kit answered for her. "I fear we indeed lost poor Rowley." He related the dreadful events in the churchyard.

Henrietta's eyes widened. "You—you mean there really are such things as bogles?"

"Oh, yes, and very disagreeable entities they are, too. They are foot-high goblins with rodent faces, who delight in preying upon the weak and lonely. Anyway, the one at St. Tydfa's churchyard rode poor Rowley away down the hill into Mulborough, and we haven't seen him since."

Jane stifled a sob and searched desperately in her sleeve for her handkerchief. Kit put a swift arm around her. "Don't fret, my beloved, I'm sure he will soon be back, and ambling everywhere in search of sugared almonds." The ghost paused, recalling a moment earlier in the day when he himself had searched through the castle, not for sugared almonds, but for Rowley. He had happened upon Amabel drawing on a piece of paper. He hadn't paid much attention at the time, but now recalled that her drawing had actually been a map of the coast around Mulborough.

Jane stopped dabbing her eyes and looked earnestly at him. "Kit? What is it?"

"My love, I think I have remembered something which might explain what else Mrs. Brimstone is up to—or perhaps I should call her Madame Soufre!"

"What do you mean?"

"Simply that I fear she may be the enemy in more ways than one. She isn't simply intent upon eliminating a rival for George Sutherton's worthless affections. I believe she is the person who is signaling to the *Légère*! She's a French spy!"

"Why on earth do you think that?" Jane gasped.

"Today I saw her drawing a map of Mulborough Bay, upon which I'll warrant she placed the channel and boom exactly. And if she has found out about the icehouse, that will be shown as well! Maybe she even knows about the old smugglers' landing."

"She does," Henrietta said quietly, remembering the conversation over chocolate in the conservatory, when Amabel had become so agitated about Charlotte's remarks concerning her patriotism.

Kit's thoughts raced on. "I believe Amabel's jealousy over Sutherton is merely an adjunct to her main purpose. It wasn't to make up with Charlotte that she begged Henrietta to bring her here, it was to find out what the *Légère* needs to know! Those signals from St. Tydfa's were seen after her arrival here, and Jane and I have seen her questioning the servants about the gold. Then there is her odd determination to attend that meeting concerning the boom. And what of the past, and all the accusations leveled at her husband? It wasn't Renchester who was the spy, but his wife! The evidence begins to mount. And now, not only has she drawn a map of this area, but her eye is upon the clock. Oh yes, you mark my words, she's counting the minutes to a rendezvous with the privateer. Tonight she means to deliver her information into French hands."

Henrietta knew he was right, for it all fell into place too well. "And she will do it at two o'clock," she said. "Remember the last words she said in here? *Soon it will be two o'clock, and all will be well.*"

Kit turned quickly to Jane. "We're wasting precious minutes, my love! With the snow so deep, she will have to leave soon if she is to be sure of reaching St. Tydfa's in good time. We must follow. Maybe we can even find a way to use our powers not only to stop her, but to sink the *Légère*!"

Jane gathered her skirts to hurry to the door with him, but Henrietta called after them. "Wait! I want to come too!"

Kit shook his head. "No, Henrietta, it's far too hazardous. Nothing can happen to us, but you could be harmed. Besides, if Amabel sees you, she will realize something is amiss."

"I promise to keep well out of sight."

"You'll stay here," he commanded. "Leave this to us. If we have the chance to do anything, we will. If, on the other hand, we only discover their intentions, we will relay any information to you. You may depend upon us."

Her lips parted to argue, but then she acquiesced. "Very well, if that is what you wish." But she did not mean to disobey. Having just been left for dead by Amabel, she had a vested interest in seeing what happened to that lady!

Without the formality of opening the door, the phantoms hurried away, and as soon as they'd gone Henrietta dressed in her warmest clothes, and raised the hood of her cloak and hastened to the empty room from where she herself had been observed by Marcus. Amabel would be simply observed when she went for a horse.

Marcus spoke suddenly from behind. "Turn around very slowly or I will take great pleasure in squeezing this trigger."

She turned in dismay and saw him leveling a pistol at her. His face changed as he realized who she was. "*Henrietta?* I thought it was the intruder again!"

She glanced anxiously outside, but there was nothing to be seen. The kitchen garden was deserted and there was no sound from the stables.

"What are you looking at?" Marcus demanded, putting the pistol away and coming to join her.

She knew she had to confide in him. A little anyway, since she had no intention of mentioning the ghosts. "Marcus, it's Amabel. She's not only been trying to kill me, but she is most probably the person who is signaling to the *Légère*. I believe she's about to go to St. Tydfa's to keep a rendezvous."

He stared at her. "You're serious, aren't you?"

"Never more so."

"How do you know all this?"

"There's no time to explain now, just believe that I'm telling the truth."

"Why should I trust you?"

She flushed in the darkness. "Now is not the time to carp about the past, Marcus. You can think what you wish of me, for to be sure I will do the same of you, but since we have been thrust together like this tonight, I think it best if we call a truce for an hour or two," she replied.

His gaze moved over her cloak and to the sturdy boots peeping from beneath the hem. "I take it you are intending to follow her?"

"Yes."

"I won't permit it."

She raised her chin. "And how do you propose to prevent me? By locking me up?"

"Henrietta—"

"There's no point in arguing, Marcus, for I will not listen." She looked out again and this time saw Amabel, cloaked and hooded, but still recognizable, hurrying toward the wicket gate. Jane and Kit were at her heels. "She's leaving now!"

Suddenly he decided. "We'll *both* follow her, and you can tell me all about it as we ride. I'll just get my outdoor clothes."

"Do hurry!"

"I will."

Chapter Twenty

The night air was bitter and light snow began to fall as Marcus and Henrietta rode out beneath the archway to the cliff top. Snow lay so deeply that the horses could not move swiftly, but they had the comfort of knowing Amabel's mount was similarly handicapped.

Marcus pressed Henrietta for more explanation, and she related a version of events that was entirely devoid of phantoms. It proved surprisingly easy. She told him how she had providently poured away a poisoned cup of chocolate, and had then nearly fallen asleep. She claimed to have sensed something sinister in Amabel's attitude, and to have had the presence of mind to continue to feign sleep, so that Amabel, thinking her to be succumbing to the effects of curare, felt at liberty to taunt her with the full truth.

Marcus accepted what she said, for he could believe anything of the beautiful but deadly Amabel, from betrayal of her long friendship with Henrietta to the unbelievable callousness of letting Major Renchester take the blame for her actions, and then poisoning him with curare.

There was no sign of Amabel or the ghosts as Marcus and Henrietta left the cliff top and entered the woodland, where the trees were very still, and deep snow continued to crunch beneath the horses' hooves. The icehouse was barely visible in the winter undergrowth, and when they reached the edge of the town, everything was silent except for the stirring of the horses in the livery stable as the two riders passed by, St. Tydfa's was barely visible against a leaden night sky. Amabel's horse was tethered by the lych-gate, but of Amabel herself, or the ghosts, there was still no sign. The bay below was silent and mysterious, seeming to stretch into infinity, and Mulborough harbor was cloaked in darkness. Snowflakes brushed Henrietta's face as she gazed up at the church tower. She half expected to see a light flashing, but there was nothing.

They dismounted well short of the church and left the horses in a field entrance, where a large holly tree afforded a little shelter. An owl hooted, and Marcus spoke softly. "I wonder if the Mulborough bogle is out and about tonight?"

"The bogle isn't here anymore," she replied without thinking.

He glanced curiously at her. "It's only a legend. There aren't really such things."

That's all you know, she thought.

He shivered. "Dear God, it's getting more cold by the minute. If this continues . . ." He glanced back toward Mulborough.

"If this continues—what?" Henrietta prompted.

"The harbor has been known to freeze over. I was thinking of the *Avalon*."

"I'm sure it will take much more than this."

"Maybe, I just have a feeling . . ."

Henrietta looked toward the church. "What shall we do? Wait here, or go up to the church?"

"If we go up to the church we risk being seen. Better to stay here, where the uncleared bushes offer some concealment if necessary." He took out his pocket watch. "If two o'clock is the appointed hour, it is almost that now." As he spoke, a light began to flicker in the church belfry.

Henrietta's breath caught and she turned sharply to look out into the bay. Nothing happened, but then there came a faint flash about a quarter of a mile offshore.

"Well, it would seem the lady is indeed spying for the French," Marcus said.

After a while the signals stopped. Time seemed to hang, then a figure appeared in the church porch with a lantern. It was Amabel, and as she began to hurry down the church steps toward the lych-gate, she was followed by Jane and Kit, although only Henrietta knew they were there.

As anxious to keep out of the phantoms' sight as Amabel's, Henrietta ran to the nearby bushes with Marcus close behind. They both ducked safely into hiding as Amabel emerged into the road. Stray snowflakes were illuminated by her lantern as she crossed to the very spot where they had been standing a moment before. Jane and Kit were at her shoulder, and Henrietta saw the grim expression on Kit's face. She suddenly knew what he was thinking. Amabel was at the very edge of the cliff; all it would take was the swift use of his power, and just like the cup of poisoned chocolate, over she would go. But not yet, not yet, for the ghost wanted the *Légère* as well!

Amabel swung the lantern slowly from side to side. An answering light swung in the bay, but from much closer than before. A boat was coming ashore! Amabel began to descend the path, still holding the lantern up so that the approaching Frenchmen could see exactly where she was. Without hesitation, Jane and Kit followed her.

Marcus and Henrietta emerged from behind the bushes and went to look over the cliff. They could see Amabel's lantern and hear small stones she dislodged as she descended.

"What now?" Henrietta whispered, pushing her hood back. Snowflakes touched her skin like tiny cold fingertips.

Marcus drew a long breath. "I'd dearly like to see and hear exactly what happens, but if we follow, she'll hear us, and so will anyone she meets. I have no desire to confront a party of armed French cutthroats on a steep, narrow cliff path, have you?"

"Hardly."

"So we remain here."

"Marcus, we've come here on the spur of the moment, without any plan."

"What plan is needed? Let us first see what unfolds."

"But shouldn't we at least alert the town?"

"And cause such a clamor that the French are warned? No, I think not."

"But—"

"Henrietta, please be calm. The French aren't going to capture us."

"How can you be so sure?"

"Because we will hear them climbing up, and have sufficient time to get away. *Then* we can alert the town if necessary. Not that it will avail the French of much even if they succeed in reaching the icehouse, because the gold isn't there anymore. Russell had it secretly moved to the abbey cellars late last night."

"What made him do that?"

"A timely sixth sense, I suppose."

"But Amabel was at the abbey, too, so surely she must know."

"Amabel happened to be occupied with me at the time."

Henrietta stiffened. "With you?"

"That's what I said."

"I see." Fresh hurt struck through her.

"Do you?"

"I think so."

He gave a soft laugh. "Oh, Henrietta Courtenay, what a suspicious mind you have. All we did was play billiards."

She was suddenly vulnerable, doubting the ghosts' reassurance that Amabel had pretended the entire affair with him. Maybe Russell had been right after all!

He felt the change in her. "Henrietta, if I say we were at billiards, you may be certain it is the truth, although why I should feel obliged to explain my actions to you, I really don't know."

"Is billiards all you've ever played with her, sir?" Henrietta couldn't help the question.

"No, it isn't, but that was in the past, before I met you, though I do not deny she has offered her favors since."

"And you, being noble, refused?"

"Yes, as it happens, I did." He was angry. "One thing is certain, madam, I should have taken *you* to my bed when I had the opportunity!"

"There was *never* an opportunity!" she breathed.

"Oh, yes, there was, and you know it."

She gazed furiously at him. "You flatter yourself!"

His voice remained level and quiet. "And you delude yourself. Admit it, Henrietta, you were within a heartbeat of succumbing. Indeed you would have given your all if I had not been gentleman enough to call a halt."

It was a truth that was painful enough to admit to herself, let alone be taunted with by him. "I despise you," she muttered.

"Do so, madam, and content yourself with knowing that the virtue you would so gladly have surrendered in my embrace will now be given up to Sutherton instead! I hope the exchange proves worth the trouble, and that he doesn't compare you unfavorably with dear Amabel!"

"Oh, how gallantly said, sirrah, how gallantly said," she whispered.

Deploring himself for having said such a thing, he looked away. Gallant? It had been as base as anything of which she'd accused him in the past.

She spoke again. "Well, it is of no consequence how low our opinions of each other may be, because in the morning I shall be leaving, and if good fortune smiles upon me, I shall never see you again."

There was a sound from somewhere below on the cliff and the bitterness was temporarily set aside as they both looked over the edge. Through the scattering of snowflakes, they could see Amabel's lantern, but only Henrietta saw the two ghosts caught in the swaying light. Jane and Kit knew nothing of the watchers at the cliff top, for their attention was solely upon Amabel and the approaching gig, which was now so close that the silhouettes of the rowers were revealed by the lantern held by a man at the stern. Amabel had almost reached the flat rock at the edge of the tiny inlet, with the ghosts close behind her, until suddenly the splash of the oars and the lap of the idle sea overwhelmed Jane. She halted at the very foot of the path and caught Kit's arm. "I—I can't go any further. I'm afraid."

"My dearest, we're ghosts now, and cannot be harmed. Besides, nothing can happen to us here on dry land."

"The Goodwins seemed like dry land too." Jane swallowed, recalling how everyone thought they had found salvation upon the hard golden sands that stretched for miles like an island. But then the tide turned, and the sands shook and turned to liquid as the sea roared fiercely in and engulfed them all.

Kit understood and drew her tenderly into his embrace. "We will observe from here," he said gently.

Meanwhile Amabel had picked her way across the seaweed-strewn rocks to the flat shelf right at the water's edge. She put her lantern down and waited as the gig glided the final yards. The man in the stern stood up. By the light of his lantern he was shown to be young, and very Gallic, with a patch over his left eye. His cloak parted a little, to reveal a uniform of sort beneath—a blue coat tied at the waist with a wide red sash. A cutlass hung at his hip. He called out softly, saying her name in the French way, with the emphasis on the last syllable. "*Amabelle?*"

Amabel answered, also in French. "*Charles! Mon tout cher frère!*"

At the top of the cliff, Henrietta's lips parted. "Her brother! She said she'd lost touch with him!"

Marcus had been gazing at the man. "Well, she was hardly going to tell everyone he was captain of the *Légère!*" he murmured dryly.

"He's the *captain?*"

"Yes. I once saw him only too clearly in the Caribbean. I'd know Charles Lyons anywhere."

"No one here had any idea who the *Légère*'s captain was. Maybe if we had . . . You see, Lyons was Amabel's maiden name."

"Was it? I've only ever known her by her married name. Ah, the benefits of hindsight. Anyway, in him you have the source of the curare. It's freely available in the Caribbean, and the *Légère* was certainly there." Marcus laughed, and then added acidly: "So it's sibling love that explains dear Amabel's alacrity regarding helping the *Légère*! How touching."

The sentiments of the angry ghosts at the foot of the cliffs were more or less the same as the gig nudged the rocks, and the *Légère*'s ruthless master leaped ashore to sweep his sister into his arms. But high on the cliff top, Marcus and Henrietta had been so intent, first upon their bitter argument and then upon events below, that they hadn't heard the stealthy shuffle of many footsteps behind them. They knew nothing until a torch suddenly flared into life and a gruff Yorkshire voice shouted a blunt challenge. "Identify yourselves, or we'll blast you full of 'oles!" Henrietta and Marcus whirled about in dismay and saw a large party of armed men from Mulborough. The signals hadn't passed unnoticed in the town.

The warning shout had rung loudly through the hitherto quiet night, and at the foot of the cliffs Amabel and her brother looked up in alarm. By the dancing torchlight far above, Amabel recognized Henrietta and Marcus, and realized she had been discovered. She grabbed her brother's arm, crying in French. "It's over! They know! We must escape!"

Charles Lyons's reaction was instinctive and ruthless. He drew a pistol from inside his coat, took swift aim toward the cliff top, and fired. The ball whined through the air and would have struck Henrietta had not Marcus dragged her down into the snow the moment he saw the movement of the Frenchman's hand. Shocked. Henrietta pressed into the deep layer of white. She was glad of Marcus's arm resting protectively around her, and wished fervently that it was love that made him shield her from a night that had suddenly become very frightening indeed.

Down in the inlet, the gig swayed violently as Amabel and her brother clambered in and the oars were shoved urgently against the rock. He hastily extinguished the lantern so that those on the cliffs had only shadows to aim at as the boat was rowed swiftly along the narrow inlet. In all too few moments the gig had drawn beyond the faint arc of light left by Amabel's lantern, which still stood upon the rock. Soon there was only the creak of the rowlocks and the rhythmic splash of the oars.

Jane and Kit instinctively swept into action as they saw Amabel and her brother escaping without the punishment they were due. Using all their powers, the dismayed shades elevated pebbles and strands of seaweed, making them hurtle through the air to strike the gig and those inside. Amabel screamed as a pebble thudded painfully against her shoulder, and her brother stared in confusion at the missiles raining so mysteriously out of the darkness. He was certain he and his men would have heard if anyone had descended the path behind Amabel, which meant that someone must have been hiding among the rocks before she came down! What other explanation was there? Pebbles didn't hurl themselves of their own volition, nor did seaweed uproot and fly. But then the lantern Amabel had left on the rock was overturned as more seaweed ripped itself free. Flames flared briefly, revealing—no one. "*Dieu*," the Frenchman whispered, crossing himself in fear.

The ghosts began to realize that their prey would soon be out of range, and in desperation Kit fixed his fearsome gaze upon the sea, in an effort to make it heave up into waves. But the almost smooth surface merely rippled a little, and under the cloak of darkness, the gig drew farther and farther away.

By now the dismayed Mulborough townsmen knew the extent of their mistake, and that far from apprehending French spies on the cliff, they'd inadvertently alerted the real conspirators at the landing below. But it was too late, and all they could do was stand by helplessly as inexplicable sounds drifted up through the darkness. More than one man thought of the bogle, and more than one fearful glance was cast toward the dark shadows of the churchyard.

Marcus scrambled to his feet and then pulled Henrietta up as well. "What in God's name is going on down there?" he breathed, gazing over the edge of the cliff, but seeing nothing.

"I—I don't know," she replied, although having seen a cup of chocolate float through the air, she could guess. But right now it wasn't the probable activity of ghosts that unnerved her, but the closeness of the shot Charles Lyons had fired. If Marcus hadn't reacted as swiftly as he had, she would undoubtedly have been struck. Maybe even killed.

Marcus glanced at her face, and quickly slipped an arm around her waist. "It's all right, you're safe now," he said gently.

"You saved my life."

"Don't feel obliged to thank me, for it was the least I could do after being so unbelievably unchivalrous a moment ago."

Suddenly there was absolute silence, and icy fingers began to pass down the spines of the onlookers. Then, as one, the brave men of Mulborough took to their heels, leaving Henrietta and Marcus alone. Henrietta heard a stifled cry of terror from the bottom of the cliff. It was Jane.

Chapter Twenty-one

The reason for the sudden silence and Jane's fear was very simple; the ghosts had themselves seen a ghost, and it was one that struck dread through them both.

They'd been continuing their onslaught of pebbles and seaweed against the retreating gig, when suddenly a glowing silver sloop with black masts glided across the entrance to the tiny inlet. The blue-and-gold banners of the Bourbons streamed from her masts, and her canvas billowed in a wind only she could feel. She heaved away from the inlet and suddenly her name came into view above the great cabin at the stern: *Basilisk*. It was the privateer that had run Jane and Kit's merchantman, the *Wessex*, onto the Goodwins.

That was when Jane cried out, and the moment she did, the ghost ship disappeared. As darkness engulfed them again, Kit put his arms tightly around his love, pressing his lips to her hair. "It's all right, my darling, it's all right . . ." he whispered, trying to sound strong for her, although in truth he was shaken too.

"Why is the *Basilisk* here? Has she come for us? Are we to go to Old Nick because we've failed?" Jane whispered, clinging fearfully to him.

Kit was afraid too, but as his glance moved up toward the cliff top, where he knew Henrietta still stood with Marcus, his fear somersaulted into anger. Henrietta had promised to remain behind; instead she had not only followed, but had brought Marcus too. It was their fault that Amabel and her vile brother had escaped, their fault that the *Légère* had not even come under threat. Maybe it was even their fault that the *Basilisk* had appeared!

Henrietta looked frantically down through the gently falling snow. For once her psychic abilities had failed her, for although she had heard Jane's cry, she hadn't seen the phantom privateer. She wanted to call out to the ghosts, but couldn't because of Marcus. What had happened? Were Jane and Kit all right?

Marcus gazed down as well, but sensed nothing at all. He listened carefully, but there was only the lap of the sea in the inlet. The French had escaped, and Amabel with them. It was time to return to the abbey to acquaint Russell and Charlotte with the night's startling events. He took Henrietta's arm to usher her away from the edge of the precipice, and after resisting for a second as she continued to wonder about the ghosts, she allowed him to lead her back to the horses.

In Hades, Old Nick's mood was mixed. He was ready to deal with what was to come, and had found it amusing to taunt the specters with the *Basilisk*, but he was decidedly displeased with Amabel for not seeing through the ruse with the curare. He had looked after her thus far, but she had failed him once too often, and would now be abandoned to her fate.

Henrietta and Marcus hardly spoke as they rode back to the abbey through the snowy darkness, but the lack of communication was pensive and tired rather than antagonistic. As soon as they arrived, Russell and Charlotte were awoken and summoned down to the grand saloon, where Marcus had tossed a fresh log onto the dying fire. As the eager new flames hissed and spat, and sparks fled up the chimney to the snow-filled night, the story of the night's events was related, Henrietta telling her version of how she'd found out about Amabel, and Marcus continuing the tale with events on the cliff.

Russell stood before the fire in his navy-blue paisley dressing gown, and tossed his nightcap aside in outrage as the full iniquitous truth about Amabel was revealed. Charlotte, who wore a peach robe trimmed with swansdown and was seated in a fireside chair opposite Henrietta, was aghast. "Oh, how right I was to despise and mistrust that vile creature! I was even right when I suggested in jest that she probably pushed you down the churchyard steps, Henrietta, but I did not for a single moment imagine she was capable of all *this*!"

Russell placed a slippered foot on the polished brass fender and gazed into the fire. "It seems we have had the vilest of cuckoos in our nest," he muttered.

Charlotte was distressed. "When I think back, there were so many clues. The mere fact she came here at all should have spoken volumes! She asked so many questions about the gold and the harbor."

Russell sighed. "I fancy that poor Major Renchester's death and disgrace now appear in a somewhat different light. No doubt she used curare to dispose of *him* too! Tell me, Henrietta, exactly how did you say she administered it to you?"

As she began to answer, Jane and Kit appeared angrily beside her chair. For a moment her voice dried up completely, and Marcus, thinking she was overcome, hastened to pour her a fortifying glass of cognac, which he pressed into her shaking hands. She gave a weak smile and battled on with what she'd been saying, even though at the same time she was on the receiving end of bitter ghostly recriminations for jeopardizing matters by leaving the abbey.

Kit had no compunction about laying the blame squarely at her feet. "It was ill done, madam! Just look what happened! It's really too bad!"

Falteringly, Henrietta continued telling Russell about the curare.

Jane was now angry with her too. "Amabel has escaped scot-free, and the *Légère* is able to carry on as before! And it's all your fault!"

Henrietta forgot herself. "It *isn't* my fault! The signals had been seen in the town!" she countered defensively.

The odd exclamation filled Charlotte with concern and she hastened to reassure Henrietta. "You mustn't blame yourself. No, of course it wasn't your fault."

Henrietta's cheeks flamed. "I—I feel as if it is," she said lamely, wishing the spirits would save their remonstrations for when she was alone. Maybe she *had* been in the wrong, but the men from Mulborough would have arrived anyway.

Kit hadn't finished with her yet. "Have you any idea what you may have unleashed?" he demanded.

Her eyes flew inquiringly to his. What was he talking about?

He bent down to face her, his hands on the arms of her chair. "The *Basilisk* appeared, and Jane fears she has come for us. I do not believe she would have appeared at all if you had not broken your promise to us. We risked breaking the rules in order to save you from Amabel, and in return you betrayed us!"

Henrietta stared up at him. The *Basilisk*? Her thoughts whirled. Wasn't that the name of the privateer that had chased Jane and Kit's ship in 1714? Yes, it was!

Marcus looked curiously at her, but said nothing. Russell cleared his throat awkwardly, and Charlotte prompted her. "You were saying, Henrietta?"

Henrietta pulled herself sharply together and somehow managed to complete what she'd been telling them.

Russell glanced toward Marcus and then nodded at the decanter of cognac in the corner. "I fancy a little liquid restoration would be in order for us all, mm? And it can be guaranteed free of curare, eh?" He smiled at Henrietta.

As Marcus went to pour generous measures, Kit went with him, peering longingly over his shoulder as the amber liquid splashed into the glasses. "Oh, tonight of all nights, what I'd give to down a measure or two," the wraith muttered wistfully.

The ghostly yearning communicated a little, and Marcus turned sharply. "I beg your pardon?"

Everyone in the room looked curiously at him. Russell raised an eyebrow. "No one said a word, dear boy."

Henrietta whispered to Jane. "Please go. If you must chastise me, do so later when I'm alone."

Jane knew the request was justified. "Very well, but we're very angry with you."

"That is abundantly clear."

Charlotte looked across. "Did you say something to me, Henrietta?"

"Oh, I was just thinking what a long night it's been," Henrietta replied, watching with relief as Jane took Kit's hand and led him through the wall.

Marcus dealt out the cognac, and Russell sipped his with relish before speaking again. "Right now I'm damned glad I had that gold moved. The icehouse was clever enough, but totally undefended."

Marcus gave a wry smile. "To say nothing of the close proximity of the livery stables, with all those potential packhorses."

"Don't remind me."

Charlotte sighed. "Right now I wish the wretched gold were elsewhere entirely."

"It will be shortly, my love," Russell reassured her. "The Treasury have been sitting on their hands thus far, but as soon as I inform them the French know what's hidden here, they'll act."

Marcus had been swirling his cognac slowly. "I don't wish to be alarmist, but there is the possibility that Charles Lyons and his merry men may try to catch us unawares by raiding Mulborough this very night, before we have the chance to do anything."

Russell stared. "*Tonight?* But he's already been once. Surely he won't attempt anything again right away! Especially now we've been alerted."

"He may anticipate our reaction to be just that. He's bold and enterprising, so do not leave any chink in the armor. The most gaping hole is the smugglers' path. My advice is to blow it up without further delay."

Russell nodded. "You're right. I'll take a party of men right now, and—"

"*We'll* take a party of men," Marcus corrected quietly.

"As you wish."

Charlotte got up agitatedly. "Is there anything else we should do?"

Seeing her unease, Russell was immediately concerned. He went to take her hand. "My dear, all *you* need do is return to the warmth and comfort of bed. Leave everything to Marcus and me."

"But—"

"All will be well, I promise you."

As they went out together, Marcus finished his cognac in one gulp, then put the glass down and looked at Henrietta. "If there is one thing the French do well, it's make brandy," he murmured.

"They also make successful privateers," she replied.

His eyes met hers. "So they do. Well, I hardly imagined that my impulse to interrupt my voyage south here would lead to all this."

"Why *did* you leave Scotland? I was under the impression you were going to stay there for some time."

"Instead I arrived here and spoiled your New Year. How very disagreeable of me."

She didn't respond.

"As it happens, I'm returning to London to commence arrangements for my marriage."

Henrietta's heart stopped. "Your—your marriage?"

"You seem surprised. Did you imagine I intended to remain a bachelor for the rest of my life?"

Somehow she clung to her poise. "To be truthful, I had not considered your situation at all."

"That I can well believe," he replied, then inclined his head and went out.

Chapter Twenty-two

Marcus and Russell left to destroy the path, and at dawn had still not returned. Snow was now falling very heavily and roads that had been cleared were once again impassable. The temperature had dropped like a stone, and the very air seemed to crack with cold.

Henrietta had fallen asleep in the conservatory. Shaken by Marcus's announcement, she hadn't been able to go to bed. Instead she'd wandered wretchedly through the deserted ground floor rooms, and had ended up in the conservatory, where she curled up unhappily in a chair beside one of the stoves that warmed the tender foliage all around. She knew she had no right to feel as she did, but she was completely devastated by the knowledge that Marcus was going to be married. She stared miserably past the billiard table at the countless snowflakes tumbling past the window. The terrace, which had been cleared, was white again. Gradually the warmth of the stove overcame her and she drifted into sleep.

The scent of orchids and orange blossoms filled her nostrils, and the strains of dance music echoed gently through her dreams as suppressed memories had their way again. She was at Devonshire House, and had retreated to the conservatory to try to regain her composure after forfeiting the kiss to Mark Paynson during the cotillion. Dark leaves pressed in the shadows and stars lit the summer sky. Variegated lanterns adorned the gardens, and there was glitter and laughter everywhere, except here in the quiet of the conservatory, where the orchids were so choice and magnificent that it was quite the thing to view them. But there was no one else around as she tried to collect her scattered senses sufficiently to return to the ball. Even behind her sequined domino she felt as if the world could see that it was Henrietta Courtenay who had been set completely at sixes and sevens by the casual brush of a stranger's lips.

Hearing a step behind her she turned in dismay to see the tall stranger coming toward her, removing his mask as he did so. For the first time she gazed upon the face that was almost to prove her undoing. "Would you slip away incognito, Fair Lady?" he asked softly.

"It—it was hot in the ballroom."

"True, but it is even more hot in here, don't you think?"

"I—I merely wished to be alone for a while."

"May I at least know your name?"

"Is that not flouting convention? It is a masked ball, and anonymity is the order of the night."

"I desire to know your name because you have aroused my interest as no other has before," he said quietly.

Her pulse quickened unbearably. "You have a practiced way, sir."

"Look into my eyes and know that I am speaking not with practice, but with honesty." He spoke softly, and came close enough to slide his hand around the waist of her bluebell silk gown. She was spellbound, and offered no resistance as he pulled her gently toward him.

His lips were tender, warm, and soft as he pressed her to him. She felt his body through their clothes, experienced an excitement she was to know only too well in the coming days. . . .

He drew back slightly to remove her domino and gaze into her eyes. "Who are you?" he whispered.

Her disarrayed senses fled into oblivion, and she did not have the wit—or the will—to invent an identity. "I am Henrietta Courtenay."

For a second she thought his touch wavered, but then it was sure again. "My name is Mark Paynson," he replied.

Anguish suddenly laced her dreams. Liar, oh, liar! I was fool enough to tell you my real name, but you were false from the outset! I was naive and artless; you were base and predatory!

"Henrietta?"

The muted strains of music were banished, and she awoke with a start as the sound of his voice brought dream and reality together. It was daylight, and he stood before her chair.

"Henrietta?" he said again.

She sat up in alarm. "What is it? What's happened?"

"I was merely concerned to find you sleeping in here."

Tendrils of the past crept around her again, as did the revelation about his intention to marry. She got up quickly, obliging him to stand aside. "Concerned? I find that hard to believe," she said quietly.

"Nevertheless, it is true."

She wanted to keep the conversation neutral. "Have you and Russell attended to the path?"

"Most finally."

She looked at the terrace. To her dismay the snow was now a foot or more deep against the window, and still falling heavily.

Marcus watched her. "Your journey is out of the question."

"But I *must* be in London for the wedding. I'm the chief bridesmaid."

"Henrietta, the road across the moor has quite disappeared, and Mulborough is already cut off except by horse, and if such situation has arisen here, where the air is salt from the sea, can you imagine how much worse it will be farther inland? In this you have to heed what I say."

"As no doubt your unfortunate wife will have to do for the rest of her days. I wager she will be the unhappiest of creatures."

He searched her face. "I did not know you were a betting woman, Henrietta."

"Oh, I think we both know whose great example I follow, sir."

"Riddle me, riddle me ree," he murmured enigmatically, and walked to the billiard table, where he and Amabel had left a game unfinished on the night the gold had been secretly moved from the icehouse. He picked up one of the balls and rolled it gently across the green baize. As it chinked against another and fetched up against the apron, he was reminded of the strange occurrence the first night he'd arrived. He gazed at the part of the table where the ball had so mysteriously moved of its own volition.

Henrietta's curiosity was aroused as she watched his face. "What is it? What are you thinking?"

"Oh, it's nothing really. Just a ball with a mind of its own."

"What do you mean?" She came to stand opposite him across the table.

"It was most curious, almost as if it were being patted by something," he murmured, taking another ball and rolling it over the baize.

Curious? Ghostly, more like, she thought.

"That same night I first heard the invisible dog," Marcus recalled.

Henrietta looked quickly away.

He studied her shrewdly. "Come clean, Henrietta. Charlotte told me you not only heard the dog at the ball, but saw both it and its master and mistress too."

Henrietta was dismayed. "I asked Charlotte not to tell anyone."

"She let something slip, and I caught on it. Don't blame her. Anyway, why so secretive? If you saw what you claimed . . ."

"Oh, I saw it." And much, much more besides . . ."

"Tell me about it."

"There's nothing to tell, beyond what you've already learned from Charlotte."

"Really? Come now, Henrietta."

She couldn't meet his eyes.

He smiled a little. "You see ghosts, don't you? I wish I'd known before."

"Why?"

"Because I would have told you of the things that have happened to me since arriving here."

Henrietta was taken aback. "What things?"

"Well, there was the dog, of course, including the fact that I could swear I heard it on the ceiling, not the floor. But then, from what you saw at the ballroom, the creature is no respecter of gravity." He rolled another ball across the table. "Then there was the self-propelling billiard ball. I have little doubt that it was actually being helped along by the same ghostly dog, which must have been sitting exactly there." He picked up a cue that lay on the baize and tapped the table apron with it.

Henrietta could imagine Rowley playing with the ball. She lowered her glance as she wondered where Jane's beloved little dog had gone. Had the bogle done away with him? Oh, how she hoped not, for Rowley's sake, and for Jane and Kit's.

Marcus's eyes were upon her again. "When I first stepped ashore here on the night of the ball, I had the oddest feeling someone was standing right behind me, but there was no one there. And tonight, when I was pouring the cognac, I could have sworn someone spoke. None of this surprises you, does it? You accept it all as feasible."

"As a child I saw things no one else did, so yes, I do accept it all."

He leaned his hands upon the table. "Pieces of jewelry that drop out of thin air would strike no alarm through you, would they? Because you would see it for ghostly work."

"Maybe."

"I'm led to believe that Jane Courtenay and Kit Fitzpaine are our doubles. Is that so?"

"Yes."

He smiled. "So tell me, Henrietta, how many times have they appeared to you since the night of the ball?"

Henrietta didn't want to answer.

He stepped suddenly over to her and turned her to face him. "Struggling through deep snow and an arctic dawn are inclined to make one exceedingly thoughtful. I'm no longer disposed to believe your tale of how you discovered Amabel's high treason and her monstrous attempts to murder you. You've been receiving a little supernatural assistance, haven't you? These same two phantoms have enlisted my aid at least twice now, once when Amabel struck you with the candlestick and then again when you were so ill-advised as to ride to St. Tydfa's before you were fit. I watched you very closely tonight, and I rather fancy we four were not alone in the saloon. Admit it, Henrietta."

"Very well, I admit it."

He relaxed. "So, Henrietta Courtenay is being haunted. My, one wonders what Sutherton would make of *that*."

"And what, pray, would your newly revealed bride think if she learned of your invisible dogs and flying jewelry?" she countered.

Jane and Kit were witnessing the entire meeting. After falling asleep themselves in their usual bedroom, they'd awoken and come looking for Henrietta in order to finish what they'd commenced in the grand saloon. Seeing how deep and unrelenting the fresh snow was, they now had reason to hope Henrietta would be obliged to remain at the abbey, and that accordingly they would have another chance to bring her together with Marcus. However, just as they found her asleep in the conservatory, Marcus had entered as well. They'd hidden amid the greenery, and at the sudden mention of Marcus's apparent match, Jane gave a sigh. The hidden pages, oh, the hidden pages.

Marcus smiled in reply to Henrietta's taunt. "Aren't you going to ask me who she is, Henrietta?"

"Her identity is of no interest to me." She was very conscious of his hands still upon her arms.

"No? Well, that's as may be, but I fear the identity of *your* intended spouse is very much of interest to me. Henrietta, Sutherton isn't worth the ink of your signature, but you are treasure beyond his wildest dreams! Can't you see that he is the very last man on earth you should marry?"

"Let me correct you, sir. *You* are the very last man on earth I should marry."

His hands fell away. "Well, that isn't about to arise, is it? However, if it were, you would at least have the comfort of knowing I wasn't marrying you for your fortune."

"But you wouldn't be marrying me for love, either, would you? If, by any wild chance, you *did* marry me, it would be said that you were doing so in order to swell you already overflowing purse. And that, sir, would make you no better than Lord Sutherton."

"You think you know me through and through, don't you?"

"Yes, sir, I do."

"How wonderful such cleverness must be. Well, I am about to confound you, madam, for I am in a position to assist you to become your cousin's bridesmaid after all. It seems the excessive cold threatens to freeze the harbor, which means I have to either risk the *Avalon* becoming icebound and her hull damaged, or I must move her. I have therefore decided to complete my voyage south to Bramnells, with a detour by way of London, and will leave at high tide in four hours' time. I've already signaled down to the crew, and everything is being made ready to set sail. The detour would be for you, Henrietta, because with the very proper presence of one of the Mulborough maids to protect your reputation, you are most welcome to take passage with me. Unless, of course, you cannot bring yourself to accept my hospitality."

Henrietta didn't know what to say.

"Well? I await your answer."

Acceptance and refusal struggled together on her lips, but in the end it was the former that won. "I—I gladly accept."

"Gladly? I doubt that very much. I trust you do not suffer from mal de mer? If you do, be sure to eat before leaving. Better to suffer on a full stomach than an empty one."

"I've never sailed before, so I don't know."

"Then eat anyway. Be ready to leave as quickly as possible, for it will take some time to reach the quay." With a curt nod, he turned to go.

Still hiding amid the greenery, Jane looked at Kit in dismay. "They're leaving in *four hours*?" she whispered, tears welling from her lovely eyes. "Oh, this whole wretched haunting has been a disaster! We hoped this renewed snow would give us more time; instead they're leaving by sea! On top of that, poor Rowley is lost, we've encountered a bogle, and the *Basilisk* has appeared! It's too dreadful. What are we going to do?" Without reply, Kit held her close. He couldn't add anything to what she'd said, because very word was true.

Marcus still hadn't left the conservatory. "There is just one thing. Our luggage will have to remain here at the abbey. We will have to ride down to the quay, and I certainly have no de-sire to labor with trunks as well. Just pack a single portman-teau." Inclining his head again, he went out.

A moment later Henrietta followed, and the ghosts emerged from hiding. Kit took Jane's hand and led her out on to the snow-decked terrace. "Beloved, we either have four hours left in which to accomplish something, or we could go with them on the *Avalon*," he said quietly.

Jane's gaze widened. "Go with them? Oh, no, I couldn't pos-sibly . . ."

"Do you want to go to heaven?"

"Yes, of course."

"Then we have to seize every possible opportunity to make this pair see sense. We know the snow will remain for some time yet, and if we go with them, we will stand a chance of ac-complishing our task."

"But we've just learned that Marcus is going to marry some-one else, and we have no idea whether it's an arranged match or a matter of the heart."

"If it is a love match I will be very surprised. Jane, I'm cer-tain he loves Henrietta as much as she loves him, and if we go with them, we will be able to use every opportunity to bring them together."

Jane glanced toward the sea. "I'm afraid, Kit. You do know what day it is today, don't you? It's February twelfth, the very same day that we took passage on the *Wessex*."

"I know, but Henrietta is to be taken to London, and the Thames estuary lies well north of the sands, my love. We don't have to go anywhere near the Goodwins, because we can go ashore in the capital."

"Even so . . ."

"I don't want to spend more years like this, Jane. I'm tired of being in limbo. Let us take our courage—and our convictions—in both hands, and do our damnedest to make this foolish pair see sense. We can't do anything for Rowley. Forgive me for say-ing this, my darling, but we have to face facts. We don't know where Rowley is. He may still be at the mercy of the bogle, or worse, by now he may have been taken by Old Nick."

Jane gave a cry and burst into tears. "Oh, *please* don't even think it!"

"We must hope he is well somewhere, but in the meantime we must keep trying to complete our task. And that means accompanying Henrietta and Marcus on the *Avalon*."

Jane struggled with her tears, and at last drew a long breath. "You're right, of course. Very well, let us go with them."

Down in the depths of Hades, Old Nick gave an evil chuckle. Their efforts were going to be in vain, for his new weapon would defeat them—and St. Peter—at every turn.

Rowley was aroused from sleep by the ringing of the bell. It was something to which he had by now become accustomed, but this time it was different. Urgent and more prolonged, it was accompanied by the sound of much activity. He could hear a swishing sound, as if wood were being brushed, and the thud of boots as men ran to-and-fro. Orders were being shouted and there were rhythmic chants as men hauled upon winches. The spaniel cocked his ears and put his head to one side as he listened. Would someone come at last to give him a chance to escape? As he listened, he gradually became aware of another sound, one that came from much closer by. It was the grunt and whistle of someone snoring. The bogle!

Rowley's eyes gleamed with the light of revenge and he crept down the wall, still cocking his ears to pinpoint the bogle's precise position. Gradually he drew close enough to realize it was sleeping on a pile of sandbags close to the door. Boldly the spaniel approached, his efficient nose first locating the bogle's feet, then its skinny legs, and finally its surprisingly well-padded posterior, which was providentially turned toward him. Opening his jaws, Rowley did unto the bogle what the bogle was wont to do unto others—he sank his teeth as deeply as he could. With a shriek of pain the manikin awoke, leaped to its feet, and hopped up and down, rubbing its rear.

The spaniel scuttled triumphantly back to the safety of his corner and sat there wagging his tail. He suddenly felt better than he had in a long time. Revenge, however small, was very sweet.

Chapter Twenty-three

After taking leave of a tearful Charlotte, Henrietta and Marcus set off through the ever deepening snow, accompanied by Russell. With them went the maid whose presence would protect Henrietta's reputation. The maid went very reluctantly, for she had never left Mulborough in her life and had no desire to do so now. However, apart from Charlotte's own maid, who was unwell, she was the only one at the abbey with experience of waiting upon a lady. Two invisible figures accompanied the small party, and although Henrietta knew they were there, she did not accord them so much as a glance, let alone a smile. This was because she and the ghosts had had a bitter falling out. Even though she was clearly very upset by Marcus's wedding revelations, Kit had rather tactlessly persisted in reprimanding her. There had been a heated exchange while she packed her portmanteau, and the wraiths had swept out in high dudgeon. Tempers had cooled a little now, and both sides wished certain things had not been said, but neither was prepared to be the first to back down.

The small group, both visible and invisible, made its arduous way through the heavy snow. The land was white, the trees bowed down with weight, and the winter roar of the river was muffled beneath ice. In Mulborough the smell of smoke hung in the frozen air as fires burned in every hearth, and the scrape of shovels was heard as the determined townsfolk endeavored to keep the streets clear. But the relentless snow continued to fall, with flakes so large and solid they could be heard. The tide was almost at its height and the water by the quay was thick with ice crystals that chinked and rustled as it washed slowly against the steps. The *Avalon*'s gig was waiting, the sailors rubbing their hands together to keep warm. Their breath billowed in clouds and they wore rug coats and low-crowned hats with flaps that protected their ears.

Marcus lifted Henrietta down first. Snow clung to her golden wool cloak and to the frame of curls around her face. In spite of the cloak's fur trimming and lining and the warm gown she wore beneath it, she still shivered as she watched him help the maid down as well. Then he unfastened their portmanteaus to give to the *Avalon*'s boatswain, Mr. Pascoe, who was about forty years old, had a rosy snub-nosed face and wisps of wiry hair that peeped from beneath a warm red woolen hat. Like many sailors, he wore gold earrings in the belief they would aid his eyesight. He had been Marcus's faithful right hand since being captured by pirates and marooned on a Caribbean island. Death would surely have been his lot had not Marcus seen his signal fire and risked a dangerous reef in order to rescue him.

Jane was very nervous as she stood on the quay. Oh, how she hated the sea, but she despised it even more since seeing the *Basilisk* again. She gave Kit an apologetic smile. "The last time we did this . . ."

"I know, my darling, I know."

"And this time we're trying to help a disagreeable baggage who won't even do us the courtesy of speaking!" Jane gave Henrietta a dark look.

"Well, it's my fault now. I should have realized how upset she was about the existence of Marcus's bride, and I should have admitted that she was right to point out that the townsmen had seen the signals. My dear, we were simply frightened about the *Basilisk*, and angry that Amabel and the *Légère* escaped. We vented our wrath on Henrietta, and it wasn't really fair. If I were her, I'd probably be in a huff too."

Jane couldn't repress a smile. "Well, put that way—"

"I'm sure we'll make it up with her soon. In the meantime, let us prepare to go on board."

Jane bit her lip and tried to be brave, but someone else in the party did not have such backbone. The maid's reluctance to leave Mulborough suddenly gained the upper hand. She glanced around at the thickly falling snow, then down at the freezing water, and burst into tears. "I don't want to go, please don't make me!" she sobbed.

Henrietta was horrified to be the cause of such distress. "Oh, please don't cry, of course you don't have to come," she said, trying to comfort the weeping girl.

"But—but Lady Mulborough said I must!"

"I shall manage quite well on my own. You return to the abbey with Lord Mulborough, who will explain to Her Ladyship that I decided I did not require you after all." Henrietta gave Russell a meaningful look.

He dismounted to assist the girl. "I am more than willing to say what you wish, Henrietta, but what of propriety? I mean, you will be alone on board ship with Marcus for several days, and it will not look good in society's eyes." He cleared his throat and glanced apologetically at Marcus.

Henrietta felt her cheeks flush. "It cannot be helped. I must return to London, and this is the only way."

Marcus interposed. "Have no fear that your good name will be besmirched, for no one need know you traveled unchaperoned. All that has to be put out is that on arriving the maid went straight to Mulborough House."

Russell nodded. "That should do, I fancy. Do you agree, Henrietta?"

"Yes."

Russell assisted the weeping maid on to her horse once more, then hugged Henrietta farewell. Still ignoring Jane and Kit, Henrietta followed Mr. Pascoe down the slippery steps. Jane took a huge breath to steady her nerves, then clung to Kit's arm as they followed. It took all her courage to exchange the solid safety of the quay for the swaying uncertainty of the boat, but somehow she managed. The specters squeezed together in the prow, directly behind Henrietta.

Jane put a ghostly hand on her shoulder. "Henrietta . . ."

Fearing another bitter exchange, Henrietta didn't respond by so much as a flicker. She had her emotions on the tightest rein imaginable, for in truth she was so wretched over Marcus that she felt like following the maid's example by bursting into floods of tears! She was also bitterly disappointed in the ghosts for blaming her for what had happened. She'd been wrong, but they were being unfair, and she wasn't ready to forgive them.

Marcus took his leave of Russell and came down the steps. The gig lurched so much as he embarked that Jane gave a squeak of fright and gripped Kit's arm so tightly that her fingers dug in. As soon as Marcus had taken the seat next to Henrietta, he untied the mooring rope and the sailors pushed the oars against the steps. Jane closed her eyes and whispered a silent prayer as the gig nosed away from the quay. Ice whispered in the sluggish water, and the chill seemed more raw than ever as the sailors swung into the rhythm of rowing. Mr. Pascoe, who was at the helm, tugged his hat farther down over his ears, and Russell watched from the quay until the gig faded from view in the swirling snow. Henrietta gazed back until Mulborough could be seen no more; when she turned to look forward, the *Avalon* could not be seen either. The gig could have been in the middle of an ocean, hundreds of miles from anywhere.

Marcus's sloop wasn't invisible to Jane and Kit, however. For them the snow seemed to suddenly peel back, and by an eerie silver light they saw the *Avalon* quite clearly. As they looked, she began to change shape, and instead of the sleek modern sloop, became the much older, larger *Wessex*, on which the ghosts had eloped when alive. Plain and unremarkable, the fully laden merchantman sat low in the water. Jane and Kit held hands tightly as for a moment they relived the past. Then the silver light faded and the snow closed in again. The ghosts didn't speak, but both knew something terrible was going to happen, something they were powerless to resist.

Mr. Pascoe suddenly put a whistle to his lips and blew hard. There was an answering whistle, and a guiding lantern shone through the murk. The boatswain adjusted the gig's course, and as they slid beneath the *Avalon*'s gilded prow. Henrietta saw two other fully crewed gigs waiting to haul the sloop out of the harbor. The oars were shipped, and Marcus reached out to make the gig fast to the steps against the side of the ship. Stepping out, he stretched down to take Henrietta's hand and pulled her effortlessly up to join him.

Kit assisted Jane from the gig as well, and as the two wraiths gazed up the steps toward the deck, the silver glow appeared again. They did not know if they were boarding the *Avalon* or the *Wessex*; indeed everything seem so blurred and indistinct that it was almost as if they were in a dream. Unable to move swiftly, they mounted the steps to the deck, where to their relief the illusion faded, and they found themselves only upon the *Avalon*. Hand-in-hand they ran toward the quarterdeck, beneath which were two doors, one to Marcus's private cabins on the same level as the main deck, the other to the hold and sailors' accommodation. The crew assembled on the main deck didn't see them, nor did the helmsman feel anything as they passed through him to the companionway that led down into the bowels of the vessel.

Marcus led Henrietta up from the gig, and on reaching the deck Henrietta gazed around with reluctant admiration, for there was no doubt that the *Avalon* was one of the finest vessels afloat. As a sailor ascended behind them with their portmanteaus, which he took to Marcus's quarters, the sloop's first officer, Mr. Barrington, stepped forward to salute Marcus. He was slightly older than Marcus, a lean man with a beard that he clearly groomed very carefully. His blue eyes were set above a broken nose and his straight brown hair was combed back from his forehead.

"Welcome aboard, my lord," he said.

"Thank you, Mr. Barrington. Now, please go about your business. I will be with you directly."

"My lord." Mr. Barrington turned on his heel and hurried away.

Marcus offered Henrietta his arm and led her astern. He ushered her through the door next to the one Jane and Kit had used, and she immediately found herself in his splendid main cabin. Furnished in crimson and gold, it was as grand as that of a house, with five glazed windows that faced directly astern. There were gold-tasseled curtains, gimbal-mounted candles, a long window seat that was richly upholstered with crimson morocco, and a glazed door opening onto the stern balcony, which overhung the water. Gleaming mahogany tables were fixed to the thickly carpeted floor, and there was a scent of sandalwood from the chests against one wall. A telescope on a stand was by the windows, and a costly brass sextant lay upon an escritoire, and in a corner stood a glass-fronted cupboard containing a select supply of cognac. Abundant ornamentation and gilt moldings provided an extra air of sumptuousness, and two portable stoves added a warmth that Henrietta found very welcome indeed after the rigors she'd endured since leaving the abbey.

Marcus stepped back to the door. "Mr. Barrington!"

The first officer hurried up. "My lord?"

"Where's the hammock?"

"A regrettable oversight, my lord. I will have it attended to directly."

"See that you do."

Henrietta was outraged. Surely she wasn't expected to sleep in a *hammock*?

As the first officer hastened away again, Marcus turned and saw her expression. He immediately strode to fling open a door that revealed a cabin containing a brass bed and a washstand. "Behold your accommodation, madam. *I* am the one obliged to use the hammock!"

She felt foolish. "I—I merely wondered . . ."

"If I was going to be base enough to force you into a canvas sling? No, madam, I was not."

"Forgive me."

"Henrietta, there is so much to forgive where you are concerned, that I think adding more to the list would be a waste of time and effort."

As always, her resentment flared. "Why do you persist in pretending that I was the one who committed the crime, when we both know it was you? Isn't it enough that I was tricked to the extent I was? You weren't a spurned lover, but a heartless gamester whose trickery didn't quite reap the anticipated reward!"

He was about to speak again when a harassed Mr. Pascoe

rapped on the door. "Mr. Barrington's compliments. Beggin' your leave, my lord, but the tide's ripe."

"Very well." Marcus looked at Henrietta again. "We'll finish this conversation later, madam," he said coldly, then strode out, slamming the door behind him.

In a deserted cabin on the deck below, Jane and Kit stood in each other's arms. Jane could still sense the *Wessex*'s presence and drew back uneasily. "In two days' time it will be St. Valentine's Day. Something horrid is in the offing, Kit, I can just *feel* it."

Kit pulled her close once more, sharing her foreboding.

"I do hope St. Peter is watching over us," she whispered.

They felt the sloop shudder slightly and heard shouts on deck as the gigs began to haul. Inch by inch the *Avalon* slid out of the harbor, and as soon as the gigs were safely on board again, she set sail toward the freedom—and danger—of the North Sea.

Old Nick watched with gloating anticipation. Oh, yes, something terrible was indeed about to happen, and as for that old fool St. Peter, far from watching over his beleaguered charges, he hadn't had so much as an inkling that anything was afoot!

Chapter Twenty-four

The snow stopped quite suddenly and a fresh wind got up. The *Avalon* had cleared St. Tydfa's headland and was forging south, but her motion as she cut through the white-topped waves made Henrietta feel unwell. It didn't help that the cabin was hot, so she donned her cloak once more and went up on deck.

The wind roared through the rigging and the canvas cracked and billowed. Gulls screamed and salt spray dashed the deck as Henrietta made her way to the starboard rail, from where she could see the snow-covered land a mile to the west. Marcus had ordered the setting of an extra sail and was watching the sailors scramble up the mast, but he walked over when he saw her. "Do you feel ill?"

"A little."

"I'll have the galley make you some peppermint."

"That won't be necessary."

"As you wish." He walked away again.

It had been a brief exchange, as cold as the winter itself. Tears blurred her eyes as she stared at the shore. Why had everything to be so cruel? She loved him so much, but he—and what remained of her pride—left her no choice except to behave as if she despised him. How long she stood there before she noticed the odd little sound, she didn't know, but suddenly she became aware of it. Barely discernible above the racket of the sea and ship, she heard a faint moan from somewhere below deck. No, it wasn't a moan, it was a howl. Yes, that was it, a howl, as if an animal were in distress! She looked around in puzzlement and realized it was coming from a hatch that had just been opened. Slowly she left the rail and looked down the companionway that led into the hold. The howling ceased, but she had heard enough to know it had been made by a small dog. A King Charles spaniel, perhaps? Her lips parted. Was it Rowley?

Her motion sickness was swept aside as she gathered her skirts to climb down to investigate, but almost immediately Marcus strode over. "Where exactly do you think you're going?" he demanded. "There are many hazards down there for someone who does not know her way around a ship."

"Marcus, I heard something."

"What did you hear?"

She looked away. "A dog."

For a moment he didn't speak, but then he drew a deep breath. "I'm beginning to recognize the way you avoid my eyes sometimes. Are we talking about *the* dog?"

"We may be. I don't really know."

"But you think it is."

She nodded.

He was unexpectedly philosophical. "Well, where things otherworldly are concerned, you are uncomfortably reliable, and since I have had an experience or two myself, it would ill become me to heap scorn upon what you say. Tell me, apart from the dog, do we have other ghostly company on board?"

"Yes, Jane and Kit are here somewhere, but I don't know where." Mentioning Jane and Kit made her pause. Had they heard the howling? Could it have ceased because they'd found Rowley? Oh, how she hoped so.

Marcus exhaled slowly. "So I have stowaways, do I?"

"In a manner of speaking, although I could be wrong about Rowley. He disappeared some weeks ago, you see."

"Disappeared?"

"Yes, he was . . ." Her voice trailed away, for it was one thing to tell him about ordinary ghosts, quite another to bring bogles into it.

"How did Rowley disappear?" Marcus prompted.

"He was kidnapped by the bogle," she said reluctantly.

"By the *bogle*?" he repeated. "You mean, there really are such things?"

"Yes."

Marcus held up his hands in a gesture of surrender. "After what went on at the abbey, I think I'd believe anything under the sun." The howling dog began again, and this time he heard it as well. "Was that it?"

"Yes. Jane and Kit can't have found him. Oh, can't I go down and look?"

"We'll both go down, but you must tread carefully. As I said, the hold of a ship is hazardous."

He helped her down onto the companionway, and then climbed in after her, closing the hatch behind him. Immediately the sound became more clear. Henrietta glanced frantically around. Where were Jane and Kit? Surely they *must* have heard.

But the ghosts were at the stern of the ship, where the sound didn't carry.

Marcus unhooked a gimbal-mounted lantern and led the way toward the forward section of the crew's quarters, in the direction from which the howling seemed to emanate. But by a storeroom door, the howls became much more clear. "In there?" Marcus inquired.

Henrietta nodded, and then called out. "Rowley? Rowley, is that you, boy?"

The howling was immediately replaced by delirious barking. Henrietta's face broke into an overjoyed smile. "It *is* him! Oh, please open the door, Marcus!"

As the door swung back and the lantern light flooded in, Marcus saw only the storeroom, but Henrietta saw Rowley running up and down the ceiling, barking. She also realized why he didn't come down, for awaiting him on the floor, its sharp teeth bared, was the bogle. For a moment Henrietta was too shocked to react, for the bogle, although small, was really quite horrid. Then she recovered and reached for a nearby broom.

The manikin didn't realize it was visible to Henrietta, until she advanced menacingly with the broom. For a startled moment it held its ground, but as the broom jabbed forward, the bogle gave a furious shriek, and dashed to the farthest corner, where it vanished behind the jumble of stores. Henrietta immediately discarded the broom and held her arms up to Rowley. "Come on, quickly!" she cried.

The spaniel jumped down to her, but she felt nothing. In fact she could see right through him, but he was safe enough as she bore him out of the storeroom. "Close the door quickly, before the bogle gets out!" she cried to a bemused Marcus.

As the door slammed shut, Rowley was beside himself with gratitude. His tail wagged nineteen to the dozen, and he tried to lick her hand. He'd been rescued, and the bogle was still locked away!

Henrietta didn't feel the spaniel's tongue or the quivering of his happy little body, but she could see everything. Her face was alight with pleasure as she cradled him. "Oh, Rowley, Jane and Kit will be so relieved to have you back safe and well!"

Marcus had only seen Henrietta performing some very odd movements with a broom, but he could certainly hear Rowley's delighted snuffles. "Good God, you really have got him, haven't you?"

"Yes."

He stretched out a tentative hand to where he knew Rowley must be, but he felt nothing.

Henrietta glanced back at the door. "I wonder how long he's been locked up in there with the bogle? He may have been there since the day you rescued me from the church tower. That's when he disappeared, anyway. I wonder how he got here?" Suddenly she remembered that day at the church. When she had dismounted at the lych-gate, she'd seen a gig preparing to come ashore from the *Avalon*, and later, after Rowley's disappearance, she had seen the same gig returning to the sloop. Rowley and the bogle must have been aboard. How she didn't know, but it seemed the likeliest explanation. She thought of Jane and Kit again and smiled at Marcus. "Come, we must find the others. We'll go up on deck and put Rowley down. He'll find them."

Marcus led the way back to the companionway, and as soon

as they emerged from the hatch, she placed Rowley on the scrubbed deck. "Find Jane," she urged.

With a pleased yelp, he dashed away toward the stern, and Henrietta and Marcus followed. On reaching the helm, the spaniel halted by the second door until Marcus opened it, then he leaped down the steps and began to bark. Jane and Kit immediately appeared through a wall. Their faces lit up with joy when they saw Rowley. The spaniel was scooped up by his sobbing mistress, and all thoughts of the quarrel were forgotten as Henrietta explained how she'd found him.

Marcus leaned against the staircase trying to imagine exactly what was happening. All he could see was Henrietta's strange conduct. It was, he thought, like watching an actress performing without the rest of the cast. There she was, laughing and speaking to people who weren't there! Yet, at the same time, they *were* there, for although he couldn't hear them, he could still hear Rowley, and if the dog was there, why not the other two as well? Who was he to question the supernatural?

The initial joy over, Kit considered the bogle. "We must think how to get rid of the bogle, which if it chooses can wreak untold havoc on a ship. Tell Marcus he must make sure the store is padlocked."

She turned and relayed the message to Marcus, who nodded his assent.

His clear acceptance of the situation made Kit raise an eyebrow. "My descendant clearly believes in ghosts," he said approvingly.

Henrietta smiled. "To deny hearing Rowley would be to deny the evidence of his own ears," she said with a smile.

Marcus gazed at Henrietta's animated face, and then smiled a little himself. She was quite unique, as he'd realized at Devonshire House. Masked and dominoed, she had still arrested his attention as no other woman ever had. What was it? The tilt of her head? The softness of her lips? The graceful but rather nervous movements of her hands? Whatever it was, her spell still wove around him now. She wasn't a woman any man could easily forget, especially not once he'd kissed her.

Kit had been observing Marcus, and being a man himself,

could read the hidden pages. He took the arm of a rather startled Jane, and then smiled at Henrietta. "Forgive us, but we'd like to be alone with Rowley for a while. Please explain to Marcus."

"Yes, of course."

Kit opened the door of the empty room, ushered Jane and Rowley through, then went inside himself. The door closed, and Henrietta was alone again with Marcus. She turned. "They've gone. They wished to be alone with Rowley."

He nodded.

She smiled bashfully. "You have no idea how pleased I am to have found Rowley."

"I can see how delighted you are."

"Even if you couldn't see anything else?" She gave a quick laugh. "How unruffled you are by all this."

"In common with the residents at Bedlam, I've discovered I hear things. All I can do now is learn to live with it."

She smiled. "Do you think you are mad?"

"No."

"Or that I am?"

He looked into her eyes. "No."

She smiled again.

He studied her. "Being at odds does not suit us, Henrietta." He held up a hand as her lips parted defensively. "No, don't repeat that *I* am the one in the wrong, nor will I cast aspersions upon you. Something went very awry between us, and the time has come to get to the bottom of it. We need to talk, and tonight there will be nothing to distract us. Will you dine with me? I can promise more than ship's biscuit, for the *Avalon* boasts an excellent cook."

She met his eyes. "I think I would like that."

"Then the matter is settled."

Chapter Twenty-five

It was after nightfall, and the *Avalon* still ran before a good wind. The snow clouds had disappeared, but in spite of a clear winter sky and a full moon that gave visibility for miles, the temperature had risen unexpectedly. It was no longer necessary for all ropes, winches, and pulleys to be checked every half hour to see they were running freely, and a lookout could be sent up the mainmast without any danger of him freezing to death. At last it seemed the great frost might be over.

Jane and Kit rested in each other's arms in a corner of the crew's mess room. They had found a comfortable pile of blankets and Rowley was snuggled up contentedly with them, sleeping deeply for the first time in a month. About six of the sloop's crew of thirty were playing cards at a table, while one of them sang a slow sea chantey to the grind of a fiddle. No one realized the specters were there.

Now the joyful diversion of Rowley's return had quieted, Jane and Kit's thoughts returned to the bad omens they'd witnessed. Something evil was at hand, and all they could do was wait for it to strike. They tried to talk about something more cheering, especially their renewed hopes of a happy outcome between Henrietta and Marcus, but the awful feeling of apprehension remained.

In the main cabin, the dinner à deux was almost at an end. Henrietta had done the best with her appearance, putting up her dark hair as stylishly as she could, and donning the second of the two gowns she'd brought with her. It was made of lavender wool that matched her eyes, and had white fur at the throat, cuffs, and hem. Usually when she wore it, she felt confident and at ease, but from the outset tonight she'd been self-conscious and unsure. She'd examined her recent actions in the minutest detail, and found herself wanting. *Why* was she flirting with danger all over again? Her dealings with Marcus in London had broken her heart and put her reputation in peril, yet here she was once more, unchaperoned and considerably at risk from her own weakness. Being her cousin's bridesmaid wasn't all *that* important; indeed everyone in the family would have understood if she'd stayed on at Mulborough because of the weather. Instead she had not only accepted Marcus's offer, she had even persisted when the maid had cried off.

In her heart of hearts she knew she was a fraud. No amount of pretense could disguise the simple truth; she was doing it all because she wished to be close to the man whose caresses she still craved. Nothing had changed since that first moment at the masked ball. She'd fallen head over heels in love with him then, and was still head over heels in love with him. Not only was she foolishly playing with fire, she was doing it willfully. It seemed she would *never* learn how dangerous this man was to her peace of mind and reputation!

Having already found it difficult to accept that she was still in love with him, it was even more difficult to accept that she was still prepared to risk so much just to be with him. Throughout the meal she had nervously deflected the conversation from anything sensitive or delicate by asking a barrage of questions about the sloop, but now, as they sat at the table, separated by the glow of a candle, she was only just maintaining her poise. She was also running out of questions.

Marcus was quietly amused and patiently answered everything she asked, no matter how trivial, but when, after floundering about for inspiration, she lighted upon the unlikely topic of compasses, he sat forward and interrupted. "Henrietta, are you *really* interested in such things?"

"Yes, of course."

"I could discourse at some length on the mysteries of sea charts, then go on to describe how a sextant works, and even how to pick up a pen and make an entry in the ship's log, which I'm *sure* you are eager to learn, but instead I'm going to draw the line upon all things nautical."

"I *am* interested, truly I am."

"You cannot humbug me, Henrietta Courtenay. You're doing your utmost to avoid talking about us."

She looked away. "There is no use. The past is over and done with."

"Is it?"

"What point is there in chewing upon old bones?"

He smiled. "Old bones? Forgive me, but the bones did not seem so old when we came on board today; in fact you chewed upon them with considerable ferocity. As I recall, I was accused of being a heartless gamester whose trickery didn't quite reap the anticipated reward."

"And so you are."

"What, exactly, am I supposed to have done?" he asked quietly. "You see, if my memory serves me correctly, and I'm certain it does, I sought your hand in marriage, but after accepting, you sent me a very curt note terminating the matter, and then flung yourself into Sutherton's predatory arms instead."

"Your résumé is more notable for its omissions than its content," she replied.

"What omissions? Your abandoned conduct in my arms, perhaps?"

She colored. "How like you to say that."

"Do you now *deny* your passionate response?"

"No, but then I was gullible and naive, was I not? In fact, I was the perfect prey for a predator such as you."

"*Prey*? Oh, come now . . ."

"What of your own conduct, sirrah? If mine was abandoned and passionate, how would you describe yours? And before you answer, perhaps I should remind you that I *know* you entered into the liaison simply to humiliate me! Being a thoroughgoing Fitzpaine, you decided a mere Courtenay had to be humiliated and then ruined socially. My seduction was the object of the exercise, and in order to achieve it, you lied about your identity.

On top of that you set the whole shabby business in White's betting book for all to see!"

Marcus stared at her. "You cannot honestly believe any of that," he said then.

"I believe every word." Tears stung her eyes and she flung her napkin on the table, then got up to go to the windows facing over the sloop's creaming wake.

Slowly he rose as well, and came to stand behind her. "Henrietta, I swear upon all that I hold dear that I am innocent. I didn't set out to humiliate or ruin you, and I certainly didn't place a wager of any sort in White's book."

"Don't lie, Marcus. You used me most foully, and if Sutherton had not told me—"

"I didn't do it, Henrietta, and if anyone is a liar in it all, I suggest you look to Sutherton. Look at me, damn you!" He caught her wrist and whirled her about to face him. "The only thing of which I stand guilty is calling myself Mark Paynson, and that I did because immediately after the cotillion I made it my business to learn your name. On discovering it to be Courtenay, I feared you would spurn me if you knew the truth. But Henrietta, I *swear* that although I came to you under a false name, I was not also under false colors. Everything I did was on account of my love for you, and on the day you ended things between us, I had been on the point of calling upon you to admit my birthright."

"How can I take the word of someone who lied so very smoothly in the past?"

"Why do you refuse to believe me, yet accept everything Sutherton says as if it were gospel?" He released her wrist.

She looked at him. "Perhaps because I cannot see how he could have found out about us, if not from the betting book. I certainly didn't tell anyone, and we were always discreet, even when we met in Hyde Park."

"Ergo *I* must be guilty? Henrietta, I'm relieved your sex is barred from the judiciary, because if you are an example of female reasoning, I vow there would never be a fair verdict!" He turned away.

"Oh, I think a fair verdict was delivered in this case, sirrah, for you did not succeed in your shabby game."

"No, but Sutherton succeeded in his!" He ran a hand through his fair hair, and then paused. "Actually, I *did* tell one person, a friend who has now gone to India, but I would trust him with my very life. My only conclusion is that Sutherton must have overheard that conversation."

"I suppose it does not matter *how* he found out, simply that he did."

He faced her again. "It *does* matter, Henrietta, because if you continue to believe this business with White's book, then you continue to believe in my guilt. Think about Sutherton, I mean really think. He is a two-faced liar with debts so monumental he needs a fortune to bail him out. How can you possibly take his word? Especially when all the time he was paying court to you, he was bedding Amabel!"

"I know what he is."

He faced her again, his eyes bright. "And *still* you intend to marry him?"

She drew a long breath and shook her head. "No, not anymore."

He was startled. "Do I hear correctly? The match with Sutherton is off?"

"That's what I said, although of course I have yet to tell him."

"Oh, to be a fly on the wall when you do! I'll warrant he's been running up countless new bills on the promise of funds after marriage."

"I trust that is not the case."

"Then you trust in vain. Oh, Henrietta, I thought you would never see sense."

"Of what possible concern can it really be to you? You've embarked upon marriage negotiations of your own, remember?"

"Have I?" He gave a slight laugh. "Well, maybe where that is concerned, I *was* indeed a little dishonest."

"Dishonest?"

For a long moment he looked at her, and then exhaled resignedly. "Maybe the time has come for complete honesty. Henrietta, my bride is a figment of my imagination, created in the hope she would cause you some of the pain Sutherton caused me."

She stared at him.

He cleared his throat. "You may as well know it all, and do with it what you will. Henrietta, I haven't looked at another woman since you. Oh, I've reached the bedside on more than one occasion, but as to slipping between the sheets, you are the only one with whom I wish to do that." He hesitated, then put his hand gently to her cheek.

Her heart missed a beat. Surely she couldn't have misunderstood? He had just told her he still loved her! When she did not pull away, he slid his fingers to twine in the warm hair at the nape of her neck. She closed her eyes as the old, forbidden sensations began to swirl unstoppably through her veins. Oh, what feelings they were, and once learned, they could never be forgotten. She had no resistance, no resistance at all. . . .

Pulling her close, he found her lips in a kiss that ignited her entire being. Flames raced through her veins, reducing her pride to ashes. Why pretend anymore? Why adopt an attitude when this was what she wanted? Her body ached to be consumed, and she was moving further and further into the heat. Pride, honor, vanity, all were consigned to the blaze as she gave herself to the desire that had smoldered through her days and nights ever since they met.

His kiss became more imperative, and he cupped her breast through her gown, at the same time drawing her more tightly against his hips so that she could feel the hard contours of his body. She gasped with pleasure. Her flesh was beginning to melt, and she was at desire's mercy. If he were to carry her to the bed in the adjoining cabin, she knew she would make no protest.

Marcus longed to do just that. To lie naked with her, to intoxicate her with pleasure, to take her rosebud nipples into his mouth, to sink his needful virility into that sweet fastness no other man had entered before, those were the dazzling prizes that were shone before him now. Oh, dear God, how close he was to abandon . . . But he couldn't, he mustn't, for to give in to his senses now would be wrong. Everything had to be right, *right*!

With a huge effort, he drew back from the brink. His eyes were dark with his emotion and his face was flushed. "Do you still doubt me?"

"No," she whispered, her eyes brimming with tears.

"Then—"

Before he could say anything more, the first officer knocked urgently at the door. "My lord?"

"Yes, Mr. Barrington?"

"Sail astern! The moon is full, and the lookout suspects it's the *Légère*!"

"Summon all hands! I'll be with you promptly, Mr. Barrington!"

"Right, my lord."

The first officer shouted an order, and almost immediately the shriek of the boatswain's whistle carried clearly into the cabin from farther along the main deck. Marcus stepped swiftly to the telescope, took it from its stand, and then went to open the door leading to the stern balcony. The noise of the sea swept in, as did the cold. The sudden draft made the solitary candle dance and flicker, although thankfully it did not go out. Spray dashed up, as white and icy as snow, and Henrietta shivered.

Marcus braced his legs against the wind and motion of the ship, then trained the telescope on the moonlit horizon. The pale glimmer of a sail was just visible; to the lookout high on the crow's nest, it must have been very clear indeed. His face set, he came back into the cabin and closed the door on the winter sea and the night.

As the candle flame steadied once more, Henrietta looked anxiously at him. "Is it the *Légère*?"

"I believe it may be." He returned the telescope to its stand before drawing her close to put his lips to hers once more. This time the kiss was tender, a loving caress intended to reassure. Then he grabbed his greatcoat and strode from the cabin. The bitter cold swept briefly in again, and the candle fluttered be-

fore the door swung to behind him. As the candle steadied, she
could hear the pounding of her heart.

She took the telescope and stood on the morocco window
seat to see what she could. There was a speck of white in the
distance, but as she looked, it turned to luminous silver. Then
everything around her began to change. She wasn't on *Avalon*
anymore, but on another, much older vessel. . . .

Things had already changed for the ghosts. Rowley had
sensed it first, at about the same moment the lookout sighted
the distant sail. Raising his head, the spaniel gave an uneasy
whine. Jane and Kit sat up immediately. A sinister smell of sulfur seemed to drift in air that was oddly still, and they found
themselves unable to move. It was the commencement of their
unnamed dread, and their fear was almost tangible.

The sailors were still seated around the table, but looked up
sharply as footsteps ran to the mess room door. Mr. Pascoe
flung it open. "Sail-ho, lads! His Lordship's about to be on
deck, so look lively!" They got up and ran from the room.

Jane and Kit tried to hold each other's hand, but their fingers
wouldn't obey. The light around them began to change, turning
slowly to eerie silver. Then, compelled by a force beyond their
control, they rose from the pile of blankets and were drawn in
a straight line toward the stern of the vessel, as if by an invisible chain. As they passed out of sight through the mess room
wall, Rowley ran after them in panic. No straight line for him.
He had to scurry through open doors and up companionways,
but as he dashed along the open deck, at last he had them in
view again. They disappeared into the captain's quarters just as
Marcus emerged, and the spaniel slipped through the briefly
opened door.

Henrietta climbed shakily down from the window seat and
replaced the telescope on the stand. The hairs at the nape of her
neck stirred uneasily, and she felt very strange. She was used to
the supernatural, but this was very, very different. Suddenly the
light in the cabin changed. It was no longer just the soft glow
of a single candle, but had become the shimmering brightness

of several four-branched candelabra. The cabin itself had changed too, becoming much larger and more plainly furnished. An old-fashioned writing desk appeared before her, and on it lay a ship's log. She saw the vessel's name quite clearly upon the cover: *Wessex.* As recollections of Lady Chloe's journal swept chillingly over her, something made her turn sharply. Her heart quickened as she saw eight hazy figures seated around a large table. They were laughing and talking, but made no sound, and among them were Jane and Kit. The door opened and a ship's officer looked urgently in. He spoke, but still Henrietta heard nothing. The captain rose swiftly from his chair and strode toward her. She had no time to step aside, but it didn't matter because he passed right through her to go to the writing desk. He took a small telescope from the drawer of the writing desk, and just as Marcus had done but a few moments before, he went out onto the stern balcony to look at a sail on the horizon.

The tragedy of 1714 echoed through Henrietta, and she knew he feared the distant sail might belong to the *Basilisk.* Past and present had become entangled, and the *Avalon* had become the *Wessex* and the *Légère* had become the *Basilisk.* Four vessels, two of them ghosts from the previous century. But what was their fate? Were the vessels of 1814 as doomed as those of a hundred years before?

The captain came back in, spoke abruptly to the other men at the table, but still all was silent. Within moments everyone had hurried out, leaving only Kit and Jane, who held Rowley close in her arms.

Then the silver glow faded, and as the cabin of the *Avalon* returned, the ghosts were temporarily freed from the spell. Jane met Henrietta's eyes. "Old Nick has us now, and on St. Valentine's Day he will drive us on to the Goodwins again," she said quietly.

Chapter Twenty-six

As the sun rose, the lookout identified the suspicious sail on the horizon as being the *Légère*. The privateer made no progress, nor did it slip out of sight, so that very soon it was clear she was stalking the *Avalon*. Mulborough was already a hundred miles astern as the sloop ran briskly southward before the wind. The sails cracked, the wind whistled through the rigging, and seagulls screamed wildly in the cloudless sky. The temperature was above freezing, and a thaw had set in.

Overnight the sloop had been well out of sight of land as they cleared The Wash, but now the low white coast of Norfolk lay to starboard. Marcus kept the *Avalon* well inshore, where the water was too shallow for the privateer, but by now he'd guessed the Frenchman's plan. Charles Lyons was biding his time, intending to capture the sloop, not destroy her. The tide was ebbing, and the area of sea ahead was a maze of dangerous shoals and sandbanks, especially off Orford Ness. Here lay the hazard known as the Black Deeps, where beneath the water was the sunken village of Dunchurch, and it was said the church bell could still sometimes be heard tolling. No vessel would willingly risk such dangers, so Lyons was confident that even the *Avalon* would soon be forced to seek more open water, at which point he would strike. The *Légère* would crack on full sail, come up swiftly, fire a few well-aimed shots with her bow howitzers. If all went Lyons's way, it would soon be over, and the *Avalon* would be in France before nightfall. It would be some revenge for being deprived of the gold at Mulborough.

Marcus had no intention of accommodating Lyons, and so although he felt that the *Avalon* stood a chance of outrunning the Frenchman, he decided to bolt for the safety of Great Yarmouth. But even as he made the decision, the wind suddenly backed sharply, sweeping off the land and forcing him to abandon Great Yarmouth. Determined not to make for the open sea where the *Légère* could pounce, Marcus sailed as close-hauled as possible, keeping to the coast. He willed a British naval vessel to appear with the wind behind her, to force the privateer to sheer off, but no such rescue arrived. There was nothing for it but to put the sloop and his own seamanship to the test. A little cloud had begun to burgeon overhead, and if he could skirt as closely as possible to the Black Deeps, maybe he could lose the *Légère* by disappearing into a moonless winter night.

Henrietta was seated on the flag locker by the taffrail on the quarterdeck. She was wrapped in her fur-lined cloak, with the hood held in place by a scarf. Salt clung to the dark curls around her face and her hands were thrust into a muff. The *Avalon*'s identification flag flapped like a wild thing as she glanced forward in the hope of seeing Marcus, but he was out of sight by the helmsman.

She had taken the liberty of bringing the telescope from the cabin, and through it saw Amabel standing at her brother's side on the *Légère*'s deck. Henrietta gazed at the woman she had regarded as a close confidante. In truth, Amabel Renchester had always been a stranger, yet the fabrication of friendship she created had seemed the very essence of genuineness. It was chilling to think how very nearly her plans had succeeded.

Henrietta was not alone at the taffrail, for Jane and Kit were with her, as was Rowley. By now the ghosts knew how well things had progressed at the dinner à deux, but were convinced that it was hopeless. They believed declarations of love had been made, and even that a marriage proposal might soon follow, but that it was now too late. Old Nick was closing in upon them, and after toying cruelly for a while, would carry them off to a terrible eternity in Hades. Even if Marcus were to propose, and Henrietta were to accept, at this cruelly late point it would all come to nothing. They were all in the hands of the Master of

Hades, and that was the end of it. They were wrong, it *wasn't* too late, but the weary wraiths were not to know that.

However, even now they abided by the rules, leaving Henrietta ignorant of their mission because to tell her would break those rules. They only told her of the struggle between St. Peter and Old Nick for possession of their souls, and said that the Master of Hades had clearly won. Henrietta comforted them as best she could, but there was precious little she could say.

Rowley suddenly jumped from Jane's arms onto Henrietta's lap, for he had taken a great fancy to her. She took a hand from her muff to stroke him, because he liked it even though he couldn't feel anything. Jane hardly noticed the spaniel's desertion. All she could think of was that the *Wessex* and *Basilisk* had foundered at first light on St. Valentine's Day, and today was St. Valentine's Eve.

Henrietta didn't hear Marcus step up onto the quarterdeck. She only realized he was there when he appeared beside her, and steadied himself with a leather-gloved hand on the taffrail. His cloak billowed as he glanced down and saw the movement of her hand as she stroked the invisible spaniel. "We have company?" he inquired above the racket of the sea and ship.

"Yes."

He looked at her. "It's too cold out here. You should be in the cabin."

"I wanted some fresh air."

"Fresh? Well, that's one way of describing it."

"I'm hardy in spite of my delicate breeding," she replied with a smile.

He smiled too, and there was sufficient warmth in his eyes to melt polar ice.

They were silent for a moment. Then she looked astern again at the following vessel. "Do you think the *Légère* is fast enough to overhaul us?"

"The truth is, I don't know. She isn't yet giving full chase, but we have sail to spare as well."

"Are we still making for the Thames?"

"Yes, although the river itself is frozen in London, and I really don't know how far we will be able to sail up the estuary.

Hopefully far enough for the *Légère* to cry off. Why do you ask?"

"I was thinking of the Goodwins." She glanced at Jane and Kit.

Marcus had been told about the silver glow and mingling of past and present, and he knew the fate Jane had predicted. He hunched his shoulders beneath his cloak. "Old Nick can go whistle. He's not getting anything or anyone while I live and breathe."

"So there is no chance at all that we will go anywhere near the Goodwins?" Henrietta wanted to allay Jane's fears if she could.

Marcus replied, "I cannot deny that the safety of the Downs is a great temptation."

"The Downs?"

"The haven between the sands and the Kent shore. It's where all shipping coming in and out of London holes up when necessary, and is reckoned the most protected stretch of water on the east coast. But the estuary is closer and I really have no desire to test the *Légère*'s mettle."

Henrietta looked astern again. "I've seen Amabel on the *Légère*. I wonder what she's thinking?"

"Amabel? Most probably that since she's unlikely to enjoy Sutherton's embraces again, comfort will have to be drawn instead from the prospect of shining very nicely in the Paris salons on the proceeds of a prize like the *Avalon*," he replied dryly.

"What will happen to us if we're captured?"

"When the *Avalon* picks up her skirts to run, she shows a very neat pair of heels. If nothing else, we'll give Lyons a run for his money."

She noticed he hadn't actually answered her question, and she remembered that Charlotte had told her Charles Lyons offered no quarter, even to women.

Suddenly the lookout shouted down from the mainmast that the *Légère* was hoisting her full rig. As Marcus glanced swiftly at the other vessel, Jane and Kit saw everything around them begin to turn silver again. The dreadful weakness of the previous night returned, and they were no longer in control. Jane gave a sob of utter dismay, and buried her face against Kit's shoulder. They were on the *Wessex* again, and there was pandemonium on the main deck as all hands were summoned. The *Basilisk* was coming up astern and the merchantman had to flee if she could.

Henrietta experienced it all too, although she remained in the present. She saw the *Wessex* superimposed on the *Avalon*, and the *Basilisk* upon the *Légère*. There was so much panic, yet everything was silent. It was like dreaming while awake. Rowley whimpered and pushed his head deep into the folds of her cloak, trying to hide. Her arms tightened protectively around him. "You're safe with me, Rowley. I won't let anything hurt you!" she whispered determinedly.

Marcus looked concernedly at her. "Henrietta?"

But her gaze was following the past.

"Henrietta!"

The other images disappeared, as did Jane and Kit, but Rowley was left behind, kept back by the sheer force of Henrietta's determination to protect him. Marcus pulled her to her feet and gripped her elbows to search her face, which was now quite ashen. "What happened, Henrietta?"

She swayed a little as everything became normal again, but Jane's dread now enveloped her as well. "Marcus, Jane is right, we *are* going to founder on the Goodwins!"

"That's nonsense. Tell me what happened."

"I—I saw the past." Still cradling Rowley, she described it all, then looked at Marcus with frightened eyes. "It's come full circle, Marcus, and cannot be avoided."

"That's utter nonsense! I admit that there are such things as ghosts. Indeed how could I deny it?" He nodded down to the way her arms clearly enveloped the invisible spaniel. "But I will *not* accept that our fate has been decreed by some supernatural force. All that's happened is that the *Légère* has tired of stalking us, and I'm going to show Lyons just how handy a good English sloop can be when necessary!" He kissed her harshly on the mouth, then turned to stride away, shouting for Mr. Barrington as he went.

Henrietta watched him go, then looked down at Rowley. "Where are Jane and Kit? What's happened to them?"

The spaniel gazed back, and whimpered again.

As the sea chase began in earnest, the Master of Hades sat back to watch. He was safe in the knowledge that weather conditions would soon favor the privateer, and unavoidable decisions would be forced upon Marcus. St. Valentine's Day and the Goodwins awaited, and with them a very neat and satisfactory repetition of the past. And all this while dithering St. Peter was well and truly distracted by a jealous dispute among angels. How provident that angels were not always angelic!

However, in spite of his outward display of calm confidence and gloating anticipation, Old Nick was in fact quite ruffled. The reason for this lay in the outcome of the dinner à deux, for he knew how very, very close the ghosts were to success, and if that happened they would elude his grasp forever. When the whole business began in 1714, he had promised himself the eventual satisfaction of thumbing his nose toward heaven. The final snatching of their souls, one hundred years to the day, would allow him to do just that, but he would lose face entirely if they slipped through his fingers. Victory *had* to be his!

It didn't please him at all that in the meantime he felt it necessary to defend his reputation. If Jane and Kit were to get away with their effrontery, his lieutenants in hell might question his authority, and that could not be tolerated. To prevent this, he had commenced the ghosts' punishment. The year 1814 had ceased to be for them. Instead they were reliving every anxious moment of the 1714 events. They felt as if they were alive again, except that they knew exactly what would unfold in the coming hours.

His fingers drummed grimly. They might think they already knew what terror was, but when they were carried down into Hades, they would discover an eternity of something much, much worse. . . .

Chapter Twenty-seven

All day the *Avalon* fled, keeping so dangerously close to the land that at times it seemed she must founder among the shoals and sandbanks, but somehow she slipped safely through. The much larger *Légère* did not dare follow her example, so sailed a parallel course in deeper water, and slowly but surely began to overhaul the sloop.

Henrietta had nothing to do except watch and wait. Rowley did not leave her arms, but by his cowering manner, and the way he whined wretchedly from time to time, she knew he was seeing things that for some reason were now denied to her. Rowley himself was her only link with the supernatural; she neither heard nor saw anything else. Of Jane and Kit there was absolutely no sign, nor was there a reoccurrence of the silver-shaded echoes from the past, and although Henrietta prayed that one or other of her ghostly friends would appear, she waited in vain.

In fact they were enduring Old Nick's callous punishment. As Henrietta gazed back from the *Avalon* toward the *Légère*, the phantoms gazed instead from the *Wessex* to the pursuing *Basilisk*. Their feelings weren't those of the past, however, for instead of the anxiety they'd experienced then, they were weighed down by an overwhelming sense of impending doom. Every second that ticked away was an agony of fear and suspense.

Marcus had too much on his mind to be concerned about Jane and Kit. He longed to make a run for a port, but the strong offshore wind denied him the opportunity. Nor did help come in the form of other vessels. The horizon remained empty, and not so much as a fishing boat sallied forth from the snow-covered land. It was as if the sloop and its hunter were the only ships afloat, and all the time the Black Deeps loomed ever closer. When dusk fell, the *Légère* was barely a quarter of a mile astern and the perils off Orford Ness were only five miles ahead.

With darkness came a quirk of the wind that carried a snatch of sound from the *Légère*. Marcus distinctly heard a burst of idle laughter from the privateer's crew, and knew they weren't as vigilant as they should be. Overconfident, he thought, and with a shrewd smile ordered all lights on the *Avalon* extinguished. Then he changed the sloop's course to avoid the Black Deeps, veering due east so that the offshore wind was now directly behind her. With barely two hundred yards to spare, she cut directly across the *Légère*'s path. It was a risky business, relying heavily upon the Frenchmen's unpreparedness, and everyone on the *Avalon* held their breath as they waited for the shouts that would signify the privateer's realization, but none came. The *Avalon* sailed on eastward, and the lights of the *Légère* continued south. Marcus hoped Amabel's brother would run his vessel into the Black Deeps, but knew that was very unlikely. Lyons was probably dining at this moment, but his eye would be upon the time. He could not help but know about the Black Deeps, for their whereabouts were very well charted, and in a while he would toss his napkin aside and come up on deck. His crew might be less than alert, but it wouldn't take him long to realize his quarry had gone or which direction she must have taken.

Therefore, after two hours Marcus changed course again, this time to beat southwest across the wind toward the Thames estuary. There was a risk they might encounter the privateer again, but he guessed Lyons would crack on as much sail as possible to surge east, and wouldn't expect what amounted to a doubling back. Even supposing the Frenchman realized the trick, and veered about as well, he would have to beat across the wind as much as his quarry. The *Avalon* only had to stay ahead of him for the night hours. By dawn she would be in the estuary, where there was bound to be sufficient naval presence to drive the *Légère* away.

The night hours passed without event, and at dawn on St. Valentine's Day, the wind fell away to a light northerly breeze. The reassuring shores of the estuary were faintly visible to north or south, without any sign of the *Légère*. There was a strange absence of other vessels for an area that was usually thick with traffic, but no one gave it too much thought. All that mattered was that the British mouse had eluded the French cat. There were cheers as Marcus ordered the breaking out of a cask of rum.

Old Nick watched and smiled. He knew their joy was premature. They weren't safe yet, not by a long chalk.

Henrietta shared the heady atmosphere of deliverance, but—like good St. Peter before her—was guilty of forgetting something very important. The bogle was locked in the very storeroom where the rum was kept. When the sailor entered to collect the promised cask of rum, the manikin tiptoed out as slyly as it had tiptoed in weeks before. Then it set out to cause trouble, beginning with the simple delight of jumping out and biting members of the crew. It decided to be visible to them, so the men would be frightened as much as possible. Sailors were renowned for their superstition, and had even been a little uneasy when Henrietta embarked at Mulborough, because women were supposed to be unlucky on board ship. Thus the sight of a hideous little goblin was sure to cause chaos.

The celebrations came to a shocked halt as the bogle went about its wicked business. It leaped from an open hatchway and bit Mr. Pascoe's calf. As the boatswain howled with pain and dropped his cup of rum, the other crew members whirled in time to see the manikin dashing back into the hatchway. For a moment they doubted the evidence of their eyes, but then the ship's cook erupted from a doorway. With a quivering finger he pointed back, and gibbered something about a gnome. As a stir of alarm spread along the deck, the bogle reappeared farther along the deck, this time treating the unfortunate Mr. Barrington to a sharp bite. After that there was mayhem. The bogle darted here, there, and everywhere, sinking its teeth into ankle after ankle, and there was nothing Marcus could do to restore calm.

At this point, Rowley entered the fray. When Mr. Pascoe was attacked, Henrietta had been standing by the taffrail with the ghostly spaniel in her arms. As incident followed hot upon incident, Rowley's hackles rose and his hatred for the odious goblin increased. Then, with a growl of pure vengeance, he jumped down to charge after his tormentor. With a volley of barks he chased it into the hold.

For a moment Henrietta was frozen with dismay; after all, it was through chasing the bogle that the spaniel had been lost before. Remembering how she'd dealt with the bogle in the past, she was galvanized into action. Ignoring the bemused gaze of the frightened seamen, she seized one of the brooms that had recently been used to keep the sloop free of snow, and hastened down to the main deck. Sooner or later the bogle would come on deck again, and when it did, she would be ready! Holding the broom firmly in both hands, she glanced swiftly at the likely doors, hatches, and ports.

Rowley's muffled barks suddenly became yelps of fear that emanated from one hatch in particular. The yelps grew louder and Henrietta advanced with the broom, oblivious to the watching crew. Rowley's yelps were very close now, and then a second sound carried too—evil, high-pitched laughter. The spaniel burst onto the deck with the bogle on his back, and Henrietta had only a split second in which to act. She swung the broom with all her might. The bogle's laughter ended on a choke as it was knocked heavily from the spaniel's back. Over and over it rolled, squealing and cursing as foully as the lowest tar.

Henrietta swept the helpless manikin along the deck. She was as brisk and purposeful as a farmer's wife cleansing a dairy as she rolled it toward the rail. But as she attempted to force the loathsome creature overboard, it grabbed a wooden fire bucket that stood nearby. For a moment the bucket wedged against the rail, with the wriggling bogle holding on tightly as it dangled above the water.

Marcus stepped forward then, and with a deft kick sent

bucket and bogle into the sea. Henrietta dropped the broom to
gather Rowley gladly into her arms again, and the spaniel covered her face with licks she could not feel. The relieved crew
dashed to the rail and watched the bogle clamber into the
bucket. As it bobbed away astern, it brandished a clenched fist
and hurled abuses that would have made a coal heaver blush.
The bemused sailors could only stare at it, but then, much to the
bogle's gibbering fury, a man slightly bolder than the rest
shouted something appropriately insulting in return. There was
a ripple of laughter, and the atmosphere lightened perceptibly
as the bogle began to jump impotently up and down in the
bucket.

But as the manikin and its makeshift craft slipped farther and
farther away, carried out to sea by the tide and unseen current
of the mighty Thames, something else in the water caught Marcus's attention. He leaned over to look more closely, then stiffened. "Ice floes," he breathed, then looked a little farther away,
and saw more.

Henrietta watched him. "What is it? What's wrong?"

Before he could reply, there was a shout from the lookout.
The *Légère* had appeared on the horizon and was coming
up at a speed that suggested she had the advantage of the
breeze.

Beneath his breath, Marcus uttered an expletive of which the
bogle would have been proud. Henrietta looked at him in puzzlement. "What does it matter if the *Légère* comes now? We're
sailing farther into the estuary all the time, and must surely be
safe?"

"I wish it were that simple. There are ice floes. The thaw and
high tide must have broken up the Thames ice. No wonder there
aren't any other vessels around. The estuary is dangerous to
shipping."

"What are you saying? That we may not be able to continue
to London?"

"Yes, I'm afraid that's exactly what I'm saying." He cupped
his hands and shouted urgently up to the lookout to forget the
Légère for the moment, and have regard instead to what lay
ahead.

The man did as he was told and everyone on deck saw how his face changed. "Ice floes, my lord! Large ones, and plenty of them!"

There was an uneasy stir among the crew, and Marcus bellowed at the helmsman. "Come about, and be swift about it!"

Mr. Barrington shouted as well. "To your stations, lads, unless you want us to become a French prize! Jump to it!" The bogle was forgotten as heavy sea boots thudded on the deck. The *Avalon* began to swing around, heeling over alarmingly as the wheel was turned to its limit. The sails cracked and billowed, and orders were roared.

Clinging to the rail, Henrietta glanced back at the *Légère*, which was already perceptibly closer. She looked uneasily at Marcus. "Where will we go now?" she asked, although deep inside she knew the answer.

He met her eyes. "No one is going to come to our aid, Henrietta, so we have to look after ourselves. I'm going to try for the Downs."

"Is there no other choice?"

He hesitated. "Yes, but I want to put an end to the *Légère*."

"But if there are other choices, surely—"

He silenced her by putting a finger to her lips. "I will not let ice or Frenchman harm you. Trust me in this, for I know something I am certain Lyons cannot yet know," he said quietly, his voice almost lost in the noise of the ship and crew. Then he took her face in his hands and put his lips tenderly to hers. It was a lingering kiss. His lips were warm and pliable, and yet strong as well. For a moment she felt the tip of his tongue slide against hers, then he released her and strode away toward the helm.

Rowley glowered after him and growled, his canine jealousy aroused as much by this relationship as it was by that between Jane and Kit. Henrietta tapped the spaniel's nose, just as Jane was wont to do. "Stop that, sir," she murmured.

Rowley gave another disgruntled growl, but then fell silent.

Henrietta remained on deck as the *Avalon* came about, and struck east-southeast toward the jutting North Foreland of Kent, some fifty miles away. The sloop leaned to starboard as the northerly breeze filled her sails, and Henrietta saw the distant *Légère* come about as well. The privateer still had the weather gauge, and her astonishing spread of canvas made her seem to fly toward them like a hawk swooping on a sparrow. Whatever Marcus's plan was, it would have to be very good indeed if the sparrow was to escape those savage talons.

Chapter Twenty-eight

The *Avalon*'s nimble maneuvering was her salvation, and as she forged toward the North Foreland, not even the *Légère* carried enough sail to cut her off. It wasn't for lack of trying, and the activity on the privateer's decks was furious as the crew strove to slice across the estuary and close the way to the sloop. The *Avalon* slipped through the gap with barely a hundred yards to spare, and when the *Légère* fired her forward howitzers at the sloop's rigging, intending to disable her rather than sink her, the shots flew wide. The privateer was forced to check and come around again, and while she was doing this, the sloop picked up her skirts and fled.

As the *Légère* took up the chase once more, Charles Lyons was aggravated considerably. He was as prideful as he was handsome and had expected to make sure of this particular prize long before now. Instead she'd led him a merry dance. On top of that his crew had let him down. They should have been more careful the night before, but by their negligence had let the British sloop slip away in the darkness. It was a state of affairs to which the French captain was unaccustomed, and his temper was foul.

Amabel kept out of his way, for he had been further irritated by the crew's consternation at having a woman on board. She'd gone briefly on deck the previous day, but had met with such hostility that she'd soon retreated to Charles's cabin again. She was devastated by what had happened at Mulborough. Instead of securing the Treasury gold for France, and at the same time

ridding herself of Henrietta, she had been forced to flee ignominiously. Her plan had been to return to London—George
Sutherton—there to resume her agreeable social existence,
while at the same time continuing to spy for France. Because of
Henrietta and Marcus, that was all at an end. There would be no
more George, and instead of the freedom and pleasures of London, there would be the less certain atmosphere of Republican
Paris.

The need for revenge contorted Amabel's face as she sat
alone in the cabin, dwelling upon her misfortunes. She prayed
the *Avalon* would be captured so that those who'd done this to
her could be made to suffer for their interference, especially
Henrietta. Oh, how she loathed her old school friend now. The
vapid creature had everything, while she, Amabel, had lost all!

If Amabel and her brother were in foul moods, so was the
bogle, which did not know how it was going to get out of its
watery scrape. The Thames tide had changed at about the same
time the *Avalon* had gone about, so that the current now bore
the bucket in the same direction as the sloop. The bogle sat dis-
consolately in its unlikely conveyance. Maybe it would float
aimlessly like this for weeks! Then something thudded against
the side of the bucket, and the bogle peered out. Its wicked little eyes widened as it saw an ice floe, and then several more
nearby, one of them disconcertingly large. The bogle swallowed, but then heard the telltale rush of a ship's bow slicing
through the water. The manikin's eyes nearly popped from its
head as it saw the *Légère* bearing down on the tiny bucket at a
rate of knots as she tried to cut off the *Avalon*'s escape.

The privateer was only yards away when she opened fire
with her howitzers. The bogle squealed and flattened itself at
the bottom of the bucket, its hands to its ears. As the shots whistled overhead and fell harmlessly into the water, the manikin
peeped out again The *Légère* was upon it, and as the bucket
spun uncontrollably along the privateer's hull, a hanging net
came providentially within reach. Lunging up, the bogle hauled
itself to safety and climbed through one of the many open gun-
ports on the main deck. There it crouched beside the nearest
cannon. Its fear was soon a thing of the past as it watched the

French crew dashing to-and-fro about their business. The wicked gleam returned to its eyes and it rubbed its bony hands together in glee. But first a little rest after suffering ordeal by bucket. It would commence its troublemaking in a little while. Slipping invisibly across the deck, it vanished through a hatch into the hold, where it soon found a comfortable corner in which to doze. But the doze became a deep snoring sleep, and it was to be some time before it wrought the same havoc among the French sailors that it had among the English.

Throughout the long morning, as the *Avalon* managed to keep ahead of the *Légère*, Marcus gave more thought to his plan to rid British shipping of the privateer. It all depended upon the shift of the sands, for just as at Mulborough and the Black Deeps, the currents and channels around the Goodwins could never be relied upon. A single bad storm could shift countless tons of sand, sometimes to devastating effect. Channels closed and new sandbars appeared where none had been before, lurking beneath the water to trap unwary vessels. Just one such spit had been detected a month ago by a naval survey, and he himself would not have known of it had he not encountered the captain of the frigate that came weekly to Mulborough to escort the packet vessel. They had fallen into conversation, and knowing that the Marquess of Rothwell's country seat was on the coast facing the Goodwins, the man had mentioned the matter.

Marcus felt certain Charles Lyons could not yet know anything. The *Légère* had been in northern waters for some time, and although smugglers, French and English alike, were likely to exchange such navigational information, they avoided that particular area of the sands since it was too far to the north for their purposes.

Marcus pursed his lips thoughtfully. What was needed was for the *Avalon* to reach the place concerned as the tide was falling, which, by his reckoning should be toward the dusk. With her shallow draft, the sloop would pass safely over the hidden peril, but if the *Légère* attempted to follow, she would strike it hard. The tide would retreat apace as always it did on the sands, and the privateer would be left high and dry, soon to break her back. The only risk to the *Avalon* was that the sand had moved again since the survey, and either disappeared or been raised that fatal foot or so to trap her as well. It was a chance that he had to take.

He summoned the senior members of his crew to his cabin to tell them what he intended. With Rowley asleep on her lap, Henrietta sat on the window seat as the men pored over a sea chart, and the stratagem was unfolded. She lowered her eyes as she imagined Jane's reaction to learning they were to make for the Goodwins after all. Henrietta knew her own resolve was frail. She wanted to place her complete faith in Marcus, but ever since the phantoms' disappearance she had been forced to share Jane's conviction that the past *was* going to be repeated. If Jane was right, not only would the *Légère* suffer the *Basilisk*'s fate upon the sands, but the *Avalon* would perish as the *Wessex* had perished. And so would all on board.

Mr. Barrington's voice interrupted her thoughts, and she looked up. Marcus had finished outlining his plan, and asked if the others had anything to add. "Well, my lord, in theory it seems infallible."

"But?"

"But we can't be sure of getting to the spot at the right time. If the tide's gone that bit too far, we'll strike fast as well."

"I know, but I've calculated that we should be able to get it right. And if we keep our course and speed steady at this, the *Légère* clearly can't close on us sufficiently for capture *before* we reach the sands. Provided the weather doesn't change, I think we stand a good chance."

"The tides are untrustworthy once we round the North Foreland, my lord," Mr. Pascoe reminded him.

"I grew up with those tides, and I think I know them well enough," Marcus replied, studying the chart again.

Mr. Barrington studied the chart as well. "My lord, how can we be sure the *Légère* will risk coming that close to the Downs? There is a constant naval presence, to say nothing of the batteries on the Kent coast."

Marcus glanced up and smiled. "I think I have the measure of Lyons's arrogance. Remember how audacious he was at

Mulborough? By the time we reach the Downs, he'll have given up attempting to take us as prize. Instead he will be intent upon sinking us. By my figuring, he should just have us within range as we have the Goodwins in sight, and he'll fire with everything he has forward."

"Which is considerable," the first officer observed quietly, thinking of the privateer's formidable howitzers.

Marcus nodded philosophically. "Yes, and we have nothing mounted astern to give as good as we get, but he'll have to be accurate immediately because in a very short time we will have sailed safely into the Downs. If he's to sink us before that, he will have to gain the measure at the first few attempts, and in my experience very few vessels manage that. We must sail on as if the channel ahead is absolutely clear. On no account must Lyons be alerted, for the *Légère* is nimble enough to extricate herself even at the last moment. She must be lured right into the channel, where it is impossible to turn until the very edge of the Downs. Then, while we glide serenely over the hidden sandbar, he should pile up most fatally. With her immense spread of spar and canvas, the *Légère* demise should be a sight to behold."

Mr. Pascoe smiled. "I will follow wherever you lead, my lord, for I owe you my life. Besides which, I think it an excellent scheme."

"Thank you for that vote of confidence, Mr. Pascoe."

The boatswain spoke again. "One last thing, my lord. Assuming it works, and the *Légère* is wrecked, what if there are survivors?"

Marcus straightened from the chart. "In conditions like this, the good men of Kent will no doubt put out in their luggers to rescue them. The wreck will be plundered, then Lyons and his crew will be flung in jail, where they belong."

Another man grunted. "The captain of the *Légère* has hoisted a red flag enough times to be undeserving of any mercy. I'd leave him and his cutthroat crew to the justice of the sands."

"There won't be any mercy for them once the authorities have them. The hangman's noose awaits privateers," Marcus reminded him.

Henrietta spoke. "And what if Amabel survives?"

Marcus turned and met her eyes. "She's a traitor and a spy, so I cannot answer what fate will befall her. Don't waste your pity, for she deserves none of it. She was the most false of friends, even to the extent of attempting to murder you." He glanced at the men again. "That's all. I think we know what to do."

As they nodded and filed out, he rolled up the chart and put it away. Then he came over to take Henrietta's hand, but as he did so, Rowley awoke. The spaniel immediately took jealous exception to the intimacy and growled. Marcus looked down toward the sound. "So I'm trespassing, am I?" he murmured to Henrietta.

"It would appear so."

"Have I understood correctly that this particular ghost cannot pass through closed doors?"

"Yes."

"And that he has a passion for sugared almonds?"

"Yes."

"Then how fortuitous that this cabin not only possesses cupboards with doors that close tight, but also a supply of said sweetmeats, for which I also happen to possess a liking." Marcus went to the cupboard concerned, flung the doors open, and took a little bonbon dish from the top shelf. Opening it, he placed it on the bottom shelf of the cupboard, then turned to look at Henrietta again. "Will you do me the inestimable service of placing our spectral friend in here?"

"You mean to shut him in? Oh, Marcus, I can't—"

"My need is greater than his, believe me," Marcus replied softly, looking deep into her eyes.

Without another word, she gathered Rowley into her arms and got up. Before the spaniel knew it, he was shut in. Initially his clamor of protest was tremendous, but then he scented the sugared almonds. His noise was silenced, and instead came the scrape of the dish as he moved it around in his endeavors to consume the contents.

Marcus smiled at Henrietta and took her hand once more. He drew her close and slipped an arm around her waist. "We are at a perilous moment, Henrietta, and approaching danger is a most efficient clearer of the mind. I will be honest with you. I left Scotland early and called at Mulborough with the sole hope of seeing you again. I knew you would be there, and I wanted to win you back."

Down in the depths of hell, Old Nick had been watching the proceedings with increasing alarm. What was this? A proposal? Surely victory wasn't going to go to St. Peter at this eleventh hour? His hand tightened upon his pitchfork and he held his breath.

Marcus smiled into Henrietta's eyes. "I love you, and I believe you love me too."

"I do, oh, I do."

He crushed her tightly to him, bruising her lips with the passion of his kiss. Hungry emotions tumbled through them both, and as his hands roamed lovingly over her body, she felt how aroused and needful he was. His virility excited her senses and she longed to satisfy a desire that turned her blood to fire. It was a hunger that could be denied no longer, for it had ached through her ever since the masked ball. He was the only one for her, and always would be. Now they were sailing into danger, and maybe it would all go wrong, maybe they would not survive. What price propriety then? What good would have been served by denying themselves the love they yearned for?

She drew back and looked into his eyes. "Make love to me," she whispered.

Chapter Twenty-nine

Marcus smoothed Henrietta's hair back from her forehead. "Make love to you? How shameless you are."

"I'm in earnest."

He gazed at her. "I want to more than you can know."

"I do know, Marcus, for I feel it too. Please, for this is the right moment, and I think we both know it."

"The sin against propriety would be cardinal," he reminded her.

"I no longer care," she said recklessly.

He put his hand to her cheek and drew his thumb lovingly across her lips. "You have always been temptation beyond endurance, my darling," he breathed, "but I will continue to resist. One day soon the circumstances will be right, but until then . . ."

Tears filled her eyes. "But I need to be with you now, with you in a way we haven't been before."

He smiled and lifted her into his arms. "Kisses and intimate embraces we can share in abundance, my dearest, only the final act of love must wait." He carried her into the adjacent cabin.

Old Nick remained uneasy. Wait for what? The marriage bed? How could it be anything else? And if that was in Marcus's mind, how easily he might suddenly put it into words! And how clear it was that Henrietta would accept! Hell's overlord watched intently as they lay together on the bed, where Marcus's caresses soon made her sigh with pleasure. A satanic eyebrow was raised at the extent of Marcus's skills. Had he worn a collar, the Master of Hades would have run a bony finger around it. The Marquess of Rothwell was devilishly accomplished in the art of love, and had he been of a more wicked disposition, he would have made a superb diabolic agent.

But Old Nick's anxiety was unnecessary, for Marcus left her a short while later without proposing. As he stepped outside to the deck and stood beside the helmsman, he marveled that he had restrained his passions. Surely even a saint would have fallen by the wayside, and the Marquess of Rothwell was certainly not a saint! Except, perhaps, where Henrietta Courtenay was concerned. A tender smile brushed his lips. For her he would face the fury and damnation of hell itself!

Henrietta lay drowsily on the bed. A delicious warmth enveloped her, and Marcus's kisses still caressed her body. Oh, such sweet, sweet pleasure, such wonderful emotion, such aching desire. To feel as she did now was to eradicate all fear and unhappiness. For these few minutes she was oblivious to everything except her love for him. And his for her. If only she had never listened to George Sutherton's lies. If only she had followed her heart, all this and more would have been hers by now. . . .

A reproachful whine sounded from the cupboard in the main cabin, and Henrietta's eyes flew open. "Rowley? Oh, Rowley, I forgot all about you!" She slipped swiftly from the bed and hurried through to let the spaniel out. As he jumped up into her arms again, she glanced down at the bonbon dish. It was empty. Somehow he had actually managed to eat the sugared almonds!

After rounding the North Foreland, where a warning lighthouse had stood for centuries, hunted and hunter at last drew near the dreaded Goodwins. The winter afternoon was beginning to draw in, and the tide had been ebbing for some time as the telltale ripple of shallows a little to port ahead revealed that the sea was retreating over miles of submerged sand. Ahead on the starboard side, in the sheltered stretch of waters between the Goodwins and the land, nestled a forest of masts, for provided the fearsome "ship swallower" sands could be avoided, the Downs was the safest of havens. But from the carefully selected angle at which the *Avalon* was approaching, leading the unsuspecting *Légère* in her wake, this sanctuary could only be reached through the narrow channel upon which Marcus pinned his hopes.

He stood on the deck of *Avalon*, taking meticulous readings from the old wooden hulk that was permanently moored at the northern head of the sands, and from various landmarks on the Kent shore, some six miles away to the west. These landmarks included his magnificent Palladian residence, Bramnells, from where he had so frequently observed ships foundering in these dangerous waters. He knew his measurements had to be accurate to the very last yard, for the margin between safety and shipwreck was very narrow indeed.

His calculations complete, he glanced back at the pursuing privateer, which was barely three hundred yards astern, well within range. He was puzzled that Lyons hadn't commenced firing, but as he looked there was activity as men at last rushed forward to the howitzers. He also saw an ominous red flag being raised. No quarter. He turned to his own crew. "Brace yourselves, lads, for the fun is about to begin."

The reason for the *Légère*'s delay was very simple; half an hour earlier, the bogle had awoken and commenced its attack. It first victim had been Amabel, who was in her cabin. After another fracas with the superstitious crew, her brother had ordered her to remain out of sight. No respecter of sex, the manikin dug its teeth into her calf, and she screamed not only with pain, but with shock from seeing what had bitten her! Still screaming, she caught up her skirts and ran up to the deck, where the dismayed sailors forgot their tasks and drew back in alarm from a woman who appeared to have gone completely mad. Their eyes nearly popped from their heads when the wicked bogle emerged from a hatchway and glanced around for its next victim. It chose the ship's boy, who was so terrified that he scrambled over a store of cannonballs, and accidentally released them across the deck. Amabel's brother dashed from the quarterdeck to see what was happening, and he too received a bite or two for his pains.

Within moments, just as had happened on the *Avalon*, there was utter chaos. The panicstricken crew clambered up the rig-

ging to get out of the way, and no one would come down as
Lyons furiously attempted to restore order. He was as unnerved
as anyone by the sight of the ugly hobgoblin, but his first and
only consideration remained his ship. However, his bellowed
orders were lost in the renewed clamor of Amabel's screams as
the bogle returned its attentions to her. All this happened as the
Avalon came in sight of the Goodwins and Marcus commenced
taking measurements to plot the exact position of the channel.

Amabel's brother was at his wits' end. Nothing he said or did
would budge his men from their places of safety. He glanced
ahead past the fleeing *Avalon*, and saw the clustered masts of
anchorage. There was very little time left before the sloop
reached safety. Capturing her was now out of the question, but
sinking her certainly was not. But to do that, he needed his
men!

At that moment the bogle tiptoed unwisely close, being of a
mind to bite the French captain again. Amabel's brother was superstitious, but not to the extent of losing face! Sinking the
Avalon had become such a matter of honor that a mere hobgoblin wasn't going to get in the way. With a curse that would
never have been tolerated at the Versailles of his and Amabel's
youth, he dealt the bogle a kick that sent it spinning along the
deck like one of the cannons that already rolled in all directions.
Then he drew his cutlass and advanced after it. The bogle sat up
and stared at him in horror. Glancing desperately around, it saw
salvation—another wooden bucket!

With a squeal it scrambled up, pushed the bucket through an
open port, and launched itself out too. Bucket and bogle hit the
water together, and after some frantic splashing the manikin
managed to haul itself to safety. Again it bobbed away astern of
a vessel upon which it had caused mayhem, and again it shook
its fist and screeched abuse of a most shocking nature. But this
time many weeks were going to pass before it scrambled
aboard another unsuspecting ship, and many months would
ensue after that before it reached dry land again. By then troublemaking would be the least of its considerations. All it would
want to do would be to find a smelly corner or rubbish heap in
which to sleep—and mind its own business, which was all it

had been doing in Mulborough churchyard until Rowley disturbed it!

Even though the bogle had gone, Amabel continued to scream hysterically. Her brother strode irritably over to her and delivered an ungentlemanly slap that resulted in instant silence. Wide-eyed, she stared at him, but he was unrepentant as he ordered her back to her cabin. The last thing he needed was for her to keep the crew up the rigging! With a choked sob she obeyed, and then he turned to confront his cowering men. Slicing his cutlass warningly through the air, he promised to disembowel them one by one unless they returned to their tasks without further delay. Slowly they climbed down from the rigging and went sullenly to their posts.

Lyons glanced grimly ahead again. If there was one thing he was going to do, it was sink the cursed sloop that had caused him such exasperation! He could make an attempt to sink her before she entered the channel, or he could pursue her into it. He smiled. How good it would be to slip into the fine haven by which the British set such store, sink the *Avalon* right in front of the batteries on the shore, and then come about to sail out once more! That would show how little the *Légère* feared anyone or anything! He snapped his fingers scornfully at the coastline, then nodded at a man who was waiting with a flag that was to be run up the mainmast. Plain red and implacable, it was immediately hauled aloft, then Lyons cupped his hands to the men now manning the howitzers in the bows. "Fire!" he shouted in French.

The howitzers boomed and the shot fell short, plunging into the water well astern of the sloop. Lyons shouted again, and after the trajectory had been adjusted, the howitzers fired once more. The shot fell much closer this time, sending spray up over the windows of the *Avalon*'s stern cabin. With a low curse, Amabel's brother strode forward to take aim himself. For a third time the howitzers fired, and this time the shot crashed through the sloop's rigging and fell into the water in front of her. Still cursing, Lyons worked feverishly to get the aim just right. There was no other thought in his head, for he knew that in order to negotiate the channel, his helmsman only had to follow the *Avalon* . . .

That was all Old Nick thought too. Leaning back interestedly on his hellish throne, he set his pièce de résistance in motion. With a languid wave of his hand he summoned the *Basilisk* and the *Wessex* to escort the two modern vessels to their doom. Oh, how delightful this moment of revenge was going to be. St. Peter had just solved the problem with his quarrelsome angels, and was belatedly beginning to realize what was going on. But it was too late now. The time for nose-thumbing had arrived!

On the sloop, Henrietta stood in Marcus's arms as they both looked back at the pursuing privateer. Rowley was hiding beneath her cloak and peeped from under the hem now and then. He knew something was about to happen, and he was afraid. He whined and withdrew as the howitzers fired. Henrietta flinched, and flinched again at the second shot, then she hid her face against Marcus's shoulder as the third shot whined through the rigging, driving a hole through a sail and splintering a spar. For her sake, and the sake of his men, Marcus gave no sign of his anxiety. He watched the *Légère* as if totally unconcerned, but his heart was thundering and he was prepared to promise the Almighty anything at all if only He would spare them all now. Just let the sand spit be where he'd calculated.

Rowley gave a sudden anxious whine, and Henrietta raised her head swiftly. Everything around her had changed, shining once more with the silver light, and there was an unearthly silence. She saw the *Wessex* again, the faces of her crew filled with dread as they stared ahead at the Goodwins, which had suddenly emerged from the sea to stretch for miles. They knew they were doomed, and could only wait for the moment the merchantman drove herself on to the rock-hard sand. Astern, the *Légère* had become the *Basilisk*, and was bearing down at an unstoppable speed. In his eagerness to take the *Wessex*, the privateer's captain had made a fatal error, and now he and his crew knew they could not escape the fate they themselves had caused. A single sound broke the silence. It was Jane sobbing. Henrietta drew from Marcus's arms as she cast around for the source of the sound, but she saw no sign of her ghostly friends. Rowley whined and crept from beneath the cloak. Henrietta bent to gather him into her arms, then again looked desperately around for Jane and Kit.

Marcus watched her, and knew she was seeing things that were invisible to everyone else on the *Avalon*. He heard Rowley whine and saw how she bent to pick up the spaniel. He caught her elbow then, and drew her close once more. "It's all right, my beloved, it's all right. What you're seeing isn't really there at all, but *I'm* here, and we're going to be safe."

"I can see the *Wessex*, Marcus, and the *Légère* isn't the *Légère* anymore, but the *Basilisk*. The sands are above water, and in a few seconds . . ." Her whisper died away and her eyes widened as she braced herself for the impact that would break first the merchantman's back, and then the privateer's.

Marcus rested his cheek against her hair. The sands were not above water, and wouldn't be for another hour; all he could see was the *Légère*. There had been silence since the third firing of the howitzers, and men were working frantically on the guns. Something had jammed on both, and they were trying to free it. Marcus smiled, but then became alert as he detected a change in the sound of the water beneath the *Avalon*. It was barely perceptible, but was the difference between deep water and that which allowed only a foot or so beneath the sloop's hull. It seemed that an age passed, but at last the sound changed again. The submerged sandbar had been crossed, and the channel was deep once more.

For Henrietta and Rowley everything suddenly fell into turmoil. In a blur she saw Jane and Kit at last. Jane was sobbing in Kit's embrace, and all around them there was panic as the merchantman's crew realized their fate.

Henrietta was frightened. With Rowley nestling deep in her arms, she whispered to Marcus. "Hold me tighter. Don't let me go."

"I will never let you go again."

Mr. Barrington called out suddenly. "My lord, two patrol frigates are coming to our aid!"

Still holding Henrietta, Marcus turned sharply and saw that

the first officer was right. Pennants streaming, the frigates were peeling away from the small convoy of merchantmen they were escorting north through the Downs. They were at least two miles away, with the wind against them, but their approach would unsettle Lyons. He looked back at the *Légère* and saw Amabel's brother step up on to the rail. Lyons gripped a rope to steady himself as he gazed past the *Avalon* toward the frigates. Marcus knew he was wondering if he would have time to deliver a fatal broadside once his vessel and the sloop reached wider water. Or would he be better advised to turn the moment he could, and beat a hasty retreat? Marcus smiled. It didn't matter which course the Frenchman decided upon; now the *Légère* was committed to the channel, the sandbar would claim her anyway! "You've been gulled, my fine strutting fellow, you've been gulled," he murmured.

Henrietta still saw the past. She experienced the wreck of the *Wessex* on the same spit of sand that had appeared one hundred years before. The merchantman's deck became a devastation of rending wood, falling spars, and torn rigging, but Henrietta heard not a single sound. It all happened in a deadly silence. Within seconds, the *Basilisk* perished as well, driving full on to the unforgiving sands within yards of her prey. In the present, the *Légère* came to a shuddering halt as she too buried her bows in the submerged bar. With a grinding and crushing of timbers, she held fast on the steep-sided spit of sand that would crack her hull as the tide retreated. Then past and present were rent asunder. Alone of the four vessels, the *Avalon* could sail on. She parted from her ghostly alter ego, and continued serenely on toward the welcoming safety of the Downs.

With a grunt of disbelief, Old Nick sat forward. How could this be? How could the sloop escape what was meant to be the inevitable? Too late the Master of Hades remembered the small matter of the *Avalon*'s shallow draft.

Chapter Thirty

Everyone on the *Avalon* cheered ecstatically as the sloop glided on unharmed. Caps were tossed into the air and no one felt any sorrow at the demise of a privateer that had wrought such terror on the seas. Henrietta gave a sob of relief. She gazed back at the other vessels, two phantoms and one that was only too real. The *Légère* had struck fast upon the sandbar and was already beginning to break her back.

Marcus's arms tightened around Henrietta. "Don't be anxious, my love, for the tide is falling apace now, and the sands will soon be exposed. Everyone on the *Légère* will escape."

"And be rescued?"

"Of course."

She raised her eyes to gaze at him. "Oh, Marcus, I love you so very, very much," she whispered.

"It's St. Valentine's Day, my darling, so what better occasion could there be to ask you to marry me? Become my marchioness, Henrietta, and make me the happiest man on this earth!"

Old Nick almost choked.

She stared at him. "Oh, Marcus . . ."

"Just say yes."

Hell's overlord leaped to his feet. No, don't say yes! Don't!

"Of course I will marry you," she whispered.

Old Nick gave a howl of anguish.

Rowley suddenly jumped from Henrietta's arms. Barking and wagging his plumey tail, he dashed along the deck. Henrietta turned from Marcus's arms to see Jane and Kit hurrying toward her across the deck. Jane was laughing out of sheer happiness, and Kit caught one of Henrietta's hands to draw it dashingly to his lips.

Jane gazed gratefully at her. "You've saved us," she said. "We had to bring two of our descendants together in love, and now that love has been properly declared, we can go to heaven, instead of to hell."

"Is *that* what this haunting has been about?"

"Yes." Jane quickly explained about St. Peter's error and Old Nick's annoyance. "But we were forbidden to confide anything in you," she went on. "We did our best to bring you and Marcus together, and we waited and waited for you to realize how much you loved each other, but you both were so stubbornly determined to nurse grudges that we quite despaired. Then we thought we were doomed anyway, because Old Nick imprisoned us on the *Wessex.* . . ."

As Jane shivered, Kit put his arm around her. "It's all over now, my darling. Our hundred years of haunting is at an end. Look up at the sky."

Jane did as she was told, and saw the glittering portals of heaven shimmering in the sky. Henrietta looked up as well but saw nothing, and when she looked at the ghosts again, they were more indistinct than before. In fact they were fading before her eyes.

Jane bent to take Rowley, but the spaniel shrank back. Jane's joy was checked. "Rowley?"

Kit caught her arm. "There's no time, beloved, we must go now."

Rowley looked around at Henrietta, and she knew he wanted to stay with her. She smiled at Jane. "I'll look after him, Jane, truly I will."

Jane hesitated, but then hastened forward to brush a ghostly kiss to Henrietta's cheek. Then suddenly both she and Kit faded completely. Henrietta gazed at the spot where they had been, and bit her lip to stop herself from crying. She knew she would never see them again.

Old Nick, already beside himself with spluttering fury, now

became positively apoplectic. He hurled his pitchfork to the ground, and vented his spleen by jumping on it. His temper was not improved by the sound of holy laughter, and he shook a fist aloft. Truth to tell, he put St. Peter very much in mind of an angry bogle.

The saint closed the gates of heaven, and then drew a satisfied breath. What was the old adage? Better late than never? Well, maybe a lack of concentration in previous times had led to this sorry business in the first place, and more recently disputing angels had caused a lengthy and tiresome distraction, but all was now satisfactorily concluded! Two very good, long-suffering souls were now where they should have been all along, and Old Nick would have to swallow the bitter pill of defeat. And of sly whispers in the ranks of his underlings.

All these goings-on, both heavenly and hellish, remained unknown to Marcus, who saw only Henrietta's unshed tears. He put a gentle arm around her shoulders. "What has happened?"

"Jane and Kit have gone to heaven at last. I've seen them for the last time." Mastering her mixed emotions, she explained what Jane had told her.

"You mean, it's been down to us all along?"

Henrietta managed a smile. "Not all along, for it's been going on for a hundred years! Just since New Year's Day, when it began to snow." She glanced toward the Kentish coast, where the land was still white.

Rowley whined and pawed at her hem. Marcus gave a start. "Don't tell me we still have the dog!"

"I fear so. He didn't want to go with them." Henrietta gathered the spaniel into her arms again.

Rowley snuggled contentedly. Now that he had discovered he could still eat sugared almonds, he had no desire whatsoever to go to heaven, where he was sure such things would not exist. He glanced slyly at Marcus, just as he had once looked at Kit. Certain rules would have to be established, not the least being that a lady's pet dog, ghostly or not, came before her gentleman. Now, if that gentleman were to provide a constant supply of sugared almonds, no doubt a satisfactory compromise could be reached.

* * *

Marcus was proved correct in his prediction that everyone on board the *Légère* would be rescued. As the tide fell and the Goodwins were exposed, to a man—and woman—they scrambled onto the sands. One of the patrol frigates then took them safely off. After that, when the water was its lowest, the *Légère* broke up on the bar and the good men of Kent plundered her most thoroughly. The privateer's crew and captain were flung ignominiously into Deal jail, and as soon as the thaw was sufficient to make the roads passable, Amabel was taken to London. There she too was imprisoned while the authorities considered what to do with her.

Henrietta's reputation remained intact when she and Marcus let it be known that a maid had indeed been with her during the voyage, but had left immediately on landing. A new maid was taken on without delay, and no one in society ever realized anything had been amiss. When George, Lord Sutherton, was confronted with his unfaithfulness with Amabel and his lies about Marcus, he could think of nothing to say in his own defense. He was so alarmed about Amabel's espionage, fearing he might in some way become implicated, that it was some time before he realized his financial dilemma was now even worse than before. He had been spending lavishly on the promise of the Courtenay fortune, and now his need for an heiress was greater than ever. Like the conscienceless rat he was, he set about lying his way into another poor creature's life, but he came sadly unstuck when on his wedding night he discovered that his bride was a schemer like himself, and had married *him* in the hope of solving her own financial problems! They unrichly deserved each other, which was perhaps as it should be.

Another wedding, that of the Marquess of Rothwell and Miss Henrietta Courtenay, was one of the social highlights of spring 1814. The beau monde flocked to the ceremony at St. George's, Hanover Square, and at long last the bride and groom's respective families deigned to be agreeable toward each other. In fact, the feud was all but set aside, except in the case of a few stalwarts like Uncle Thomas, who to the end of his hidebound days would find it hard to forgive his niece for marrying a Fitzpaine!

But then, very little in this world mattered to Uncle Thomas, except perhaps when the next Tattersall's sale would be held.

Henrietta and Marcus spent their wedding night at Bramnells. When the April sun set at the end of the most wonderful day of her life, she stood at the tall window of the principal bedroom. All she was wearing was a flimsy pink muslin robe that frothed with lace at the throat and cuffs, and her dark hair was brushed loose about her shoulders. She gazed out toward the distant Goodwins, exposed now, and pale and mysterious beneath the crimson of the dying sun. Of the *Légère* there was no sign, for the sands had long since claimed every trace of her, sucking her down into their mysterious depths as if she had never been.

As Henrietta watched, the tide began to turn. The sea came in at a fearsome rate, and in only minutes, the miles of sand had become a maelstrom of crashing surf. She glanced up at the sky, wondering about Jane and Kit, and then turned back into the room, where Marcus lay watching her.

He was dressed in a blue brocade dressing gown, which was open to reveal the unexpectedly dark hairs on his chest. He wasn't alone on the bed, for Rowley sat determinedly at the bottom. The ghostly spaniel's gaze was fixed upon the man with whom he was competing for Henrietta's attentions. Marcus couldn't see the dog, but he knew he was there. Indeed, Rowley was *always* there these days!

Henrietta knelt on the bed beside her new husband and put warm fingertips on his chest. "We are alone together at last, my lord," she said softly.

"So we are, my lady," he replied, his gaze moving over her. The delicate muslin did not conceal her figure, and his blood was already stirring with his overwhelming desire for her. He put a hand up to touch her breast.

Rowley growled. They ignored him as Marcus caught her hand to pull her down into his arms, but Rowley growled again, louder this time. The spaniel was past master at this game; he'd done it enough times to Kit to know exactly how to put a damper on proceedings. But Marcus wasn't Kit. After drawing Henrietta's hand to his lips, he got up from the bed.

Henrietta looked at him in surprise. "What are you doing?"

"I'm going to deal with Master Rowley."

Henrietta's eyes widened. "Deal with him? Oh, Marcus, I'm sure he's only looking after my honor."

"Is he indeed? We'll soon see. He is about to be faced with a dilemma, and I'm pretty certain your honor won't figure in his decision." Going to a drawer, Marcus took out a large dish of sugared almonds, which he placed on the floor. Then he returned to the bed and lay down once more.

Rowley gazed at the sugared almonds, then at the bed, then back at the sugared almonds. His mouth watered and with a sigh he jumped down. As the almonds began to rattle, Marcus gave a sleek smile. "So much for your honor, my love," he said softly, pulling her down into his arms.

"But my lord, I was going to surrender my honor anyway."

"Oh, you were, my lady, you were," he breathed, and drew her lips to his.

The sweetest of ecstasies consumed her as he made her his at last. Never had any woman enjoyed a sweeter initiation, or known more pleasure. She sighed when he drew her nipple into his mouth, and she cried out when he entered her. She had not dreamed it could be like this, and she knew she would never spurn him again, or misunderstand him, never doubt or question him, never turn from his kisses. He was part of her now, and they would never part again.

Afterward, when they lay in each other's arms, their love consummated at last, the only sound in the room was the crunching of ghostly canine teeth upon another sugared almond.